GW00775844

Brenda Clarke was born in Bristol and educated at The Red Maid's School, Westbury-on-Trym. She is married with a son and a daughter, and one granddaughter.

LAST OF THE BARONS

A descendant of kings, but not in direct line of succession to the throne, Richard Neville, Earl of Warwick, saw himself, nevertheless, as the person most competent to rule England. He was the man chiefly responsible for wresting the crown from the feeble Henry VI and setting up his cousin, the Earl of March, as Edward IV. Edward, however, was not the politically inept young man that Warwick believed him to be and his marriage to Elizabeth Woodville alienated almost the entire Neville family. From then on, Warwick's life degenerated into a struggle for political power that eventually led him to the fatal field of Barnet.

Books by Brenda Clarke
Published by The House of Ulverscroft:

THE FAR MORNING
A ROSE IN MAY
WINTER LANDSCAPE
UNDER HEAVEN
RICHARD PLANTAGENET

BRENDA CLARKE

◆

LAST OF THE BARONS

Complete and Unabridged

ULVERSCROFT
Leicester

First published in Great Britain in 1998 by
Severn House Publishers Limited
Surrey

First Large Print Edition
published 1999
by arrangement with
Severn House Publishers Limited
Surrey

British Library CIP Data

Clarke, Brenda, *1926 –*
Last of the barons.—Large print ed.—
Ulverscroft large print series: general fiction
1. Warwick, Richard Neville, Earl of, *1428 –
1471* —Fiction 2. Great Britain—History—Wars
of the Roses, *1455 – 1485* —Fiction
3. Historical fiction
4. Large type books
I. Title II. Honeyman, Brenda. Kingmaker
823.9'14 [F]

ISBN 0–7089–4143–5

Published by
F. A. Thorpe (Publishing) Ltd.
Anstey, Leicestershire
Set by Words & Graphics Ltd.
Anstey, Leicestershire
Printed and bound in Great Britain by
T. J. International Ltd., Padstow, Cornwall

This book is printed on acid-free paper

LIST OF BOOKS CONSULTED

Warwick the Kingmaker Paul Murray Kendall

Richard the Third Paul Murray Kendall

The Yorkist Age Paul Murray Kendall

The Reign of Edward VI Eric N. Simons

The Plantagenets John Harvey

Wars of the Roses J. R. Lander

The End of the House of Lancaster R. L. Storey

The Paston Letters, Everyman edition

The Travels of Rozmital. Edited by Malcolm Letts for the Hakluyt Society

The Waning of the Middle Ages J. Huizinga

Life in Medieval England J. J. Bagley

The Popes. Edited by Eric John

Dictionary of National Biography

Part One

'PROUD SETTER-UP . . .

1455 – 1464

1

He stood in the meadows outside the town of St. Albans, flanked on either side by the men of his household; armed, and in open rebellion against his King.

On this twenty-second of May, 1455, Richard Neville, Earl of Warwick, was twenty-six and a half years old; a tall young man, in whose face blended the features of Neville, Beaufort and Plantagenet. One of his great-grandfathers had been that much-married and prolific prince, John of Gaunt, whose mistress, Katherine Swynford, had given birth to three sons and a daughter. When, late in life, Gaunt had made Katherine his third wife, his nephew, King Richard the second, had legitimatised his brilliant Beaufort cousins, thus enabling Joan to marry the widowed Earl of Westmorland, Ralph Neville of Raby. These two had reared a family of eleven healthy children, the eldest of whom was Warwick's father and the youngest, a daughter, Cicely, who had married her cousin, the Duke of York. It was on behalf of his uncle, York, that Richard Neville now stood beneath

3

his banner of the Bear and Ragged Staff, waiting for the return of the herald who, in a last-minute attempt to avoid open warfare, had been sent to King Henry within the town. The long and cautiously-worded missive which their messenger had carried, had been prepared earlier that morning by Warwick, his father, the Earl of Salisbury, and York, but although much time and thought had been expended by the three lords upon making it as circumspect as possible, in the end it was nothing more nor less than a demand for the arrest of Somerset.

Edmund Beaufort, Duke of Somerset, grandson of Gaunt and cousin of sorts to York, the Nevilles and to the King, himself, had been swept to power ten years earlier, when, together with the Duke of Suffolk, he had arranged for the marriage of the French Princess, Margaret of Anjou, to Henry the sixth of England. The marriage had been disastrous in every respect. The self-willed young Queen had soon gained complete ascendancy over the mind of her feeble young husband, who, even then was beginning to show the signs of madness inherited from his maternal grandfather, King Charles the sixth of France. Within two years, Henry's uncle Humphrey of Gloucester, sole surviving

4

brother of King Henry the fifth, was dead; murdered, it was whispered, on the orders of the Queen.

The people had been roused to fury. Oblivious to the short-comings of a somewhat rash and turbulent character, they had christened Humphrey their 'Good Duke' and the rumours of his murder had confirmed their hatred of a marriage which had brought no gain to England except an unwelcome truce with France. At a time when they had started to lose the concept of themselves as a part of Christendom and to emerge as an insular and bellicose nation, the English had been forced to watch the gradual loss of all their territorial gains in France.

A month or so before Warwick's birth, in November of 1428, Joan of Arc had raised the siege of Orleans and although, two years later, she had been burnt at the stake, the French had continued to gain ground. In 1449, Somerset had surrendered Rouen to the French and the armies of Charles the seventh had driven the English from Norman soil.

Humiliated, bewildered, the English had simmered with discontent until, in the spring of 1450, the general dissatisfaction had boiled over into open rebellion. A howling mob had demanded the death of Suffolk and when

5

Henry had merely banished the favourite to France, the people had taken the law into their own hands. By word of mouth the order had passed, carried along the rutted tracks by pedlars, beggars and thieves, until, at the end of April, Suffolk had been hacked to death by the Channel pirates, head and body left to rot on Dover sands.

As the year wore on, there were more murders and risings, culminating in June and July in the rebellion of the Kentishmen who, for two days and nights, had held London just as their grandfathers had done seventy-nine years previously. The leader of the rising had been a certain Jack Cade who, like Wat Tyler before him, had found it impossible to hold his peasant army together for more than a short space of time. The need to reap and lay up stores for the winter months, had proved a greater enemy to both leaders than the forces of government. Cade, however, unlike Tyler, had claimed some semblance of authority for his rebellion and, by insisting to the last on being called John Mortimer, had implicated the Duke of York in the revolt.

The name of Mortimer had connotations of which most people were only too well aware. When, at the end of the previous century, King Richard had been deposed by Henry of Bolingbroke, he had been childless. His acknowledged heir had been Roger Mortimer, the grandson of his uncle, Lionel of Clarence, Edward the third's third son. Roger Mortimer had been murdered in Ireland and it was while investigating the death of his heir in that country that Richard had received the news of his cousin's invasion of his realm. He had returned to England, to captivity and death and with him, in Pontefract castle, had died the hopes of a Mortimer succession.

The murdered Roger Mortimer, however, had left two children; a boy, Edmund, and a girl, Anne, who had eventually married her cousin, the Earl of Cambridge. Cambridge had lost his life in a futile attempt to reassert the regal claims of his brother-in-law, betrayed to the King by Edmund Mortimer, himself. He had been executed at Southampton as Henry the fifth had embarked for France. His estates had been forfeit to the crown and his wife and family left destitute.

A few weeks later, however, a dazzling change had taken place in the fortunes of Cambridge's eldest son. The Duke of York, the Earl's older brother, had died at Agincourt, and as he had no children of his own, his title, estates and wealth all passed to his nephew. In a moment, the five-years-old Richard Plantagenet had become one of the richest and most important men in the country. His wardship had been granted by the King to Ralph and Joan Neville of Raby and it was in the Neville household that Richard had spent most of his childhood and all of his youth, playing and working with his Neville cousins and finally falling in love with the youngest and loveliest of them, Cicely, the Rose of Raby.

Unlike most of their contemporaries, Richard and Cicely did not marry until they were well into their twenties, a circumstance largely due, Richard had always felt, to the reluctance of Joan Neville to consent to her daughter's marriage. For Joan, shrewd daughter of old Gaunt and the astute Lady Swynford, although well aware of the advantages of such a match, had experienced serious misgivings. Richard might have inherited great wealth and position from the spear-side of his family, but from the distaff-side he had inherited something far more dangerous. Since the death of his uncle Edmund in 1425, he had been the holder of the Mortimer claim, which made him, by the rules of primogeniture, rightful king of England.

Had Richard shown any signs of wishing

to press this claim, Joan might never have consented to the match. But the Duke of York had been a stolid, phlegmatic young man, contented with his lot. Nor in all the vicissitudes of his life following Joan Neville's death in 1440, had he ever shown any inclination to demand the crown which many considered to be rightfully his.

There had been some who had hoped that the birth of a son to Margaret and Henry in the October of 1453, would have stirred York to assert his claim, but most people were glad he had not done so. At the time of the Prince's birth, Henry had been completely insane and York was Protector of the realm. Yet, ineffectual as his rule was, the people were fond of their King and for York to have seized power at such a moment would have scarcely endeared him to his fellow countrymen. As it was, he enjoyed more respect than most of the other barons, not only in England but also in Ireland, where his eighteen-months rule as Lord-Lieutenant had earned him the loyalty of the Irish.

It was possible that York's strong hand on the reins of government, together with the support of the people, might have brought peace to a land torn by baronial factions and inundated by the return of the now unemployed soldiers from France. It was not to be, however. The implacable enmity of the Queen and her favourites for one who stood so dangerously near the throne, had brought about a schism in the ranks of the lords and ensured that York became the focal point for every disaffected magnate in the country.

As long as Henry had remained insane and York at the head of the government, an uneasy truce had prevailed. But the preceding Christmas, Henry had regained his senses and Somerset his power, thus leaving York in a perilous position . . . just how perilous he had realised in the early part of this year when his spies had brought him word of a secret conference to be held at Westminster with the Queen and Somerset presiding. This, to York, had meant only one thing: that he, Salisbury and Warwick were about to be arrested and impeached for high treason.

From his castle at Sandal, near Wakefield, the Duke had sent messengers to his brother-in-law and nephew on their Yorkshire estates, urging them, at last, to arms; with the result that by the time the Queen, together with Henry, Somerset and her army left London in the middle of May, she found her enemies in full battle array, barring her path at St. Albans.

Warwick shifted his feet among the sweet-smelling grasses, crushing a clump of butter-cups and grinding the fragile gold petals into the earth. He was impatient for the battle to begin, for he had small doubt that with Somerset at one elbow and the Queen at the other, Henry would be forced to refuse their terms. And he was glad, because on this warm spring morning of brilliant sunshine and dappled shadows, Richard Neville felt in himself a need for action; anything to release the pent-up energies of a healthy and vigorous body.

There was little hope nowadays of gaining glory in France, where, for the last hundred years, ambitious young men had been able to earn fame and fortune; and there was no doubt that the Earl of Warwick was ambitious. He had not always been so in spite of his high degree and Plantagenet blood for, as his mother had pointed out to him, he had held no special position in the scheme of things. There were few nobles who could not claim some kinship with the King, and Warwick's marriage to Anne Beauchamp had not been a brilliant match, the lady having had a brother who had inherited their father's earldom. Even

11

when the young Earl had died in the summer of 1447, he had left an heiress in the person of his four-years-old daughter. But when, two years later, the little girl had also died, Richard Neville had suddenly found himself married to one of the richest women in the kingdom.

In his wife's right, he was invested with the titles of Earl of Warwick, Baron of Hanslape and Elmley, Lord of Glamorgan and Morgannoc. The vast lands of the Beauchamp and Despenser families were his; lands which stretched from Cornwall to Northumberland and from the Welsh marches to the Wash. At last he was someone in his own right, not merely the Earl of Salisbury's eldest son and his ambition grew apace. He could no longer be content with the quiet life, but was on fire with a sense of destiny which events so far had done little to justify. During York's brief Protectorship, he had been a member of the Royal Council, but with the waning of his uncle's political fortune, his own had waned also, until here he was, forced to stake everything on an act of open rebellion.

It had been by no means certain that, in this first moment of conflict, Salisbury and his sons would have found themselves ranged side-by-side with the Duke of York. True,

York was the brother-in-law of one and the uncle of the others, but this meant little or nothing in a society where almost everyone was related by marriage or by blood. It would have been impossible, a year before, to have predicted which side any but the principal protagonists would have favoured on this May morning outside St. Albans. In the shifting loyalties about the throne, few were motivated by anything other than complete self-interest. Twice in past years the Nevilles had been ranged against their kinsman, York, and only the increasing influence of Somerset upon the Queen — a direct threat to their own power — had at last forced them to support the Yorkist faction.

And because Salisbury had, at one time and another, championed two of his tenants in their quarrels with their neighbours, the Parrs and the Thornburghs also supported the Duke of York, while their antagonists, the Bellinghams and the Crackenthorpes, gave their loyalty to King Henry. It would, therefore, merely need a change in Salisbury's affections to alter not only those of his followers, but also that of their enemies. It was a pattern repeated over and over again on both sides and meant that neither the King nor York could be certain of their supporters from day to day. Much better to negotiate;

to form an alliance, however uneasy, as the Duke of Buckingham was even now urging upon Henry, seated in his quarters at the Castle Inn.

But it was not the King who answered Buckingham. The Queen, eyes flashing, breasts heaving, whirled like a fury upon the elderly Duke.

'We all know, my lord,' she said, 'that your wife is sister to Salisbury and the Duchess of York, so if you wish to join your Neville in-laws, you may do so. But do not ask it of me, or His Grace of Somerset, or the Earl of Wiltshire here.'

She really was a magnificent creature, thought Buckingham; wasted, of course, on a monk like Henry. Was it true, he wondered, that Wiltshire was her lover? He glanced contemptuously at the handsome, slightly effeminate, young man who stood behind her. James Butler, Earl of Wiltshire, turned away, pulling nervously at his belt: a broken reed, reflected Buckingham, if there were to be any fighting.

He turned back to the King. 'Your Grace, I beg of you . . . ' But Henry was not listening. Instead, his attention was fixed on the uncovered bosom of his wife's lady-in-waiting and he put up a hand to blot out the offensive sight.

'Take that woman away and cover her,' he ordered in a trembling voice. 'It is a sin against the Holy Ghost for women to flaunt themselves abroad next door to naked.'

Wiltshire gave a quick, high-pitched titter and Somerset sneered. Margaret, ignoring him as though he had not spoken, bent to draft her reply to the Yorkist lords.

It was not a reply likely to mollify any of them and caused York to indulge in a bout of obscene oaths which brought a look of unaccustomed admiration to the eyes of his eldest son, Edward, Earl of March.

Edward, a tall, fair boy of thirteen, who had been allowed to leave his school books behind in Ludlow and accompany his father for this, his first taste of battle, was not usually roused to admiration for anything that the Duke did or said. Warwick, watching him now through half-closed lids, had long ago come to the conclusion that there was a veiled hostility between father and son. There was no doubt that York was fonder of his second son, Edmund, and Warwick wondered idly if the stories rumoured about at Edward's birth had had any foundation in fact.

Edward had been born at Rouen in 1442, when York had been Lieutenant-General in France. Stories that he was the son of

15

an archer named Blackburn, a bowman of the Duchess of York's guard, had been current at the French court at the time and had been whispered on and off ever since. Very few people, even the scandalmongers, themselves, really believed what they were saying and for a very good reason. It was not, Warwick reflected, that it was impossible to imagine the Duchess being unfaithful to her husband, fond of him as she was. It was simply that no one could picture her being unfaithful with a bowman of her guard. For Cicely, like all the Nevilles, was fiercely proud, had a high sense of family and was deeply conscious that to be a Neville was to be unique. No one, Warwick thought, could imagine his aunt even considering a common bowman as her lover and yet . . . Perhaps some doubts did linger on in the mind of her husband, who must have heard the stories, although he had never been known to mention them. Certainly no rumours had clouded the births of their other children and Cicely and Richard of York had had eleven — of whom seven had survived infancy — and their twelfth child was expected this coming summer.

Warwick suppressed a sigh of envy. He had only one child so far, a daughter, Isabel, born three years ago, not long after the birth of the Yorks' youngest child, Richard. He wanted a son; a son like Edward, healthy and handsome and dutiful, smiling now at his cousin, Warwick, with a charm and deference that were delightful. Yes; one could manage a son like Edward, a good-humoured, malleable boy; mould him into whatever one wished.

It was to be Warwick's tragedy that the years ahead were to prove this impression of Edward totally false.

* * *

It was eleven o'clock. York raised his arm and the charge began. Barriers had been erected by the defenders across the entrances to Holywell street and St. Peter's street and it was against these barricades that the Duke and Salisbury led the main attack. Warwick, in a supporting position, was to create a diversion in the gardens of the houses in Holywell street and it was with nothing more than this in view, that he plunged with his men across the defensive palisade and ditch into a garden where the apple-blossom drifted in pink and white clouds about their mailed feet. A man erupted hastily from the privy and disappeared into the house like a frightened rabbit. The smell

17

of crushed herbs made Warwick sneeze and ever after reminded him of this moment when he achieved his first, and unexpected, triumph.

A messenger, pushing his way to the Earl's side, informed him that his father and uncle had been repulsed: everything was now up to him. Warwick smiled. The blood beat more quickly in his veins as he realised that his destiny was upon him; fame and glory within his grasp. He signalled to Sir Robert Ogle, his Captain of Archers, and the next minute the air was alive with the hum of arrows and the twang of bowstrings. Then, with a great shout of 'A Warwick!' 'A Warwick!' the footmen crashed through the gardens, leaving a churned mass of mud and stalks where, only moments before, neat flower-beds had been. In the rush, several men fell down the wells and had to be helped out, swearing and screaming, by jeering comrades, or left to lie there until the battle was over.

And over it was in less than half an hour. Somerset lay dead outside the Castle Inn; Henry Percy, Earl of Northumberland, and Lord Clifford were dying; Buckingham and Dudley, both injured, had taken sanctuary in the Abbey; Wiltshire had fled. The Yorkist lords were victorious thanks mainly to Warwick, and it was in recognition of

18

this fact that York graciously motioned his nephew to his right hand as they approached the bewildered Henry, standing in the doorway of his inn.

The King had been hit in the neck by an arrow and was vainly trying to staunch the trickle of blood which was staining the collar of his coarse grey tunic; a garb which, together with his square-toed, country shoes, earned him an amazed and contemptuous glance from his young cousin, Edward, Earl of March.

The Duke and the three Earls fell on their knees; their followers did the same. There was the rustle of skirts as Margaret, white-faced, more arrogant than ever in defeat, joined her husband in the doorway. Now twenty-five years old, she was still an extremely handsome woman with the dark hair and eyes of her Angevin father, Duke René. But in her ways, the Queen closely resembled her mother; a strong-minded woman who had fought her husband's battles while he wrote poetry, organised tournaments and dabbled with music. She, too, had known defeat, but like her daughter, it left her undismayed.

'And now, my lords?' Margaret's voice snapped out over their heads. 'What do you intend?' Her voice cracked as she caught sight of Edmund Beaufort's lifeless body.

First Suffolk, now Somerset had been taken from her.

'We intend no harm either to His Grace or to yourself,' York answered, rising. 'My brother-in-law and I merely wish to take our rightful places in the government.' He felt a movement beside him and added: 'My nephew, the Earl of Warwick, will also deserve a place. His actions here today were largely responsible for rooting out the traitors that surrounded Your Highnesses.'

Margaret's eyes lifted suddenly to Warwick's. A long look passed between them; a look of hatred and challenge.

'Richard Neville shall come by his deserts,' was all she said, but the moment was charged with an emotion that hung heavily upon the air and imprinted itself on the memories of everyone present . . . except the King.

Henry, still unsure of what had happened, his mind clouding yet again by this reversal in his fortunes, allowed himself to be led away. Margaret watched him go, then clapped her hands to summon her women. Salisbury stepped forward to escort her to her litter, but although she placed her hand in his it was at his son that she was looking. Their eyes met once more, but this time the challenge went deeper.

A duel to the finish, thought Warwick, and in that second was born an enmity which, in spite of everything that was to happen in the years to come, would only be ended by death.

2

The September sunlight forced its way between the over-hanging rooftops of the London streets, crowded now with people, cheering their hero, the Earl of Warwick.

Four years had passed since that day outside St. Albans when Richard Neville had first made his mark in the world, during which time the fortunes of the House of York had see-sawed uncontrollably between power and fortune, shame and despair.

In the October following the battle, Henry had again become insane and York had reassumed the title of Protector of the Realm. Then, in February of 1456, the King had recovered sufficiently for Margaret and her favourites to take control of the government once more and Richard Plantagenet's power had gradually dwindled away. In the autumn of the same year, York and Warwick had been trapped at Coventry and just escaped with their lives from an ambush laid by the sons and relatives of those lords who had been slain at St. Albans. York had sought the shelter of his castle at Sandal, while Warwick, with his wife and two little girls — a second

22

daughter, Anne, had been born earlier that year — fled across the Channel to Calais, of which city he was now Captain.

In England, matters had gone from bad to worse. The mercers rioted because, they said, the Italian merchants were taking all their trade. At the beginning of 1457, the French, under the leadership of Margaret's close friend and admirer, Piers de Brézé, sacked Sandwich, leaving it, in the early hours of a summer's morning, a mass of smoking, roofless houses. The English howled for blood, accusing Henry and Margaret of doing nothing because the Queen, herself, was one of the hated French. In order to placate the angry mobs, the title Keeper of the Seas had been grudgingly bestowed upon the Earl of Warwick, who had successfully defended Calais against the marauding de Brézé. The people were delighted and when, in May of the following year, 1458, Warwick had met and routed almost the entire Spanish fleet, he had become the darling of England. 'There has not been such a great sea-battle for over forty years,' one of his sailors wrote home enthusiastically. And when, a month or two later, Warwick severely trounced a Hanseatic fleet for failing to dip its flags in honour of the Captain of Calais, national pride had known no bounds. Finally,

Warwick, together with his own men and the men of Sandwich, had sailed boldly into Tilbury harbour and confiscated three Italian ships. In so doing he had won for himself a permanent place in the hearts of his countrymen.

None of this, however, had made any difference to his standing at court. Indeed, it had, not unnaturally, had the opposite effect and in the November of 1458, during a brief visit to Westminster Warwick and his servants had been physically attacked. Uneasy at this sign of Margaret's increasing power, he had retired yet again to Calais and in the early months of this year of 1459, had visited Burgundy with a view to enlisting its Duke's support against the increasing depredations of the French.

Duke Philip the Good had been a reluctant ally of the English ever since his father had been assassinated by the French on the bridge at Monthérau in 1419. His court was the most civilised in Europe and hedged about by rigid protocol (which, in centuries to come, would be inherited by his Spanish descendants). He had received the Earl civilly enough, but between his son, Charles, and Warwick there had been immediate antipathy. But one person above all others at that glittering court had impressed himself upon the Captain of Calais; the Dauphin of France, who had been a fugitive in Burgundy ever since his long-suffering father had driven him from his homeland.

Louis, now thirty-six years old, was one of the ugliest men Warwick had ever seen, with a huge, bulbous nose and protuberant eyes. He had one of the most fertile and cunning minds of his generation; had a passion for politics which transcended all other emotions; hated pomp and show; wore a motley collection of clothes more suited to a mountebank than to a prince; and, in short, was everything that Warwick was not. Yet the two men had taken to each other on sight and, in the first few moments of their brief meeting, had forged a bond of friendship and admiration which was to last for the rest of their lives.

Warwick had returned to Calais to find messengers from his uncle and father anxiously awaiting him. Queen Margaret was gathering an army in the Midlands with the palpable object of challenging the Yorkist lords. Warwick was bidden to join his kinsmen in York's Welsh castle of Ludlow, bringing with him as many of his garrison as could possibly be spared. And on this September day, he was passing through London on his way to meet them there.

Little Richard Plantagenet, seven years old, and, since the death of his sister, Ursula, once more the baby of the York family, lay flat on his stomach in Ludford meadows. The warmth of the September sun fell across his back, heavy like fur, and the long shadows cast by Ludlow castle crept slowly over the grass, reaching out for him with a gigantic black hand.

He had been at Ludlow since the summer, when the Duke of York had decided that his three youngest children, Margaret, George and Richard, should be removed from Fotheringay Castle and brought here to Ludlow, the home of his two eldest sons, Edward and Edmund. Until that July day of their arrival Richard had never set eyes on either of his older brothers, but from the moment of his first meeting with Edward, Richard had been smitten with an admiration and devotion that was to last him his whole life through. This did not please ten-years-old George who had so far been the only hero in his little brother's world, and he looked upon the youthful Earl of March with a somewhat jaundiced eye; a circumstance highly amusing to Edward, who did not yet realise the extent and depth of George's prejudices. Richard, young as he was, did and was worrying now about this rift in his brothers' relationship when he heard his name called.

'Diccon!'

He raised his head from his arms and saw George, a splash of scarlet against the green, running across the meadow towards him.

'Horsemen coming!' panted George. 'Might be Warwick!'

Richard scrambled to his feet. He was agog to see this famous cousin of his, whose exploits had so captured his imagination. The two boys ran eagerly up the slope and in at the postern gate. The courtyard was already crowded with stamping horses and dismounting men and the Duke of York emerged from the bailey door to greet his guest; not Warwick, but his father, Salisbury.

The Earl's brilliant blue eyes were glittering with laughter and his voice, loud and jovial, boomed out before his feet touched the earth. He waved a gnarled hand to indicate a stretcher party behind him.

'Ambushed, by God! At Blore Heath!' His squires ran to steady him as he rocked to the ground. York hastened forward, anxiously.

'Ambushed? By whom?'

'Audley and Dudley! But Audley's dead and Dudley's our prisoner. Although' — and his elation vanished a little — 'they've got Thomas and John.'

York became aware of the absence of his nephews and looked his concern, but Salisbury only spluttered with laughter and wagged his grey head.

'They won't hurt them,' he said. 'They are too valuable as hostages.'

Cicely had appeared from the cluster of buildings at the northern end of the courtyard and came towards them, worried, yet still with that cool, remote air so characteristic of her, an air which always made her appear aloof and divorced from the mundane considerations of her fellow-creatures. Nevertheless, she was interested now.

'What happened?' she enquired.

'Ambushed!' Salisbury repeated, easing his feet one after the other. 'Near Market Drayton! I got the men into the shelter of some woods but they were fairly spoiling for a fight. They routed Dudley's troops, only Thomas and John pursued the enemy too far and got themselves captured.' His eyes clouded; then he shrugged philosophically and continued: 'We got away in the dark.' He grinned, his eyes snapping with amusement. 'What do you think? Some goddam friar appears out of nowhere and offers to fire off the cannon to cover our retreat. Of course I agreed and to judge by the sound of it, he was going at it most of the night. Giving them hell!' Salisbury shook from head to foot with gusts of laughter. Richard and George stared at him in wonder.

Becoming conscious of his nephews' scrutiny, Salisbury swooped towards them, poking his face into theirs, staring at each intently.

'So these are the young ones, are they? This one' — he stabbed at George with a stubby forefinger — 'is like the rest of them, but this one . . . ' He straightened abruptly. 'He looks too damn puny to be one of yours.'

Cicely was an indifferent mother, but criticism of any of her brood aroused all her maternal instincts. Her eyes sparkled dangerously.

Salisbury, oblivious of his sister's anger, continued blithely: 'Skinny little devil! Sallow, too! What he needs — '

'Richard!' The word dropped into their midst like a stone.

Immediately, husband, brother and son, all answering to the common name, glanced towards her, but Cicely was glaring at her brother. Little Richard watched, fascinated, as the colour surged up under Salisbury's fair skin. It was reassuring to know that his uncle stood as much in awe of his mother as did everyone else.

'Yes, well . . .' grunted the Earl. 'I daresay he'll live.'

'He will probably outlive you, my dear uncle,' said another voice and Salisbury wheeled round to confront his eldest nephew, who was looking coldly down at him from his already considerable height.

Edward, Earl of March, was seventeen years old and although over six feet, had not yet finished growing. He was generally acknowledged to be an extraordinarily handsome young man, genial, lazy, with sensual eyes and a full-lipped mouth. But under this easy-going exterior, hardly apparent as yet, ran a vein of stubbornness as hard as diamonds. He was angry now because of his uncle's thoughtless remarks about this youngest brother of his, of whom he had grown so fond during the three months he had known him. This thin, under-sized boy had won for himself a place in Edward's affections which no other person, man, woman or child, would ever rival.

Salisbury shifted uncomfortably, suddenly finding himself an object of disapproval.

'Pooh! I suppose he will! Probably as strong as an ox, eh, young fellow?' and he gave his blustering laugh. 'Warwick not here yet?' he enquired, changing the subject. Then, as York shook his head: 'Daresay he'll be here very shortly,' Salisbury predicted.

He was right. Warwick and his Calais men rode into Ludlow a day or so later and, like Salisbury, brought with them some wounded, injured in a skirmish near Coleshill with the Duke of Somerset's troops.

'Somerset is out for my blood,' Warwick said grimly as he greeted his father and uncle. 'He still holds me personally responsible for his father's death at St. Albans.' He passed his hand across his forehead. 'It was a near thing! God's Bowels, it was a near thing! If we hadn't had such good horses we should never have done it.'

But this mood of despondency, alien to an ebullient nature like Warwick's, could not last, especially in view of the tumultuous reception he had received on every stage of his journey. It now being four o'clock in the afternoon, and therefore suppertime, he spent the meal in regaling his relatives with details of his triumphal progress across the southern counties; to the great delight of his younger listeners and to the annoyance of his uncle, who wanted to discuss the fortifications to be erected in the Teme valley, and to the irritation of his father, who wanted to tell of

31

his exploit at Blore Heath.

Cicely watched them with a faint smile on her face and said nothing, except to admonish Margaret and George for giggling and Richard for gobbling his food. But while she listened to the loud, confident male voices around her, she wondered uneasily whether it would be as simple as it all sounded, and how this second armed clash with Margaret and Henry would really end.

She raised her mazer of ale to drink and stared absently at the table immediately below her own. After a moment, she was aware of being watched and, focusing her vision, found herself looking into a dark, swarthy face, topped with a thatch of curling black hair. The man was wearing scarlet livery and the badge of the Bear and Ragged Staff, so she touched her nephew, lightly on the arm.

'Who is that man?' she asked and Warwick followed the direction of her eyes.

'That? Why, that's Andrew Trollope, my Captain of Archers and one of the most famous men to come out of the wars in France.'

'And is he reliable?' Cicely enquired, causing Warwick to throw back his head and laugh.

'Reliable? I'd trust him with my life!'

Andrew Trollope, from his vantage point on a small knoll of ground, watched the erection of an earthwork across the Teme valley and the Leominster road.

An unusually fine October day was making his men sweat and grunt with fatigue as they shovelled the warm, dry earth into a steadily rising embankment. After a while, Trollope disappeared behind some bushes, ostensibly to relieve himself, but in reality to re-read a letter which he had received some weeks earlier.

He withdrew it now from the inside of a rather unsavoury shirt, for he was not a man of cleanly habits. He was loud in his support of those doctors who argued that bathing made men more susceptible to the plague; he sympathised with merchants who were imprisoned for allowing their apprentices to go verminous to bed; and he had never been known, when in London, to take advantage of either of the public wash-houses, provided by that city, for its men. The only occasion on which he had been induced to enter the water had been in Bruges, but that, after all, was different. No man in his right mind would visit the Burgundian capital without calling at the famous — or infamous — Waterhalle, where a man and woman could bathe together, naked, and where, provided the woman was masked and did not reveal her identity, they could spend the night together with the blessing of the state.

A fleeting memory of that time lifted Trollope's face into a lascivious grin before he spread the crumpled paper on his lap and carefully read the message which he knew almost by heart. The letter was from Somerset, urging Andrew to return to his rightful allegiance and not to bear arms against the King.

A breeze sprang up and little clouds came chasing across the sky in an ever-changing vista of shapes and the grasses rippled in patterns of silver and green. Trollope, however, saw neither and sat hunched over his knees, his face creased into a frown, until a sudden movement by his side made him start quickly to his feet, crushing the paper in his big hand. But it was only John Blount who, after a quick, conspiratorial glance behind him, motioned Andrew to resume his seat on the ground.

'What news?' Trollope muttered and Blount answered in an equally subdued voice: 'The Queen has reached Worcester with the King, and she has offered a general pardon to anyone who will go over to her side.'

It was what Andrew had expected. He stared abstractedly before him, his lips pursed; then he said: 'Sound out the men — carefully, you understand — find out how many of them would come with us if we were to go.'

Blount nodded obediently. 'You think we should stay loyal to the King?'

Trollope shot him a sidelong glance, then grunted his assent. It was an explanation which would do for Blount, although there was far more to it than that. Andrew was more devious than most people, seeing only the blunt, rough soldier, gave him credit for being. He was tired of living in exile in Calais; he wanted to come home; to live with honour and prosperity on the winning side. As far as he could see, the coming conflict could well end in stalemate, with the Yorkist lords sat snugly behind their defences in Ludlow castle, while the royal party camped outside until another unsatisfactory compromise had been reached . . . and no guarantee that he would not be back in Calais within three months.

But now he was being offered a free pardon and in return, he, Andrew Trollope, could decisively alter events to suit himself. If, he reasoned, he and most of his men — the bulk of Warwick's troops, in fact — defected to the King, then it would not only drastically deplete the Yorkist garrison, but ensure its defeat. For who knew better than Warwick's captain all the secrets of the Ludlow defences? Under his direction it could be taken in an hour.

'Less,' he muttered as he heaved himself to his feet. With Blount he began walking towards the castle, still keeping its impregnable watch over the little town below.

★ ★ ★

Edmund, Earl of Rutland, crouched on his haunches by the fire and spread his hands to the blaze. The soft, warm breeze of three days before had changed to a north-easterly wind, bringing with it the sharp, dank smell of early autumn. Edmund, in spite of his weight and height, felt the cold intensely and was glad that here, in Ludlow, they still had the old open hearth in the middle of the room. He felt certain that the new-fangled wall fireplaces which, his mother had told him, were becoming all the rage in London, could never give him the same comfort.

The smoke, which eddied and billowed in a hundred small draughts, made him splutter and cough, but as many people believed it was good for the health and contained medicinal properties beneficial for rheumatism and sore throats, it failed to worry Edmund. Not that he suffered as yet from rheumatism, but it ran in the family. His cousin, Warwick's wife, was prone to it, while his eldest sister, Anne, was a martyr to cramps and colds.

Edmund had never seen either of his two elder sisters, Anne and Elizabeth, but it never occurred to him to think it strange. It was the custom for children to be sent away from home at a certain age to be brought up in the households of other families. (Foreigners thought the custom barbarous. 'Typical of the English,' they said.) Edmund's sisters had been no exception to the rule and Anne, who was now twenty years old, had been married since the age of eight to the Duke of Exeter. But, thought Edmund, if his father had hoped to wean Henry Holland from his allegiance to the House of Lancaster by this alliance, he had been doomed to disappointment. Exeter was rumoured to be with the royal troops who, even now, were camped at the other end of the Teme gorge. They had appeared earlier that afternoon and were the reason why York, Warwick and Salisbury were huddled in conference at the far end of the room and why Edward was out, inspecting the defences.

Edmund was angry. He should have been allowed to accompany his brother and had it been left solely to his father, Edmund knew that he would have been permitted to do so. He glanced under his heavy lids to where York was sitting; a short, stocky man with a moustache that drooped across the corners of his mouth, giving him a somewhat sullen expression. Edmund knew that he was his father's favourite and had often wondered why. Another boy might have taken advantage of the fact, but the young Earl was too lazy and too guileless to profit from a situation out of which his younger brother, George, would have made immediate capital.

There was a flurry in the doorway. Edmund looked up to see Edward, wind-blown and dishevelled, with a look of fear and incredulity on his face. For a moment he stood silhouetted against the flickering torchlight in the passage behind him; then he plunged forward, the swirl of his cloak causing a cloud of smoke from the fire.

'Trollope and his men! They're gone!' He seized his father and cousin by the shoulders, shouting a little as they stared uncomprehendingly. 'They've gone, I tell you! Deserted to the Queen!'

'Impossible!' Warwick exclaimed and laughed, but his laugh broke uncertainly in the middle.

York had started to his feet. 'They know all our defences,' he began, but got no further. If confirmation of his son's words was needed, it came with the sound of distant screams and cannon-fire. Cicely entered, her three youngest children behind her, her eyes alarmed and questioning. York turned towards her.

'Trollope has deserted to the Queen. He knows our plans and our defences.'

Few words were needed for Cicely to grasp the urgency of any situation. She had lived all her life in an atmosphere of treachery, precipitate flight and sudden death. It was she who voiced the words which York was loth to speak.

'You must leave the children and me behind. You will travel lighter if you travel alone.' She saw the reluctance in his face turn to relief and smiled enigmatically. 'Don't worry. Henry won't allow harm to come to women and children, not if they are his own kith and kin. What will happen in the town . . . that is another story.' Her smile this time was grim. 'Where will you go?' she added, almost as an afterthought.

'He will come to Calais with us.' Warwick answered for him, but York shook his head.

'It will be better to split up. If I can make it in safety, I shall go to Ireland. Edmund can come with me.'

'Edmund?' Cicely's tone was sharp, but her husband had already moved away, shouting for his squires. After a pause, Cicely said to her nephew: 'Will you take Edward with you, Richard?' and Warwick nodded his head.

They were ready to leave within the hour. As Edward embraced his mother, he noticed his sister and two small brothers huddled together, shaking with fright. He knelt and pulled George to him.

'You are the man now. Look after our mother and sister and Diccon. They are in your charge.' It was a moment's handling of George such as he was never to achieve again. As he left the hall, he looked back and saw that George had stopped trembling and was standing with his arms about Margaret and Richard.

Behind Edward's head, the night sky was already turning red with the glow of fire.

★ ★ ★

Cicely stood in Ludlow market-place, her three children by her side. The smell of

40

burning and charred flesh was all around them and the roofless houses echoed with the cries of the dying. Margaret and Richard had both been sick at the sights they had seen, but George, like his mother, was furious. Cicely, however, felt something else besides anger; shame that these people who had looked to the castle for protection had been abandoned to their fate. It went against her Neville nature to blame either her husband or her brother and she therefore transferred their guilt to the woman who now rode towards her through the market-place.

Margaret of Anjou, at the head of her troops, was flanked on one side by her husband and on the other by her son, a strong, well-built child of six years, with the long nose and heavy, pouting underlip of his uncle, the Duke of Calabria. There was little of his father in him and, as she forced her own children to their knees, Cicely wondered if there were any truth in the stories that he was the son of Wiltshire or the late Duke of Suffolk.

'Your Grace,' Cicely said, addressing herself directly to Henry. 'I throw my children and myself on Your Grace's mercy.'

'Yes! Yes, of course!' Henry stared vacantly before him. He forced his mind to concentrate on things around him and tried hard not to let it wander off, as it had a habit of doing, into some grey, remote world of its own. He was thirty-eight years of age, but appeared older. Looking at him, it was difficult to believe that he was the son of the militant Harry of Monmouth; grandson of the powerful Bolingbroke; great-grandson of the magnificent Gaunt; or cousin to the wily Dauphin of France.

'Yes, indeed, we must be merciful.' Margaret's voice sounded cold, but triumphant. 'Especially as our cousin of York has no man to protect her. These Nevilles' — she half-turned in her saddle, so that the men behind her could hear more clearly — 'know their own worth. They know that they must save themselves first and leave women and children to fend for themselves.'

There was a shout of laughter and Cicely's eyes burned under her lowered lids. George felt her tremble.

Suddenly, another voice, sharp and shrill, cut through the cold morning air. With the handle of his whip, the little Prince of Wales pointed at Richard.

'Who is that?'

Richard tried to speak, but fear choked the words in his throat. Cicely was forced to answer for him.

'And how old is he?'

Again Cicely replied for her son.

Edward of Lancaster gave a crow of laughter. 'He is a year older than I am. Why is he so small and weak?'

There was more laughter and George's anger became so intense that it felt like a hard, round lump in his chest.

'Swine!' The word, soft and sibilant, hissed between his lips, causing his mother to grip his arm in consternation. No one, fortunately, had heard him, because Henry was speaking, telling them in his slow, difficult way that they were to be put into the custody of the Duchess of Buckingham, one of Cicely's many sisters.

But as the royal party moved on its way, past the dead, eyeless houses, they left behind them an agony of hatred in the mind of one small boy. George Plantagenet would never forgive Margaret of Anjou and her son for the insults they had offered his family on this dreary October morning.

3

On a January afternoon in the year 1460, Sir Richard Woodville, Lord Rivers, rode into Sandwich accompanied by his wife and eldest son. The townspeople who crowded to watch, gained, however, an entirely different impression; namely, that the two men and their army of servants were in attendance upon the lady. This was hardly surprising as Lord Rivers' wife, whilst being a devoted mate and doting mother, never allowed any member of her family to forget that she had been born Jacquetta of Luxembourg; was a descendant of Charlemagne; had married Henry the fifth's brother, John, Duke of Bedford; and was aunt-by-marriage to the King.

Jacquetta had been no great age when, in 1433, she had been chosen by the Regent of France to become his second wife. Her pride and her ambition had been gratified, but her heart, understandably, had remained untouched. Bedford, worn out and exhausted after years of unrewarding struggle to hold his brother's French possessions intact, and dedicated to the memory of his first wife, the pious, childless Anne of Burgundy, had been an unsuitable husband for a young and ardent girl, anxious to love and be loved. Her roving eye had soon alighted upon the very personable form of one of her husband's gentlemen, Sir Richard Woodville, and her affections, once touched, had remained surprisingly stable in one so young and volatile.

Bedford's death in 1435, while it proved an irremediable loss for England, had been an event of unalloyed happiness for his widow, who, as soon as she had compounded for the offence of marrying so far beneath her, had settled down to produce for her Richard what she had been unable to produce for her John; a large and healthy family of five sons and eight daughters. Her late husband's nephew, King Henry, had been persuaded to accept the marriage and had made Sir Richard Woodville a baron, granting him the title of Lord Rivers.

This unlikely union of twenty-four years standing had proved extremely happy, largely due to Rivers' unacknowledged conviction that he was obligated to his wife for marrying him and that he must, therefore, allow her all her own way. And if this attitude had made Jacquetta spoilt and overbearing, it was not a criticism ever levelled at her by her own children, who admired her passionately and were nearly all as arrogant and as sybaritic as herself. The exception to the rule was the eldest child, Anthony, now a man twenty-four years old, as ardently devoted to pleasure and the good things of life as any of his family, but in whom worldliness vied with austerity, sensuality with asceticism. He had inherited from some source other than his parents, a sense of humour and as he rode beside his mother's sumptuous litter, through the cobbled streets of Sandwich, he reflected with amusement how little they must present the appearance of a raiding party.

Nevertheless, this is what they were. Queen Margaret had sent Lord Rivers and his son to organise an attack on Calais and bring back — preferably in chains — the traitorous Earls of Warwick, Salisbury and March, who had been sitting snug and safe behind their stronghold's walls since they had escaped from Ludlow three months earlier. The Duke of York and his son, Edmund, had, in spite of many traps, reached Ireland — where they had received a rapturous welcome — and were, therefore, out of Margaret's reach, but she was determined to ensnare those whom she could. It was Rivers' job to commandeer such ships as he would need to transport himself and his men to Calais and, consequently, later that day, having seen his wife suitably bestowed in the town's largest inn, he and his son walked briskly along the quay-side.

The morning had been cold and as they had passed through the rimed and rutted by-ways of Kent, their horses' hooves had splintered each frozen puddle into a cobweb tracery of cracks. Now, perversely, there was a hint of spring in the air and the sky was tinged with the pale, cucumber-green, usually seen in April. Lord Rivers, looking at it, said gleefully: 'We shall have a fine night and a clear dawn. We should be up and away by five.'

Anthony regarded him thoughtfully. 'You're sure of that?' he asked.

It was Rivers' turn to stare at his son. 'You heard what the ship's Master said. A fine night and — '

'I didn't mean that.' Anthony paused, drawing his sable-lined cloak more firmly about him. For a moment or two he said nothing, apparently absorbed in watching a sailor climb the ship's rigging to direct the furling of a sail. Then he went on: 'Didn't it surprise you that the Captain was so obliging? Didn't you expect some difficulties in chartering a ship?'

'Obliging? Difficulties? What are you

47

talking about?' Rivers, genuinely puzzled, preceded his son off the wharf.

Anthony ran his hand along the rough stone surface of a wall, feeling the cold burn into his fingers. 'Your mission here can hardly be a secret,' he answered patiently. 'Your avowed intention is to capture Warwick on a charge of treason, which can only lead to one end. These people here in Sandwich love him; worship him. Yet you met with no opposition when you wanted to hire ships to fetch him from Calais.'

'Pooh!' Rivers exclaimed scornfully. 'You see shadows round every corner. That man was far more interested in the gold I had to offer him than in saving Warwick's life.'

It was on the tip of Anthony's tongue to warn his father not to judge others by himself, but he bit back the unfilial comment and followed Rivers into their inn. They found the Duchess in a peevish mood: she fancied an almond-fish soup and the fool of a landlord had no almonds. Anthony thought how like their mother was his sister, Elizabeth. How often had he seen Elizabeth's husband, Lord Grey, and her two little boys, Thomas and Richard, soothe her in just such a manner as he and his father were using now towards Jacquetta. There was no real vice in either mother or daughter, he reflected; they

48

were just two spoilt, self-centred beauties who should have been slapped instead of cajoled; bullied instead of placated.

At any other time, Anthony might have imparted his fears to the Duchess, for she was far more astute than her husband, but when his mother had been deprived of something she wanted, it absorbed all her attention until the matter had been remedied. Still uneasy, Anthony went to bed, but lay awake for a long time, listening to the faint lap of the water as it smacked gently against the harbour wall. Now and then would come the shrill blast of a trumpet and a man's voice announcing the direction of the wind. Tonight, because the weather was fine, each shout was followed by the muffled closing of doors, subdued whispers and the pad of feet on the cobbles as merchants made their way to their ships, to ensure that all was ready to sail on the first favourable tide. There was a moon and the reflection of the light on the water rippled over the walls of Anthony's room until he felt as though he were in an underwater cave, drifting . . . drifting . . .

He sat up, suddenly alert. As he struggled to clear a mind clouded by dreams, he tried to identify the noise which had awakened him. Had he heard a grunt, a thud or, more probably, both? There it was again; the sound

49

of a blow and a body falling to the ground. Anthony was out of bed, reaching for his sword, but those few seconds' deliberation had cost him his freedom. As he wrenched back the bed-curtains, a greasy arm, smelling of garlic and sweat, slid silently about his neck and he found himself held in a vice-like grip.

'Not so fast, my fine buck-o!' breathed a voice in his ear. 'The Earl of Warwick wants to see you.'

★ ★ ★

The Duchess groaned loudly. The ship into whose cabin she, her husband and son had been cramped throughout the day, was still riding at anchor in Calais harbour. It had been there for some hours and it was growing dark. From his position near the tiny window, Anthony had watched the busy comings and goings during the day, but now the great Tower of Rysbank which overlooked the quay-side, was turning slowly into a black, one-dimensional shape, silhouetted against an opaque, pewter-grey sky. A faint echo reached his straining ears as the city's massive gate was slammed shut, for no one, not even the King, himself, was allowed entry by land after dark. For half an hour after the curfew bell, silence reigned over the town and over the twenty or so square miles of territory, all that remained of the once vast English possessions in France.

The Duchess groaned again. Her husband patted her hands in a sustaining manner and glanced fretfully at his son. 'You seem to be taking this very calmly,' he said. 'Don't you care what dreadful things can happen to us? You might show concern for your mother, at least.'

Anthony turned his head. 'I don't think anything very dreadful will happen to any of us,' he answered. 'Humiliating, perhaps! But dreadful, no!'

'I'm glad to hear you speak so confidently,' snapped the Duchess. 'On what do you base your assumption?'

'Well, they have fed us and wined us' — Anthony nodded towards a pile of empty wooden dishes — 'and generally administered to our bodily comforts. They have — '

'They have also gone to great lengths to bring us here,' his mother interrupted, waspishly. For a moment, indignation triumphed over fear. She continued: 'And I have never been so mistreated in my life! Hauled from my bed and forced to dress with some greasy lout breathing heavily on the other side of the bed-curtains. Me! A descendant of Charlemagne!' A shout from the deck made her jump, recalling her to reality and her sense of outrage died. 'Are they going to kill us?' she asked, twisting her hands in her lap.

Anthony crossed to her side and took both her hands in his own. 'I don't think so,' he said, reassuringly. 'But if they do, they do. Death comes to everyone sooner or later and we must accept our destiny with fortitude.'

Rivers looked sharply at his son. He had noticed before in Anthony this tendency to fatalism, so at variance with the daily necessity of self-preservation. It came, Rivers thought irritably, from reading tracts by mystics like Richard Rolle and from the younger generation's predilection for such books as *The Cloud of Unknowing* and Walter Hilton's *The Scale of Perfection*. They had had better things to do in his young days than fill up their heads with such nonsense.

The cabin door banged open and a man, whom Rivers recognised as Sir John Wenlock, entered. Wenlock had fought for the King at St. Albans, but had been so won over by Warwick's charm of manner that, ever since, he had been that nobleman's closest friend and ardent admirer. He had come now to escort Lord Rivers and his son to Calais

52

market-place, where the three renegade Earls awaited them.

The square was a blaze of light. Nearly every man, woman and child in the city had pushed into the confined space and many had been provided with candles. (Later, Warwick's chandler calculated that this piece of extravagance had cost his master about sixty pounds, or the price of a year's supply of lighting.) Anthony, who had not yet found his land-legs, felt slightly sick. The smoke made his eyes weep and the flickering candle-flames bellied into pale, watery circles with scalloped, iridescent edges. The crowds were held in check by men-at-arms, carrying torches which illuminated faces full of dislike, even of hatred, for these representatives of the Queen.

The merchants of Calais had suffered for years at the hands of the government; had seen the court favourites and the Italians granted licences to deal in wool, previously the monopoly of the Calais staple; had had their ships plundered by the Channel pirates at the instigation of the magnates; and had suffered the retaliation when those same pirates had attacked foreign merchant vessels. Warwick had righted many of their wrongs; had trounced the hated foreigners; and so, like the men of Kent, the men of

53

Calais loved him for it. They would protect him with their own lives and were only too happy to demonstrate their loyalty to him and their detestation of his enemies.

Warwick stood on a small dais in the middle of the square and as the two Woodvilles were brought before him, he cleared his throat preparatory to making his carefully planned oration. But Salisbury could not wait for such niceties and, leaning forward, spat in Rivers' face.

'Son of a knave!' he yelled. 'Do you dare to come after us as traitors?' He gobbled with indignation, spitting out his words like a mouthful of plumstones. 'You and your son are the traitors! We are loyal servants of the King.'

There was a cheer from those standing near enough to hear, which was taken up by the people behind them and then by the people behind again, until wave after wave of sound rolled and echoed round the market-place. Warwick, exasperated, turned on his father and silenced him with an imperious gesture of his hand.

When order had been restored, he again cleared his throat and began.

'What right have you, Lord Rivers,' — he succeeded in making the title sound like an insult — 'to try to arrest any member of

54

my family as a traitor? What are you? What were you? I'll tell you! A common squire who made his fortune and his name by going to bed with his master's widow!'

A tide of colour surged into Rivers' unshaven cheeks and he started forward furiously. Anthony laid a restraining hand on his father's arm and whispered: 'Let it be! Don't play his game by letting yourself be baited.'

He glanced up to find the Earl of March steadily regarding him, a gleam of amusement, almost of approbation, in his eyes. But whatever appreciation Edward might secretly have felt for the prisoners' control, it did nothing to soften his own diatribe when it came to his turn to speak.

'My cousin is correct, Lord Rivers,' he said coldly, 'when he labels you a common squire. You are a nobody! A nithing!' The old Saxon word of scorn and contempt flashed out in derision. He continued, arrogantly: 'Every one of us here on this platform can claim kinship with the King. Like him, we are all descendants of the mighty Gaunt. For myself, I can claim descent from three of Edward the third's five sons.'

Warwick shot Edward a sudden, surprised look, not lost upon Anthony Woodville, who smiled inwardly. Until this moment, he had regarded Warwick as the leader of this group; March and Salisbury as his shadows. But that little flash of self-assertion which he had just witnessed, suggested an independence of spirit not immediately apparent in the young Earl. As Anthony and his father were led ignominiously away at Warwick's command, to serve a term of imprisonment in the fortress of Guisnes, he decided that Edward, Earl of March, was a man to watch in the future.

★ ★ ★

In the spring, Warwick sailed to Ireland to consult with York about their projected invasion of England. He found his uncle and cousin living like kings in the draughty halls of the faithful Irish chieftains. Indeed, York's whole attitude had become extremely royal and Warwick felt some concern.

'The sooner York and Edmund leave Ireland, the better it will be,' he confided to Edward and Salisbury on his return to Calais. 'York was talking of claiming his rights.'

While he had been away, his family circle had been enlarged by the arrival of his father's brother, Lord Fauconberg, a vigorous little man who had proved his worth to

Warwick and Salisbury on many previous occasions. Sitting astride a joint-stool, he looked up now to enquire: 'You don't think that this might be the answer?'

'No!' said his nephew, emphatically. 'I do not. Ruling the country through Henry is one thing. Trying to depose the son of Harry of Monmouth is another.'

Edward set his cup of wine down on the table and looked thoughtful. 'Don't you feel that the Agincourt legend has worn a little thin? My father is, after all, the rightful king and people are tired of misgovernment.'

'No,' Warwick repeated. 'The people, however much they may dislike Margaret, are fond of Henry for his own, as well as his father's sake. They would never follow York.'

He sounded sincere; he looked sincere; but, deep in his heart, he knew that there was another reason for his determination to prevent York from claiming the throne. Hardly acknowledged, even to himself, was the feeling that he, Richard Neville, was more fitted to rule England than any of his kinsmen. But Warwick was orthodox; not for him the action of a Bolingbroke; the setting-up of a parvenu dynasty. He could no more put the House of Neville on the throne than he could fly. Nevertheless, the idea of ruling by proxy had long ago taken root in Warwick's mind, but he had sense enough to know that such a contingency was unlikely if his uncle York obtained the crown. He stood a far better chance of putting his talents to the test if he secured the person of the King. Whosoever had possession of Henry, was virtual master of the realm.

There was, of course, another possibility. He looked across at Edward who was sharing a bawdy joke with Fauconberg. If anything should ever happen to York, then, Warwick felt, would be the time to forward the pretensions of his uncle's House. He could never manage York, but he had no doubt whatever that he could control York's indolent, easy-going son.

If Edward were the King, Warwick could be the true ruler of the country; he would govern while Edward played. His cousin's little display of independence in the market-place, along with many other similar instances, had faded from Warwick's mind. He was an uncomplicated man, who accepted people at their face-value. First impressions were everything to Warwick and then, because he could never admit that his judgement might be at fault, he failed to revise his opinions until it was too late. He had one great interest in life, himself, and was unsubtle enough to assume that other people found the subject of Richard Neville equally fascinating.

Wenlock came into the room. 'Did you have trouble on the voyage?' he enquired and Warwick crowed with laughter.

'Exeter tried to intercept me at Dartmouth, but his sailors mutinied rather than attack me and he had to put back into port.'

'My precious brother-in-law will be spoiling for your head,' Edward grinned. 'The sooner we come to grips with Margaret and all her party, the better.'

'Well, there is no need for delay,' Warwick answered. 'Everything is ready here and your father is only waiting for a favourable tide.'

Three weeks later, in the worst June weather in living memory, Warwick, his father, his cousin and his uncle Fauconberg knelt before Becket's tomb in Canterbury Cathedral to ask God's blessing on their enterprise. They had been received in Kent as saviours and their army was augmented daily with new and eager recruits. All that was needed now, was spiritual approval of their mission.

In the evening light, the saint's tomb gleamed with hundreds of precious stones, so thickly encrusted that the solid gold in which they were set was well-nigh invisible.

Above the tomb hung Becket's hair-shirt and, to the left, was a small spring which had been seen to run with milk and blood. In the crypt, behind it, was housed one of the swords which had killed Thomas; also, the nails and right arm of St. George and some of the Holy Thorns. In the choir, adorned with yet more jewels and large, creamy pearls, stood a picture of the Virgin, which — so the story ran — had talked with the saint when he was alive.

As he rose from his knees and turned to leave, Edward threw a last look over his shoulder. The enormous ruby, the Regale of France, given by King Louis the seventh, glowed like liquid fire and the candle-light struck blue sparks from sapphires and diamonds. He could not know that within eighty years — the span of a man's life — it would all be gone, the Regale adorning the hand of his grandson.

4

Warwick and his army had spent the night encamped on Blackheath while the Londoners debated whether or not to give them right of entry. Lord Scales and the court party had naturally urged the Mayor to keep the gates shut, but the citizens had always been pro-Warwick in temper and it had needed little pressure from the Earl's brother, George Neville, Bishop of Exeter, for them to grant admission to the Yorkist host.

'Thank God,' muttered Edward to Fauconberg. 'I was beginning to feel like Jack Cade.'

A little man with bright, darting eyes and restless hands, slewed himself round on his horse. This was the Apostolic Legate, Francesco Coppini, who had accompanied Warwick from Calais and represented the official papal blessing on the enterprise.

This recognition by the Pope was a feather in the caps of the Yorkist lords and the result of two differing political ambitions running together for a while on a parallel course. Coppini was diplomat first, Bishop second, and worked hard for his master, the Duke of Milan. The Sforzas' present ally, King Ferrand of Naples, was being challenged for his kingdom by the House of Anjou, the latter being aided and abetted by their liege-lord, Charles the seventh of France. Sforza and Ferrand, therefore, wished for an English invasion of France to divert the French from their purpose. It was one of Coppini's many tasks to bring this about and, finding Margaret and Henry, not unaccountably, averse to his proposition, he had persuaded Pope Pius the second that Warwick and York were the two men most likely to bring peace to the war-torn realm of England.

Pius the second, born Aeneas Sylvius Piccolomini, and occupier of St. Peter's chair for the past two years, was a man of crusading spirit; a man to whom the doing was more invigorating than the achievement. The father of several illegitimate children, he openly admitted that in his search for the carnal pleasures of life, he had loved a great many women, but had grown tired of them as soon as he had won them.

Since becoming Pope, his burning ambition had been to lead a crusade against the Turks, who had captured Constantinople in 1453. For this, however, he needed the whole-hearted support of the princes of Christendom and little had so far been forth-coming. It was up to Pius, therefore, to bully or cajole his spiritual vassals into backing him. When considering the problem of England, His Holiness realised that nothing was to be hoped for from that quarter until the country's internal disputes had been settled. And so, when Coppini had assured him that the Duke of York and the Earl of Warwick were the men most likely to bring peace and prosperity to the kingdom, he had armed the effervescent little Italian with full authority to promote the Yorkist cause. Coppini had hurried to Calais and had been just in time to embark with Warwick, Salisbury and Edward for their invasion of England.

Everything about England fascinated him. He had been overwhelmed by the glory of Becket's tomb; thought the island's inhabitants the best dressed and best fed he had seen anywhere in Europe; was amazed at their continual grumbling and dissatisfaction; had been enchanted by the cherry and apple, plum and pear orchards of Kent; and was alert now to every sight, smell and sound of the London streets. Edward's reference to the rebellion made him say now: 'Who is this Jack Cade?'

As they started across London bridge, Edward pointed to the badly mended holes in the road. 'This is some of Cade's handiwork,' he answered. 'He was a Kentish rebel and his biggest battle was fought on this bridge. He and his men captured London ten years ago.'

'The revolt of your peasants, that, too, began with the men of Kent,' Coppini said, pleased to be able to air his knowledge. 'Why are these Kentishmen so . . . so . . . ' His English eluded him and he spread his hands in a frustrated gesture.

Edward considered the matter, not out of any particular deference for the Legate, but because he found it useful to know what motivated his countrymen.

'Perhaps,' he said, after a pause, 'it is on account of the fact that, in Kent, there is a system which we call gavelkind: that is, a man may leave his property equally divided amongst all his sons. This makes every man a landowner of sorts. Also, there is no villeinage in that county. To say a man is a Kentishman is to say that he is free. Probably this makes him more independent and intractable to authority than his fellows.'

Coppini hooted. 'All Englishmen I've ever met are like that,' he said. 'It's what makes them such a thorn in the flesh of the Holy See. Every Englishman must think and doubt for himself.'

Edward smiled. 'Is that such a bad thing?' he asked. 'Abelard said that to doubt is to seek, to seek is to find.'

'Oh, as to Abelard — !' Coppini rolled expressive eyes. 'He's just the man to appeal to a lustful nation like the English.'

'The ravishing Eloise,' murmured Fauconberg.

Salisbury gave his great roar of laughter and said: 'The ravished Eloise,' whereupon even Coppini grinned.

'You see!' The Italian shrugged his shoulders. 'You find everything a joke. But too much doubt and independence of thought can lead to a nation of heretics; to innumerable little sects, each believing that his way of worship is the only way.' He looked again at Edward. 'Your great-great-grandfather, King Edward the third, did not burn Wycliffe. Who knows what consequences that may one day have?'

Before Edward could reply, an enormous crowd of people rushed on to the bridge to bid their hero welcome. Warwick smiled and waved, but Coppini became frightened as he was pushed and jostled against the walls of the houses and the sound of the swiftly rushing water, pouring through the nineteen arches of the bridge, sounded ominously in his ears. He crossed himself and sent up frantic prayers until, finally, they got safely to the other side, but the crossing had not been without its casualties. At least two knights had fallen, brought down by the uneven surface of the road, and now lay crushed by the mob. Death, however, was too common an occurrence for anyone to waste his time on the unfortunate victims and the bodies were left for the bridge's two wardens to dispose of.

Warwick took up his quarters at the Greyfriars' House where, over dinner, his brother, George, a glib, rather self-satisfied, young man, made his family conversant with all that had been happening before their arrival.

'Scales has had word,' he informed them, 'that the King has raised his standard near Northampton. Exeter, Somerset and Buckingham are already with him and others are joining him fast. No time should be lost in engaging him in battle.'

Warwick flushed a little at this unsolicited advice, but he was fonder of George than of his other brothers, recognising in him a kindred spirit of ambition, so he let the matter pass, merely remarking: 'It will be more prudent if we first take an oath of allegiance to King Henry. The people must be satisfied as to our motives.' Then, seeing his brother's face fall, he added: 'But the first contingents of foot-men can be ready to leave at dawn.'

George's eyes sparkled with the anticipation of action, but Salisbury had other things on his mind. 'Where are Thomas and John?' he demanded, as he noisily drank his brawn soup, a concoction swimming with pine-cones, almonds and cloves.

'In the Tower,' George replied, nibbling delicately at a fish tart, then spitting it out on the rushes. 'That eel is bad!' he exclaimed wrathfully. 'Those water-bailiffs aren't doing their job properly!'

It was the business of the water-bailiffs to search all the eel-ships at Marlowe's Quay every morning and throw back into the water any fish which were not up to standard.

'God's Nails!' thundered Salisbury. 'Don't be so goddam finicky. A nice fop I've raised in you. What's going on at the Tower?'

'Scales and the court party have retreated inside and are holding it for the King.' George eyed his father with contempt, but Salisbury was impervious to the opinions, spoken or conveyed, of any of his sons.

'Then I'm just the man to root them out,' he snorted and Warwick confirmed this opinion.

'And so you shall, Father. You and

Wenlock and Cobham can stay and win us the Tower.'

That afternoon, at St. Paul's, Warwick, Edward, Salisbury and Fauconberg swore on the Cross of Canterbury to uphold their sovereign's cause and reaffirmed their loyalty. It was only for the country's good that they wished to bring Henry under their control and the sole reason why the streets now echoed to the sound of soldiers' feet as they marched northwards to do battle with the King.

★ ★ ★

It was the wettest July anyone could remember, although Coppini confided, with a droll look, to one of his companions: 'Always when I have come to England it is raining. And always it is the worst weather that the English have ever known.'

Nevertheless, it was extremely wet and the little Legate, following in the rear of Warwick's army, wished himself on more than one occasion, back in Italy. Certainly, it rained there, but clear, sweet rain, not this murky drizzle which hung like a pall over the countryside, blurring the outline of tree and hedge and turning the roads into a sea of mud.

But whatever else was dampened, Coppini's spirits most definitely were not. As they approached Northampton, he zestfully proclaimed absolution for the Yorkists and threatened with ex-communication all their enemies. Nor did he approve of the Earl's determination to parley with the opposing side. On this point, however, the Earl was adamant and sent as his envoys a deputation of clergy. His choice of chief emissary was the Bishop of Salisbury and this, as Edward pointed out, was a mistake.

'Have you forgotten,' the young man asked, gently, 'that the Bishop was with Henry at Ludlow, last year? Our uncle Buckingham will give him very short shrift. You know how he dislikes turncoats.'

Warwick rounded on his cousin, furious at having his authority put in question. The tent shook with the sound of his anger. 'The Bishop's interests are for the King, as should be Buckingham's. We may well settle this whole matter peaceably.'

Edward shot him an incredulous and somewhat speculative glance, then shrugged his shoulders and said no more. He was slowly reaching the conclusion that Warwick was a very emotional man, fond of the theatrical gesture, the dramatic word. Such histrionic posturing, the young Earl reflected, was all very well, provided that it was part of a scheme; but to indulge in it for its own sake led to the sort of situation from which there was no turning back, as Warwick was now demonstrating. His ultimatum that he would see the King at two o'clock or die in the attempt, left no alternative but to fight when Henry, through Buckingham, rudely spurned his offers of peace.

The royal army was drawn up with the town of Northampton at its back, behind an embankment and ditch, which had been filled by diverting the swollen waters of the Nene. Unfortunately for Buckingham, the unceasing rain which had caused the river to rise, had also flooded his trench and the guns which should have wrought such havoc among his enemies, as they advanced across the intervening fields, were water-logged and useless.

Warwick's army was divided into three, himself commanding the centre, Fauconberg on the left and Edward on the right, opposing Lord Grey of Ruthyn. As the trumpets sounded, the Yorkists moved slowly forward, the heavy steel-plating of the lords proving far more cumbersome on that rain-soaked ground than the leather jackets and light leg-armour of the archers and men-at-arms. With an unnecessary warning to their soldiers to beware the spikes hidden below the waters of the ditch, Edward, Warwick and Fauconberg plunged into the muddy depths and began their assault upon the embankment.

The advance of Warwick and his uncle was halted in a shower of arrows and flying earth, but Edward met with no such opposition. Rather, he and all his company were assisted across the embankment by the eager and friendly hands of Lord Grey of Ruthyn and his men, who had decided, for reasons best known to themselves, to make a last-minute change of sides. ('Undoubtedly the fear of ex-communication,' Coppini confided later to a friend, not yet fully aware of the average Englishman's blighting indifference to threats of papal displeasure.)

Once across the embankment, there was nothing to stop Edward from falling on Buckingham's centre flank and, from that moment, the result of the battle was a foregone conclusion. The fleeing soldiers of the royal army were trapped by the river and the water turned rapidly from dark earth-brown to a dull brick-red as blood mingled with the mud and slime and seeped across the lush pastureland that bordered the Nene. At one point it was possible to walk from one river-bank to the other over a bridge of corpses, so thickly piled were the slaughtered and the drowned.

In half an hour or less, it was over. Buckingham was killed defending the King's tent. One, Sir William Lucy, who had rushed out of Northampton to help his sovereign, lay dead for another reason, hacked to pieces by his wife's lover, John Stafford, who, because of Lucy's loyalty to the King, had always supported the Yorkist faction and, by chance, had been present at this battle today.

Inside the royal tent, Henry sat, cowering in a corner, jumping at every shout and wincing visibly at the continuous clashing of steel upon steel. Margaret was in Coventry with their son and without her astringent presence, the King's courage failed him utterly. In his hands he ceaselessly caressed a pathetic memento of his childhood, a small wooden block on which his name had been carved in raised, reversed letters. He could remember the simple pleasure it had given him when a boy, to rub it in the ink and then press it on to parchment; to see his name appear without the laborious effort of writing it, himself.

His mind was clearer today, like a room swept clean of cobwebs. He had known when he awoke that morning that it would be so, lying on his narrow bed in the hilltop convent of St. Mary de Pratis and listening to the sweet, prodigal beauty of the birds' song at dawn. Presently, their shrill chorus had been augmented and enriched by the joyous, limpid voices of the nuns at early Mass, until that, too, had died away, leaving only a deep, welling silence that had made Henry shiver with happiness and catch the breath in his throat. Only to one of the King's monkish temperament, who had been forced to live out his life in the endless clatter of the English court; to one who had been its very hub, the object of every over-weening ambition and the focal point of a struggle for power ever since he was nine months old; only to such a man could the splendour of silence mean so much. Today, too, he was able to remember things; things like his coronation in Notre Dame Cathedral, the only English king so far to be crowned King of France; the burning of the witch, Joan, in Rouen market-place; and how, last Easter, he had given away his best — his only! — gown to the Abbot of St. Albans as part of his Maundy money and his Treasurer had had to buy it back for fifty marks.

The last recollection made him give one of his sudden, disconcerting whinnies of laughter, but now there was no one to be startled by it. Everyone had gone out to join in the fighting . . . Fighting! There had been bloodshed for as long as he could remember and always over him. Over him! — he, who so hated violence that he could not bear the quartering of traitors and wished no man 'to suffer such a thing for my sake.'

It had all started, he thought, sadly, with the death of his uncle, Bedford, in France and the resultant disintegration of his father's French empire. First, his remaining uncle, Humphrey of Gloucester, had fought his great-half-uncle, Cardinal Beaufort, and then, somehow, although he was never quite certain why, the long years of enmity between his wife and his cousin, York, had flared into open warfare. The Yorkist lords had been triumphant at St. Albans five years ago and now they were victorious again. Today, he could reason and he knew that this must be so, for here, crowding into his tent, came Warwick and his father and another man whom Henry suddenly remembered as Fauconberg, Salisbury's brother, and that immensely tall young cousin of his, Edward, Earl of March.

They were kneeling to him, kissing his hand, using him with every respect, but he knew that he was really their prisoner. He wanted his wife and son, but these lords were saying that he must accompany them to London and he knew that he had no

74

choice. In any case, he could not resist; his mind had begun to darken yet again; a faint aura of unreality shrouded everyone and everything within the tent. Submissively he rose, putting his hand on the arm of a man whose face was already growing unfamiliar, and allowed himself to be led outside.

★ ★ ★

The old house in Southwark had once belonged to Sir John Fastolfe, but that veteran of the French wars had died ten months earlier, leaving, in a last-minute, nuncupative will, the bulk of his property to his friend, John Paston. This had already led to litigation on the part of the Duke of Norfolk, who hotly contested such a disposal of the Fastolfe estates and the years ahead were to be fraught with much action, both legal and violent.

On this warm September afternoon, however, nothing noisier was to be heard — in the Southwark house, at least — than the laughter of children at play. John Paston was from home, but he had let his house for an indefinite period to the Duchess of York, who had arrived in state only the day before yesterday, bringing with her a small army of servants and her three youngest children,

Margaret, Richard and George.

It was three months since, with the news of Northampton ringing in her ears, she had quit the protective custody of her newly-widowed sister, the Duchess of Buckingham, that lady's bitter recriminations falling on her deaf and indifferent ears. For a while, Cicely had lingered in the west, expecting, like her eldest son, nephew and brother, to hear at any moment of York's arrival from Ireland. But as the weeks had drifted by with no sign of her husband and Edmund, she had decided to remove to London. Here, at any rate, she was at the centre of things and was in immediate receipt of any news which might arrive for Edward, Salisbury or Warwick.

The three Earls had been much occupied in the month or so since their July victory. Salisbury had won the Tower, releasing his two sons and inadvertently bringing about the murder of the escaping Lord Scales by a gang of London youths. Warwick and Edward had returned with Henry to the capital and set up a new government, secure in the knowledge that Margaret was no danger for a while.

She had fled with her son to Wales, but rumour and spies alike reported that before she had finally won through to the safety of

Harlech Castle and the protection of Henry's half-brother, Jasper Tudor, she had been set upon by thieves and robbed of everything she possessed.

The Yorkist leaders rejoiced and made another pilgrimage to Canterbury, taking with them an excited Coppini, delighted by Warwick's renewed promises of an invasion of France and hints that Pius might be prevailed upon to grant him a cardinal's hat. Warwick also crossed briefly to Calais to release, in person, his Woodville prisoners — he was not above gloating a little as he gave them the news of the King's defeat — and to patch up a truce with the Duke of Somerset, who had escaped to France.

At the beginning of August, another event made Warwick's apparent mastery of the realm even more secure. James the second of Scotland moved to besiege Roxburgh Castle, the much disputed frontier fortress which his father had failed to win back twenty-three years before. Just as it seemed that he might achieve his object, thus embarrassing the new English government, he was accidentally killed by one of his own cannon. His death left Scotland, for the second time in thirty years, with a boy king and at the mercy of all the rivalries and factions attendant upon a minority reign. Warwick's and Edward's rejoicing helped to allay their uneasiness over York's delayed arrival.

Neither man was perhaps as worried about this as he appeared to be on the surface. Beneath their protestations of concern was a feeling that all was running smoothly and that York's disturbing presence might only act as an irritant. Nevertheless, they could not ignore the fact that it was Richard Plantagenet whom the people wanted, or turn deaf ears to the ballad-mongers and their songs.

'Send home, Lord Jesus, most benign,
Send home Thy True Blood to his proper
    vein,
Richard, Duke of York, Thy servant Job,
    forbye.'

This particular ballad, sung in a harsh, throaty voice, carried clearly above the hundred noises of the Southwark streets this warm September afternoon and caused Edward to smile wryly.

'We do the work, while my father gets likened to Job,' he remarked disgustedly to his friend, William Hastings, as they turned into the Pastons' house and came to a halt in the courtyard.

Immediately there were shouts of 'Edward!

Edward!' as Richard and George came headlong out of the house to greet him. Margaret followed at a more decorous pace, but was as rough and eager as her brothers in her search of Edward's pockets.

'What have you brought us?' asked the single-minded and practical George, while Richard, now a thin child of eight, stood wrapt in adoration. Edward laughed as he stooped to pull the child into his arms.

'That's my George,' he said, patting the elder boy's head in ironic affection. 'You'll never want for the asking.' But he produced the presents, a tiny doll for his sister and sweets for his brothers, and was delighted at the pleasure they provoked. He jerked his head towards a corner of the yard and demanded: 'Whose is the horse?'

Before any of the children could answer, however, his mother came out of the house, waving a letter.

'From your father! At last! He has landed and is at Chester. He will send me word as soon as possible where to meet him.'

The summons came sooner than expected. When Edward arrived for his daily visit the following Tuesday, he found the Pastons' courtyard graced by a coach covered in blue velvet and upholstered in mulberry, the livery colours of York. Four pairs of horses snorted and stamped while the second and third carriages were piled high with luggage belonging to the Duchess. Ostlers, grooms and outriders mingled with men-at-arms and Cicely stood, directing operations. As her eldest son knelt dutifully to receive her blessing, she kissed him abstractedly on the crown of his head and said: 'Hereford!' Leaving him to make his own deductions from this cryptic utterance, she stepped into her coach and was gone in a whirl of plunging horses and shouting servants.

Edward looked after her thoughtfully. What, he wondered, did his father have in mind?

5

When the Duke of York finally arrived in London on the morning of Friday, October the tenth, he left no one in any doubt as to his intentions. Not only was his sword borne upright before him, but among the many banners and pennons fluttering overhead were some bearing the full arms of England. York had come to claim the crown at last.

The streets were crowded with people waiting for their hero, but the ecstatic cheers which greeted the advance guard of trumpeters and clarion players died away on a sigh as the forest of pennons came into view. At first, in the swirl of early morning mist, the crowds thought themselves mistaken. They identified unerringly the Yorkist badges of the White Rose and the Fetterlock; they hesitated to identify with any certainty the Lions of England, for that could mean only one thing.

And it was not for him to seize the throne that the people had prayed so hard and so long for the Duke's return. As they dispersed, pushing their way through the mountains of filth outside the houses and the piles of

81

offal outside the butchers' shops; as they cursed the pigs and dodged the goats which, legally, had no business to be within the city limits; as they shouted to each other above the constant pealing of the bells, ringing for the hours of the day, summoning people to meetings, warning them of the opening of the municipal courts and sounding a requiem for the dead; and as they jostled their way into the ale-houses, the citizens were puzzled and disturbed.

York, meanwhile, had made his way to Westminster, where Parliament had been sitting since the previous Tuesday, called by Warwick and presided over by the new Chancellor, George Neville. Indeed, it was for news of a parliamentary session that York had been waiting throughout his cross-country ride from Chester, for during his year of exile, he had had time to do much thinking. And the conciliatory, often adoring attitude of the Irish chieftains had influenced him more than a little.

'You,' the young Earl of Desmond had told him, 'are the only Englishman who has ruled this land with justice and mercy. You gave us a stability and peace that we had not formerly known. How much more you could do for your own country! Why,' he added, turning to Edmund, 'does your father not claim what is rightfully his and replace this ineffectual Henry?'

Edmund's placid features had lit with an unwonted fire and, thereafter, he and York had spent long hours discussing what they should do.

Since the Ludlow disaster, York had become increasingly aware of the invidiousness of his position. For years, he had been prepared to accept the fact that the Lancastrian dynasty was established; the Mortimer inheritance lost. He had been content to have it so, but his resolution not to press his claim of primogeniture had been severely weakened by a train of events which had started with the death of Henry the fifth, when York was twelve years old.

Had Henry the sixth grown up to be as strong a man as his forbears, all would have been well, but his naturally gentle nature, allied to the madness of his maternal grandfather, had left him subject to the domination of stronger minds than his own. And since the death of Cardinal Beaufort, the most powerful influence in his life had been that of his Queen.

Margaret of Anjou was a Frenchwoman through and through. She had settled in a foreign country but never become indigenous to it; where she was, there also was a little piece of France. She found the English barbaric and uncouth; a rough, troublesome people who never seemed to do as they were told. The magnates were no better and because, above all else, she was a dynast, she had early singled out York as her most dangerous foe. As long as she had remained childless, he had presented no particular threat. But when, after eight years of marriage, she had at last given birth to a son, York had immediately become the object of her bitterest hate.

It would have taken a more obtuse man than the Duke not to realise that for this situation there was no remedy. For years, he had struggled to preserve his place in the government, often his very life, without recourse to the most potent weapon in his armoury. When friends had urged him to assert his regal claims, he had refused. The House of Lancaster had sat on the English throne since 1399 and time had given possession an aura of legality. Now, however, things had changed: York was an attainted rebel with a price on his head. Only the victory of Northampton permitted his return, but Margaret was still at large and it needed merely a swing of the pendulum to bring her back to power. What were his prospects then? At best, they offered more fighting; at worst, exile or ignominious death. Gradually, the certainty had grown in him that his only safety lay in seizing what had always been lawfully his.

He must, however, make his claim before the assembled lords, both spiritual and temporal, of the realm and what better opportunity would present itself than a parliamentary session? With this possibility in mind, he had lingered over his journey, sending Cicely on ahead to apprise him the moment that such an event took place — with the result that he was able to make his entrance into London three days after Parliament was convened.

The lords, warned of York's approach, but not the manner of it, waited for his arrival. Edward, Salisbury and the Archbishop of Canterbury stood out from the throng, uneasily aware of the absence of Warwick, who had elected to deal with some urgent business at his lodgings. In actual fact, anger and pride had prevented his appearance in Parliament on this particular autumn morning; anger because his uncle had delayed his coming until all the hard work had been done, then descended on London like some conquering hero; pride because he hoped to convey to York by his absence, that he considered himself no longer the Duke's subordinate, but his equal.

Unfortunately for Warwick's intentions, such subtle nuances were completely lost upon York, who had other, more important things in mind and did not even notice that his nephew was not present. As he made his appearance in the crowded hall, his eyes went straight to the throne. It was empty. Henry, as he had hoped and prayed, was not there. Deaf to the welcoming speeches of his friends, his gaze fixed like a man in a dream, he shouldered his way through the press until he reached the canopied chair on its dais. For a second he hesitated, but in that moment all noise died away, leaving a silence which was almost tangible. Every man in the hall held his breath. Then, deliberately, York reached out his hand and gripped the arm of the throne, turning slowly to face his fellow peers, who stood as though turned to stone.

After what seemed an age, Thomas Bourchier cleared his throat and stepped forward. 'The King is in his apartments, Your Grace,' he said quietly. 'Do you wish to see him?'

The question only served to exacerbate York's already inflamed temper. Could the fools really not see what he was trying to do?

'No, I do not!' he shouted. 'In fact, I know of no one in the whole kingdom who could not more fitly come to see me than I go to see him.'

Yelling to his servants to follow, he strode from the hall through the long corridors where the draughts eddied the rushes about his feet and wafted the smells of the kitchens about his nose, to the royal apartments. The King's servants, hearing the tramp of mailed feet, had already put up the bars, but York was now beside himself with frustration and fury. He sent for an axe and when it arrived, ordered one of his men to break down the doors.

★ ★ ★

Warwick's black, gilded barge sped along the Thames like a great, angry swan. The swiftness of its pace imperilled the progress of lesser craft which swarmed on the river this warm Friday afternoon. Watermen shouted abuse; crane-operators paused in their work of unloading vessels moored at the wharves; and people along the banks stared sombrely at the ensign of the Bear and Ragged Staff. There was going to be trouble, of that they were sure, for if they had already heard of York's actions in Parliament that morning, how much more certain that Warwick had done so.

Warwick had indeed heard the news, brought to him by no less a personage than the Archbishop of Canterbury. He had proceeded to set the Greyfriars' House by the ears, first demanding that Thomas Bourchier should act as his intermediary with York; then, when that prelate had indignantly refused — 'I am no messenger-boy, my lord!' — called for his barge and, supported by his brothers, Thomas and John, set off for Westminster, himself.

Fear informed his actions as much as anger. If his uncle's claim were accepted, all Warwick's plans for ruling the country by proxy must be relegated to the realm of dreams. He took comfort from the Archbishop's assurance that York's actions had alienated such small support as he had had. But that the Duke had come prepared to uphold his claim by force if necessary, became apparent to Warwick as soon as he stepped ashore at Westminster. The murrey, blue and white of the Yorkist livery was everywhere; the Fetterlock and White Rose embroidered on every tunic — or so it seemed to the Earl's jaundiced eye as he was conducted to the royal apartments, where his uncle was now firmly ensconced.

York was leaning against a sideboard and, to judge by the laughter of his companions, was in a jovial mood. Edmund of Rutland was lounging on the floor, idly plaiting the rushes under his hand, while Fauconberg and Coppini were seated at a table. In the far corner, propped against the wall and a little divorced from the proceedings, stood Edward, a slight smile the sole indication that he had heard his father's quip.

The laughter died and heads were turned as the three Neville brothers made their entrance. For a moment York regarded them with a faint hauteur, then he held out his hand, saying: 'Now we only need Salisbury and your brother, George, to complete the gathering of the clan.'

Warwick ignored the hand and York withdrew it, flushing angrily.

'My father,' Warwick said, 'has gone to the Pastons' house in Southwark. He hopes to persuade my aunt to use her influence with you.'

'God's Bowels!' York began, furiously, then stopped, shrugging. 'He'll get no support from Cicely,' he said with a laugh. 'What's the matter with him? Doesn't he fancy his sister as Queen of England?'

'No! Neither he nor anyone else! I warned you, uncle, in Ireland, that this couldn't be. The people will not accept you.'

York eyed his nephew. 'The people, or the Earl of Warwick?' he enquired and it was Warwick's turn to blush.

Edmund looked up. 'My dear cousin, don't be so angry,' he begged. 'You know very well that the crown is rightly my father's. And he is determined to have it, whatever anyone else might say.'

Edward, realising that his brother's words sounded far more offensive than the mild-mannered Edmund could possibly have intended, intervened with: 'Be quiet, brother. Mind your own business and everything will be all right.'

'It is his business,' snapped York, rounding on his eldest son in a flurry of temper. 'Edmund, at least, knows where his loyalties lie.'

'Gentlemen!' Coppini rose, anxious to pour oil on troubled waters. He turned to Warwick. 'My lord,' he said, 'surely you cannot deny that His Grace, here, could provide this country with a stronger rule than King Henry's. And what a fine family of sons he has to come after him! The succession would be amply assured. Whereas the Prince of Wales — '

'If he is the Prince of Wales,' Fauconberg put in, with a grin, 'and not the son of Suffolk or Wiltshire.'

'Or even the Holy Ghost, as Henry, himself, suggested when he first saw him,' Thomas Neville added with a spurt of convivial laughter, earning for himself a look of pained surprise from his eldest brother.

'We have not come here to bandy jokes,' Warwick said nastily, causing Thomas and John to exchange a grimace of comic dismay. Warwick glared at York, longing to list his many grievances concerning his uncle's conduct. But common sense prevailed. He could do no good by an open breach with the Duke: he could do irreparable harm. A split in the Yorkist ranks would benefit no one but their enemies.

Biting his lip, he turned aside and took Edward's arm. 'I intend calling a conference of the lords at the Blackfriars' tomorrow morning. I rely on you to persuade your father to come. It is for the good of us all.' He pressed his cousin's hand significantly.

Edward nodded and sighed. He could think of pleasanter tasks than cajoling a recalcitrant parent into acting against his will. Last night, he had become deliciously aware of a new arrival at court; the curvaceous Eleanor Butler, daughter of old Talbot of Shrewsbury, and recently widowed. He would rather have expended his powers of persuasion on her. Edward sighed again. Life was very hard!

★ ★ ★

The next three weeks were ones which Warwick hoped never to live through again. He needed every ounce of diplomacy and self-restraint he could muster and to a man of his explosive temperament this came very hard indeed.

When York, in spite of his eldest son's considerable powers of persuasion, failed to appear at the Blackfriars' House the following day, a number of citizens and clergy were sent to Westminster to add their entreaties to those of Edward. They returned in haste to inform a horrified Warwick that York was holding a Royal Council, actually enthroned in regal splendour. His only answer to their representations had been that he intended to be crowned on the following Monday. Salisbury arrived hot-foot from Southwark, where he had again been visiting his sister, with Cicely's confirmation of this news and the meeting at the Blackfriars' broke up in disorder.

Warwick's next move was to get the magnates to draw up a list of their objections to York's claim. Two days later, as he rested after the rigours of the day in his lodgings, in the company of Salisbury and Edward, he received a not unexpected call from his uncle. York stormed into the room and slapped a paper down on the table.

'Do you really expect me to take this seriously?' he shouted. He thumped with his fist, making the leather wine bottle fall on its side. 'The first two items alone are enough to make an honest man spit!'

Warwick eyed his uncle uneasily. He was aware that the lords, unwilling to betray Henry, but, at the same time, reluctant to offend a man who might yet set himself up as their future king, had made a poor job of their objections. He opened his mouth to speak, but York silenced him with a wave of his hand.

'Listen to this! Item: I bear the arms of Edmund of Langley and not those of Lionel of Clarence. Of course I do! I bear the arms of my paternal grandfather. My claim to the throne is on my mother's side.'

'That doesn't stop you — ' Salisbury began, but York rounded on him in a fury.

'I know that! I'm not a fool! But each one of you knows that it was never my design to claim the throne until circumstances drove me to it.' Giving them no time to reply, he went on angrily: 'Item: That Richard the second was a usurper and Henry the fourth the rightful king because of his descent from Edmund Crouchback. God's Belly! That old story!'

Edward hooted with laughter and strolled over to his father's side, reading over his shoulder. Then he glanced at Warwick, who shifted uncomfortably in his chair. 'You must admit, my dear cousin,' he said gently, 'that this is an extraordinarily stupid objection. No one pretended to believe it when Bolingbroke was alive, let alone when he was dead.'

A rare gleam of approval shot into York's eyes and he was moved to pat his son on the arm. 'Quite right, Edward, and so I shall say. As for the rest, concerning the oaths that I've taken, I'm willing to answer for them in an episcopal court and nowhere else.' He rolled up the paper and tucked it into his belt.

Warwick got up and faced his uncle across the table. 'I warn you,' he said fiercely, 'that if you take the crown now, you will have to do so by force. Your popularity with the people, particularly the Londoners, whose support is so vital to you, will vanish for ever. You cannot hold the throne unless the people are behind you and you know this.'

'Quite right,' put in Salisbury. 'I was saying to Cicely only the other day that the

English don't like usurpers. If you do seize the crown, then you must either have the whole-hearted approval of the people or be prepared to be as ruthless as a Bolingbroke. And somehow,' he added shrewdly, 'I don't think that you are.'

York made as though to reply, then hesitated. This sign of weakness was eagerly seized on by Warwick.

'I have a plan,' he said urgently. 'A plan to which I think Parliament will agree. It offers no offence to Henry and safeguards your position for the future. Trust me!'

York, suddenly beset by self-doubt, was forced to do so.

By the end of October everything was settled and Warwick was hailed by lords and commoners alike as saviour of the realm. His compromise solution that Henry should remain King during his lifetime, but disinherit his son and recognise York as his rightful heir, was accepted with relief by a nobility caught on the horns of a difficult dilemma. The Londoners, concerned only with the fact that the threat of open warfare had been averted, could not praise Warwick enough.

York and Edmund, however, were openly dissatisfied: it was not for this that they had returned with such high hopes from Ireland.

But on October the thirty-first, together with Edward, they swore to the settlement in Parliament and pledged their word to do nothing that would end Henry's life. York was plunged in gloom, but it was not in his nature to fly continually in the face of Providence. He was essentially a practical man, concerned with the realities of life and once he realised that his actions, far from getting the support he had expected, had estranged his well-wishers, both great and small, he bowed to the inevitable. The Duke's philosophy was that there was always tomorrow and Edward, although he could not like his father, watched and learned a valuable lesson.

'Swim with the tide,' York said succinctly to his two eldest sons as they prepared for the processional march to St. Paul's which was to set the final seal on their bargain. 'Sooner or later, you are bound to come ashore. Swim against it and you'll be drowned.'

Three months later, he and Edmund were to prove to their cost the truth of his words.

★ ★ ★

It was the thirtieth of December and the momentous year of 1460 was almost out. In another week, the Christmas truce between York and Queen Margaret would expire and the Duke, with Salisbury and their two sons, Edmund of Rutland and Sir Thomas Neville, would have to leave the castle of Sandal and push on northwards to do battle with the Lancastrians.

The agreement over the succession had not been accepted by the exiled enemy lords nor by the Queen. As soon as she heard the news, she and her son left Harlech and travelled by sea to Scotland where they became the honoured guests of the Dowager Queen of Scots, Mary of Guelders. Somerset came from France to join them and, by promising Mary the fortress of Berwick, Margaret was able to augment her Welsh and Yorkshire retainers with a sizeable force of Scots adventurers, gaol-birds and ruffians.

As this motley crew began to move south, Jasper Tudor, in accordance with his promise to his sister-in-law, started raiding along the Welsh border, thus leaving the London government in the position of being menaced on two sides at once. Eventually, it was decided that Edward should lead a contingent of troops into Wales, while his father dealt with the threat in the north. Warwick, meantime, would manage the country's affairs in London.

It was not really an arrangement that suited York, but he had no choice. More and more he felt that it was his nephew and not himself who was becoming the head of their party. The leadership which had once been naturally his, was slipping away. On all sides he heard men talk of 'Warwick's government'. At last, York was beginning to realise that his prolonged stay in Ireland had done him no good. More than that, his absence from the battle of Northampton had been most damaging of all. In the opinion of the people — and no English magnate, however proud, underestimated the worth of that opinion — a military victory meant more than any diplomatic coup. And so, while instinct prompted him to demand that he should be left in charge of the government, instead of Warwick, York, nevertheless, elected to lead the north-bound army. A resounding triumph, the proof that he was as great, if not greater a general than his nephew, would restore his popularity and his place in the hierarchy.

Edmund went with York. Cicely, left behind in London with her three smallest children, said nothing. She was astute enough to see that if the younger boy was constantly in his father's company, the less remarkable would the fact become.

The Duchess had often pondered the reason for her husband's marked preference for his second son. She acquitted him of believing the stories circulated at Edward's birth. In a restricted, gossip-ridden society such as theirs, few people were untouched by scandal, whether real or imaginary. No! It would just seem that her husband had his favourite child, even as she had hers; Edmund for York, George for herself.

Leaving London on December the ninth, York had reached Sandal, just outside Wakefield, by Christmas. Sending a messenger to arrange a cessation of hostilities with the advancing Lancastrians, he had settled down to enjoy the twelve days of festivities in the company of his son and also in that of Salisbury and Thomas Neville, who had decided, at the last minute, to go with him. If the truth were known, the Earl had been finding the overbearing attitude of his eldest son more than he could stomach, while George Neville, with his airs and graces, had never endeared himself to his father. John, as sober as his brothers were flamboyant, was hardly an entertaining companion and so it was Thomas whom Salisbury selected to accompany him.

They all sat now before a blazing fire in a small upper room of the castle. Both the older men were more content than they had been for months. The increasing distance between themselves and Warwick made York once more the master of his fate, Salisbury the head of his family.

'What time do you expect the foraging party back from Wakefield?' Salisbury enquired with a yawn. The hot, flickering light of the fire had made him pleasantly tired.

'By dark.' York stretched his toes to the warmth and smoothed his hair. Before his eyes lay vistas of burnt-orange caverns and sparkling blue fountains, but he was not the man to see fairyland in a fire. What little imagination he had, he inherited from his Castilian grandmother who had also bequeathed him a streak of her Latin temperament, oddly at variance with his normally phlegmatic personality. This conflict of two entirely different natures had led to a certain instability of character in the Duke, prompting him from time to time to acts of rashness. On this cold December day it was to do so again — for the last time!

A page scurried in, but before he could speak, the Captain of the Guard pushed past him.

'Your Grace! My lord! The Queen has broken the truce! We are surrounded.'

The two men stared at him for a moment, open-mouthed, then, with a crashing oath, York was on his feet and making for the tower stairway, Salisbury close on his heels. From the battlements they had a panoramic view of the surrounding countryside; to the north, Wakefield and the Calder Valley; to the south, the woods about Chevet lake; more forests to the west; and to the east, Nostell Priory set in thickly wooded groves. Nothing, in fact, could have been more favourable for an army wishing to approach unseen than this densely afforested land. Everywhere, men were appearing through the trees, the last rays of sun glinting on breastplate and spear as they moved like ghostly shadows in the gathering dusk.

Salisbury laughed. 'If they think to starve us out, they're wrong. We're well provisioned.'

York nodded. Then Thomas Neville pointed to the north where the foraging party could clearly be seen straggling down the Wakefield road. They were immediately engaged by a troop of Lancastrian horse and it was obvious, even before York left the battlements that his men had no hope against the unexpected attack.

'We must send to Warwick for relief,' Salisbury said as he panted after York down the narrow, twisting stairs. 'One man could

101

be smuggled out. We could last out till then.'

'No!' York descended to the main hall where he summoned his captains. He felt a surging excitement as he realised that now was his moment to prove his military prowess, both to himself and to Warwick. Caution and common sense went flying to the winds as he ordered his armour to be brought to him.

'You can't mean to go out and fight them,' Salisbury protested, but the Duke's sudden burst of enthusiasm had already infected his nephew and son, who were shouting wildly for their squires. Flinging his arm around the Earl's shoulders, York said: 'Think how impressed Warwick will be when he knows that we have turned the tide, here, at Wakefield.'

An answering gleam of madness shone in Salisbury's blue eyes. It would be good to show his son that they were not dependent upon him; to put him back, once and for all, in his proper and subordinate place.

Half an hour later, the drawbridge was lowered and the Sandal garrison issued forth to do battle with the enemy. In the van strode the Duke of York, his son, Edmund, his brother-in-law, Salisbury and his nephew, Thomas Neville.

102

6

Edward lay still and silent, looking at the moonlight which seeped through a crack in the roof of his tent. It was dazzling silver. Outside, he could hear the movements of his guards, their feet crunching on the ground. The earth was like iron on this icy January night and the cold penetrated deep into his bones in spite of the heavy fur rugs with which he was covered. But it was not merely the bitter weather that made him shiver: it was the news he had received from a sweat-soaked messenger as he had approached the walls of Shrewsbury late that same evening.

Disaster such as he had never foreseen, such as even now he could scarely contemplate, had overtaken his family. His father, his uncle, Salisbury, his cousin, Thomas, and, worst of all, the playmate of his youth, the companion of his adolescence, his brother, Edmund, were all dead — killed, executed or murdered. From the messenger's faltering lips he had learned of the broken truce; of that last, mad foray from Sandal Castle; had heard of his father's and his cousin's death in battle; of his uncle's execution by

103

the Bastard of Exeter; had listened in grim silence to an account of his brother's murder at the hands of Lord Clifford, whose father had been killed at St. Albans.

Edward watched the moonlight fade, to be replaced by a sliver of palest grey. He could not sleep. If he closed his eyes, he could see his brother fleeing from that scene of carnage towards Wakefield; saw him, impeded by his armour, lumbering across the bridge to reach the safety of the town. He saw Lord Clifford, lighter clad, mounted, catching up with Edmund and seizing him by the hair, that yellow hair, so like Edward's own. He saw the dagger poised; heard Edmund's scream for mercy die in his throat as the blade plunged in; saw the glazed eyes and the blood-drenched neck.

Edward threw off his furs and got up, swaying with misery and fatigue. His squire, roused by the movement, also started to his feet, but when his master waved him back to sleep, sank down again with a thankful sigh. The slit of sky turned from grey to coral and then to flame-red. A stormy day, thought Edward, the surface of his mind continuing to note those little things which made up the normal pattern of living, while the lower reaches of his consciousness registered a procession of hideous and bloody pictures.

His father's head had been torn from the Duke's body on the orders of the Queen and sent to York, where, set up over the Micklegate bar, it had been derisively encircled with a paper crown. Edward had never liked his father, largely because the Duke had never appeared to like him and because the young Earl was not one to waste his affections where they were so obviously unrequited. Nevertheless, Edward would never have wished his father such a death and the outrages perpetrated upon his dead body were an insult not only to the Duke, but to the whole House of York, of which Edward was now the head. And Edward mourned his father the more savagely because, at the back of his mind, there was a suspicion of relief; an inchoate feeling that life would be easier, freer, now that York was dead. He burned with a desire for revenge, the fiercer because he could not love and regret his father as he felt he should.

He heard the sound of a horse and went to the opening of his tent. A messenger was being helped to alight by two of his guards, while a third stood alert for any sign of treachery. But the man was genuine enough; one of Edward's own scouts whom he had sent in advance to look for a sign of the enemy.

'My lord!' The man knelt, his breast heaving from the swiftness of his ride and the biting wind, which made his throat and chest ache. 'Pembroke has been joined by the Earl of Wiltshire. They are on the march from Wales.'

The sky was streaked with a dark blood-red and Edward stared at it like a man possessed. He had intended to return to London after he had received the news of Wakefield, but here was his chance to strike at the Lancastrians and wreak his vengeance on them if he could. Jasper Tudor and James Butler should rue the day that their Queen had ordered the desecration of York's body.

As the sun rose above the hills, the whole firmament seemed to be aflame; red, pink and orange. Then it faded, leaving a leaden, overcast sky. A blustery wind sprang up out of the east, bringing with it squalls of rain and hail; miserable weather which pursued Edward's army during the next three days as it marched south into Herefordshire. Cold, hungry and tired, it seemed to the men that they would never track down their quarry. Only Edward's determination, fired by his lust for vengeance, kept them going as they staggered, footsore and weary, across the bleak winter landscape with its leafless trees, water-logged roads and black, frostbitten hedges.

At dawn on the third of February, however, a scout caught up with Edward at Leominster to report that he had sighted the Lancastrian army encamped on a common, a few miles to the north.

'This is a good omen,' the Earl told his troops as he prepared to lead them on the march that would intercept Jasper Tudor and his men. 'Pembroke and Wiltshire have spent the night near Mortimer's Cross. I am of the House of Mortimer and this undoubtedly augers well for our success in the battle which we shall fight today.'

He stepped down from the farmer's cart which he had been using as a makeshift platform and encountered William Hastings' mocking smile. Edward grinned in return and threw his arm about his friend's neck.

'You cynical bastard,' he said affectionately. 'You may not believe it, but the men will. And they will fight the better for it, you'll see.'

An hour later, as they approached the little Herefordshire town, it became apparent that Jasper Tudor's scouts had also done their work, for the Lancastrian army was drawn up in battle array. Jasper, himself, commanded the centre and not only did he display the cognisance of the Earl of Pembroke, but he stood beneath the Red Dragon standard which his father, Owen Tudor, had adopted in order to bolster his claim that he was descended from Cadwallader. As he deployed his own men, Edward's eyes kept returning to that offending banner.

Who were these Tudors that they should set themselves up as lords of the realm and claim descent from the ancient princes of Wales? What had Owen Tudor been before he had caught the fancy of Henry the fifth's widow, Queen Catherine?

'A Clerk of the Wardrobe,' Edward hissed savagely to Hastings, who stared at him in surprise. Oblivious to the fact that he had not spoken his earlier thoughts aloud, Edward continued: 'A Welsh adventurer! And when Catherine was dead, he had the audacity to say that he had married her.'

Hastings, who had divined Edward's line of thought, nodded in agreement. 'But they put him in prison,' he said.

'And let him escape! And finally pardoned him.' While he talked, the Earl's alert gaze watched his captains as they marshalled the archers into protective, wedge-shaped formations between the two wings and the centre of the army. 'And then, Henry must make two of his half-brothers the Earls of

Pembroke and Richmond.'

'Didn't Edmund Tudor marry your mother's cousin?' Hastings enquired, but absently. His eyes were riveted on the sky, where the sun had risen in its pale, wintry splendour.

Edward nodded. 'Five years ago. He died the following year, leaving her a widow at fourteen. There's a child. A son, I believe, called Henry.'

He stopped speaking, conscious suddenly that all eyes were turned towards the heavens. Lifting his own, he saw what appeared to be three suns in the sky. He stared, incredulous. Never before had he seen such a phenomenon, nor could he imagine what had caused it. One of his captains came galloping up in alarm. The men believed it to be an evil portent and refused to fight. Similar messages arrived from other parts of the field and Edward, had he not been so heavily armoured, could have stamped in frustration. But his wits, which were always to serve him well in a crisis, did not fail him now.

'Tell the men,' he instructed his commanders, 'that this is a good sign. The three suns represent the Trinity; Father, Son and Holy Ghost. It means that God is on our side.'

The scaffold had been erected in Hereford market-place. The crowds, who had come to watch the execution, were orderly and ominously silent. The Yorkist men-at-arms, fresh from their victory at Mortimer's Cross, had nothing to do but clear a path for the condemned man and to see that everything was carried out with speed and efficiency.

From the window of a house overlooking the square, Edward watched grimly. Beside him, William Hastings was uneasy.

'You mean to go through with this?' he ventured and encountered a look of blazing fury from Edward's blue eyes.

'Why not?' The voice was clipped; the manner distant. Hastings, unused to such treatment from his normally affectionate friend, was moved to anger himself.

'Because he is an old man,' he answered, curtly. After a second, he added: 'And he has done you no harm.'

'He's Jasper Tudor's father! The King's step-father — or so he claims! That's enough for me. Margaret and her followers shall regret Wakefield as long as they live.'

Hastings fell silent. This was an Edward he had not hitherto encountered; an Edward, indeed, whom few people, before today, had known existed. William realised with a shock that it would pay him to deal cautiously with his apparently easy-going young lord. Beneath the friendly exterior was a man of iron determination; a man who could, at times, revenge not only insults and violence, but his own inadequacies and frustrations upon anyone who happened to be at hand. Jasper Tudor was the man for whom Edward had really prepared the scaffold, but as both he and James Butler had escaped into the mountains of Wales, the Earl of March would send Pembroke's father to his death with no qualm of conscience whatever. He might regret it in the future, but he would not allow that possibility to weigh with him now.

As though reading his friend's thoughts, Edward laughed. 'There's only one member of my family with a conscience, my dear William, and that's young Diccon. And it will do him no good. A conscience weakens a man when he should be strong and makes him hesitate when he should be doing. At last! They are coming!'

There was a ripple of movement in the crowds and the muffled beating of drums. Hastings withdrew his gaze from his friend and directed it at the scaffold. He had learned a valuable lesson and he would never forget it in his dealings with Edward.

Owen Tudor, meantime, had reached the foot of the scaffold. He had not really believed that Edward, of whom he had heard nothing but good, but would carry out this act of retribution and even now, as he slowly mounted the steps, he half-expected a reprieve. He was an old man; in his sixties, which was a fair age. It was one of those ironies of fate that he should meet death on the scaffold now, for no other reason than that he was Jasper Tudor's father, having cheated the executioner all those years ago, when he had expected and been prepared to die by the axe.

After Queen Catherine's death, the discovery that she had been living, not in solitary state as her brothers-in-law had imagined, but with her Clerk of the Wardrobe and borne him several sons, had caused a terrible outcry. Owen had been imprisoned, every dawn expecting that that day would be his last. He had come to terms with death in those far-off times, but it had not claimed him. Henry had shown his mercy; set him free to live in honourable retirement and given titles to Owen's two eldest sons. (A third child, named after his father, was a monk at Westminster.)

Owen raised his eyes and looked at the window directly above him. He saw a fair, handsome young man, with clear, regular features and a hard, unsmiling mouth. There was no mercy there. This was, after all, the end. Owen made his confession to the priest, but had no idea what he said. The old doubts and difficulties were surging through him as they had done long ago. What was death like? Was it, as he had always been taught to believe, the beginning of a new life, like stepping into another room? Or was there nothing beyond the grave, only an eternal darkness; a snuffing-out as though one had never been? In a few minutes he would know — or not, as the case might be. And yet, even now, he could not credit it. He reflected that to himself, every man was immortal. Death was something that happened to others.

The executioner ripped off the collar of his red velvet doublet; that doublet which he had chosen to wear in a moment of bravado. He knew that he must speak to the people. They expected it and if he failed to do so, they would think that he was afraid. But he had nothing to say; the words stuck in his throat. Finally, he said quietly: 'Let this head which used to lie in Queen Catherine's lap now lie here on the block,' and moved forward in the straw.

I am alive, he thought, and yet I am dead. And then, as he knelt and laid his head on the block, he was comforted. I am dead, and yet I am alive.

The executioner raised his axe. The crowd

stopped its murmuring; every movement ceased. The silence was oppressive and Hastings started to sweat. The blade crashed down and the headsman held up the grizzled, bleeding head. Hastings was not a superstitious man, but for no good reason he shivered. It was as though someone had walked over his grave.

★ ★ ★

The news of Owen Tudor's execution and the victory at Mortimer's Cross was brought to Warwick in a London bordering almost upon panic. Queen Margaret and her host were moving inexorably southwards, spreading destruction in their wake. The stories of murder, rape and arson which were daily brought into the city by a flood of terrified refugees, alarmed the most sanguine and had it not been for the Londoners' confidence in Warwick, must have caused an evacuation that would have left the capital almost defenceless. As it was, a certain uneasiness prevailed at the Earl's lack of action and the feeling was rife that he should have made a move to meet and do battle with Margaret before she had left the midlands.

Warwick, himself, was conscious of this fact, but the news of Wakefield had left him temporarily stunned. His father's and brother's deaths he genuinely mourned and resented. His differences with Salisbury had been of the most superficial kind. The Nevilles never probed beneath the surface of their disagreements for causes other than the obvious ones and, in consequence, never became aware of their deeper feelings for one another.

York's death, however, had left Warwick with a problem which he had been unprepared to face, and his indecision was rooted in that. He was now virtually alone in his opposition to the Queen. Apart from Edward, who was only seventeen, and Norfolk, preoccupied with his feud with the Pastons, there was no magnate of any consequence prepared, at this juncture, to risk open warfare — and the size of an army usually depended upon the number of its commanders. (Each baron brought into the field those men who wore his livery and to whom he gave his protection and who, in return, gave him their support when needed.) Moreover, Warwick's resources were now severely strained. If he went to meet Margaret, whom could he leave in London to head the government and rule in Henry's stead? His brother, George, he trusted implicitly, but there was no one else, not even Thomas Bourchier. His other brother,

John, recently created Lord Montagu, was a capable soldier but a poor politician. If Edward failed in the west as his father had failed in the north, Warwick saw nothing for it but flight once again.

The tidings of Mortimer's Cross changed many things. It meant that Warwick could do battle without the fear of another army approaching on his flank; it fired him with the desire to emulate Edward's success; and, above all, it inspired in the Londoners an admiration for the new Duke of York which highlighted the conflict now going on in Warwick's mind. Last summer, in Calais, he had considered the alternative to ruling through Henry; an alternative dependent upon his uncle's death. And now York *was* dead. Was this, then, the moment to abandon Henry and proclaim his cousin King Edward the fourth? He discussed it with George, but the wily young Bishop preached caution.

'Defeat Margaret first,' he advised, 'then you can think about Edward.'

The need to confront the Queen had indeed become the paramount necessity. Warwick, like a man suddenly awakened from a dream, realised that unless she were stopped immediately, Margaret would soon fall upon London. And so, on February the twelfth, together with Norfolk and John, he left London with his troops, taking Henry with him. By nightfall, he found himself once more outside St. Albans.

★ ★ ★

Warwick fled westwards with the remnants of his army. St. Albans, once the scene of his greatest triumph, was now the place of his most humiliating defeat.

Everything had gone wrong. His scouts had failed to return, captured by the Queen; his outpost at Dunstable had been surprised and overwhelmed; his main army had been taken unawares before his men had finished making their extensive preparations for defence. The elaborate nature of those defences had also, in part, contributed to Warwick's downfall. Like other commanders, before and since, he had been so convinced of their impregnability that he had underestimated his enemies' powers of penetration.

He had had the ground strewn with spiked iron balls and nets full of nails, but these had not stopped the oncoming hordes of barbaric Scots and Welsh, drunk with success after their victory at Wakefield. Warwick's old enemy, Andrew Trollope, had caught his foot in one of the man-traps, but still managed to kill fifteen of his opponents — a fact to which he modestly admitted when Henry knighted him that same evening.

Henry, himself, had been taken with his Yorkist guards, Sir Thomas Kyrielle and Lord Bonvile, both of whom, in spite of the King's promises to the contrary, were beheaded after the battle. Sir Anthony Woodville, who witnessed the executions, turned away in horror. He was already sickened by the outrages perpetrated during the march south and his brother-in-law, Lord Grey, had just died in his arms, which meant that his sister, Elizabeth, was now a widow. He had expected to see John Neville, who had also been captured during the battle, join his fellow prisoners on the scaffold, but Montagu's life was saved by the fact that Somerset's brother was Warwick's prisoner in Calais. As he moved amongst the dead, Anthony stooped to examine one of the new-fangled Burgundian hand-guns with which Warwick had equipped his army and which had added to the confusion by back-firing on their users.

Warwick had also provided his archers with shields studded with nails, so that, as well as protecting their owners, they could be thrown down and used to impede the enemy. These had been a partial disaster by

118

falling, as often as not, harmless side up. No, reflected Warwick bitterly, the fates had been against him today. Nothing had gone right!

He rode through the February afternoon, wet and bedraggled, his mind a confusion of racing thoughts. Later, however, when the weather cleared for a while, bringing a foretaste of spring, Warwick's mind cleared with it. A small, purple cloud stood out, sharply defined against a wash of pale, turquoise-blue sky and, looking at it, the Earl came to a sudden decision. He had lost Henry, now reunited with his war-like Queen, but it no longer mattered. Warwick had always had an alternative and now was the moment to present a new king to a people alienated at last from Harry of Monmouth's son by the ravages of his wife. Margaret had finally gone too far and in every village and town through which he passed, Warwick met with a rapidly growing hostility to the Lancastrian cause. He sent messengers galloping ahead to meet the victorious Edward, advancing from Hereford, with instructions for his cousin to meet him at Chipping Norton.

The little cloud had almost passed from sight, trailing behind it long, wispy tendrils of the same smoky purple, the colour of ling at dusk. The turquoise faded; a bank of clouds away to the west caught the last rays of the sun in a halo of flame. Then twilight descended in a flurry of rain and a chill squall of wind. But in spite of the cold and the damp Warwick travelled through the night and the next morning rode into the little Cotswolds' town to find Edward already there.

In the parlour of the tiny inn the cousins embraced, then Warwick fell on his knees and kissed the younger man's hand.

'Your Grace!' he said. 'I here pledge fealty to England's rightful sovereign. God save King Edward the fourth!'

7

London was chaotic. The news of Warwick's defeat, completely unexpected as it was, caused pandemonium. The information that a party of Scots was already looting and burning beyond the walls in the vicinity of Holy Trinity Priory, convinced even the most confident that all was lost. It seemed merely a matter of time before the main Lancastrian army fell upon the city.

Mayor Lee, wakened by these tidings in the middle of the night, hastily donned some light armour and went out into the streets to rouse his fellow magistrates and to order the militia to man the walls. His servants, laying about them with fists and cudgels, were hard put to it to clear him a path through the stampeding crowds. Everyone who had sufficient money was making for the wharves to charter a ship and, in Thames street, the Mayor recognised a servant of Cicely's, who shouted to him above the clamour that the Duchess was sending her two youngest sons to Burgundy without delay. Lee nodded his head. A sensible precaution, he thought, for if London fell, Margaret would be unlikely to spare any males of the Yorkist line.

The stretch of road from the Tower to Billingsgate, that part of the city known as Petty Wales and notorious for its endless, day-time traffic jams, was, tonight, almost impassable. Ignoring the curfew, people had poured out of their houses, adding to the confusion of carts and carriages which, piled high with their owners' belongings, were making for the quay-side. Fighting his way along Fish street, past the 'King's Head' and 'The Bull', the Mayor came at last to the Steelyard, the home of the Hanse merchants, the 'Easterlings', whose duty it was to look after and, if necessary, defend Bishopsgate.

Inside the massive, fortress-like edifice calm prevailed, a fact which Mayor Lee attributed to the complete absence of women — then glanced furtively over his shoulder as though he expected his wife to materialise, summoned on wings of flame to avenge such heresy. He spoke briefly, but urgently, to the twelve Councillors and their leader, who ruled with a rod of iron this strictly all-male community. Having impressed upon them the need for the gate to be guarded by night and day, the Mayor went on to the Guildhall, a building started by one of his predecessors, Sir Richard Whittington, fifty years earlier.

The other aldermen and magistrates were already assembled and, almost without exception, willing to vote for the surrender of the city to the Queen in return for her promise that it should not be sacked. A delegation was immediately sent to Margaret, and the next day a deputation of Lancastrian lords was allowed inside the walls to start negotiations. It was not a situation, however, which anyone relished and Mayor Lee had little doubt that if Warwick were to suddenly appear, defeated as he was, the Londoners would rally to him to a man.

But Warwick had disappeared, no one knew where. Had he gone into hiding; fled to Calais; or, as some rumours had it, marched westwards to meet the new young Duke of York? George Neville, who had prudently taken refuge in Westminster sanctuary, was inclined to this latter theory and, in order to gain time, proposed to the Mayor that he should make it a proviso that Queen Margaret withdraw the bulk of her army to Dunstable. Lee adopted the suggestion, although he had small hope of the Queen acting upon it, but, to his amazement, she complied.

The relief in the city was so great that, by Friday morning, spirits were beginning to rise. And, in the afternoon, the Londoners' natural optimism so far reasserted itself as to embolden a gang of city youths, led by Sir John Wenlock's cook, to plunder the baggage-wagons being sent to Margaret at St. Albans. They ate the food, pocketed the money and boasted of it in every ale-house from the 'Paul's Head' in Crooked Lane to 'The Tabard' in Southwark, without anyone making a move to apprehend them. On the contrary, they were fêted and applauded wherever they went and it would have gone hard with any magistrate who had tried to do his duty.

On Saturday, while negotiations with Margaret were still in progress, another party of citizens made a sally beyond the walls and, by a stroke of the greatest good fortune, put to flight a band of Welsh and Scots who had been pillaging the Fleet Street shops. They returned to a hero's welcome and their fellow inhabitants insisted on ringing the triumphal bells; those three impressive monuments to the iron-founder's art, which hung in the stone tower at Westminster and which, normally, were only sounded for royal occasions.

The news, however, that these overt acts of hostility had resulted in Margaret breaking off negotiations, had a sobering effect and might have caused another wave of panic. But Monday morning brought the first of Warwick's messengers with the glorious tidings that he was marching to the defence of the city . . . in the company of the country's rightful King, Edward the fourth.

The information left the city both jubilant and stunned; jubilant that Warwick was coming to their rescue; stunned at the possibility of a usurping sovereign. Some of the very old men could remember back sixty-two years to the time when Henry of Bolingbroke had deposed his cousin, King Richard the second, and they shook their heads sadly. All the troubles of the past five decades could be traced to that event, they said, and they stared mournfully into their ale and prophesied further doom. But the majority of the Londoners, particularly the younger element and the merchants and, above all, their impressionable wives, were delighted with the idea once they grew accustomed to it. They were tired of their pious King, his gloomy court and his hell-cat of a wife.

Even so, they would never have abandoned Henry had it not been for this last, dreadful march of the Queen's. Stories of destruction, of killing, looting and burning still filtered into the city from every part of the country through which Margaret had passed with her troops. The kind of devastation which had been inflicted upon the land was of the sort usually reserved for some conquered foreign territory which had been abnormally stubborn in its resistance. The English were in a vicious mood, thirsting for vengeance.

And now Warwick, their hero, the man who, in the people's eyes, could do no wrong, was offering them their chance of revenge. If he had waited a lifetime, Warwick could have found no more propitious moment than this to present King Edward the fourth.

* * *

It was Sunday, March the first, 1461. In St. John's fields were assembled all the notables of London; Mayor Lee in his scarlet gown and chain of office; the aldermen; the Archbishop of Canterbury and several bishops; the Duke of Norfolk, glaring balefully at Sir John Paston; the lords Scrope and Fitzwalter; William Hastings chatting to Humphrey Neville; and every citizen who could get there, dressed in his Sunday best. Pie-men and pedlars were doing a roaring

126

trade, while the ballad-mongers were doing an equally good job of selling their two latest rhymes, written on grubby sheets of paper. In one corner, some of the younger, rougher members of the crowd had joined hands and were swaying in unison, chanting:

'He who has London forsaken
Will no more to our hearts be taken.'

That was one for Margaret and Henry, thought Warwick with satisfaction, as he supervised the proceedings at a distance. It was not his policy to be much in evidence today and Edward was staying in modest seclusion behind the solid stone walls of Baynard's Castle. It was vital that the people should feel that they had rejected Henry and chosen Edward themselves and if they needed the slightest prod in that direction, then the Chancellor, George Neville, was the very person to channel their thoughts in the proper way. He was ascending the hastily-erected platform now, his clever young face alight with enthusiasm. For this important occasion he had rejected his episcopal robes and selected a rich, velvet costume in black, white and grey; a combination of colours greatly favoured, so he had always been told, by Duke René of Anjou. In sartorial matters George had no prejudice and was perfectly willing to pay this tribute to the man who was Margaret's father. He held up one of his slender, white hands for silence. A huge sapphire glowed, drawing attention to the long fingers with their beautifully-kept nails.

'My friends,' he shouted, 'I am here today to put to you two most important questions. But first, let me remind you of one of those songs which you have been buying in such numbers this morning. 'Let us,' it says, 'walk in a new wineyard. Let us,' it says, 'make a new garden in this month of March with that fair white rose, the Earl of March'.

'If all of you here today elect that 'fair white rose' as your King — and he is your rightful King, make no mistake about that — if, as I say, you choose Edward for your sovereign lord, then, indeed, it shall be a walk in a new wineyard. On that I give you my word! This country of ours shall indeed be a new garden. On that I give you my word!

'Now, I come to those two questions which I mentioned earlier. First: do you want King Henry of the usurping House of Lancaster to continue to reign over you?'

There was a moment's silence; a moment when Warwick and his brother held their breath. Then a great shout arose of 'No! No! No!'

George Neville heaved a sigh of relief. 'Do you,' he asked, 'want King Edward of the rightful House of York to reign over you?'

This time, there was no hesitation. 'Yes! Yes! Yes!' the people shouted. Someone started to clap and in no time everyone was doing the same. A few of the rowdier apprentices, not content with that, pounded on the breast-plates of the men-at-arms, to the great annoyance and discomfort of the gentlemen concerned, but to the delight and amusement of crowds who were now in holiday humour.

A delegation of citizens was sent at once to inform Edward of the outcome of the meeting and, three days later, he was hailed as King at Westminster and took his seat on that throne which, six months before, his father had tried so vainly to claim. The faithful were rewarded. Fauconberg became a Royal Councillor; Wenlock was made Chief Butler; and George Neville, retained as Chancellor, was heaped with titles and honours.

'And what can I give you, Richard?' the new King enquired of Warwick, as they sat at ease in the royal apartments at Westminster, but the Earl shook his head.

'Nothing,' he said, simply. 'I am Warwick.'

Edward's fair brows lifted a little and he regarded his cousin from sleepy blue eyes. 'And you feel that no other honour could be greater than that.'

Warwick, oblivious to the faintly sarcastic note in the King's voice, inclined his head. The gesture, Edward reflected, was almost regal, but he said nothing. At present he needed Warwick. The day might come, however, when he did not.

'To business,' he said, smiling. 'The coronation must be soon, but not before we have beaten Margaret in battle.' Odd, he thought, how one always referred to Margaret in such matters, never to Henry. 'What are the latest reports?'

'She is withdrawing northwards,' Warwick answered, 'laying waste the country as she goes.' He leaned towards the King, tapping his knee significantly. 'This is the best opportunity we shall ever have to defeat her. The people will flock to us in droves. They will support us as never before.'

'I do so love the royal plural,' Edward murmured, rising to his feet. 'I do so feel that it becomes . . . us!'

To the flourish of trumpets, he passed into the room beyond, his bedchamber. Warwick was left standing irresolute. He was disconcerted, a little ill-at-ease, but he did not know why. He had an odd suspicion that he had just been put in his place — except that such an idea was utterly preposterous.

★ ★ ★

The heavy rains of February had flooded the river Aire, rotting the wooden bridge which had for years spanned it at the appropriately named location of Ferrybridge. The retreating Lancastrians, plundering their way across Yorkshire in the bitterly cold days of late March, had no difficulty in completing Nature's handiwork, tearing down the water-logged structure with their bare hands and so gaining a much needed breathing space from the pursuing Yorkist army.

Most of Margaret's troops were still bewildered and embittered by the withdrawal. London, the Promised Land, flowing with milk and honey, had been within their grasp, but, like Moses, they had been doomed to see it only from afar. They could not understand the Queen's decision to retreat when she had had the country's richest city apparently subdued.

Margaret, herself, was uncertain why she had decided to withdraw. After her victory at St. Albans she should have been filled with self-confidence, but she was not. She was conscious that the ravages committed by her barbarian horde had alienated people from her as never before; not only those who were her avowed enemies, but many of her own supporters. Lord Rivers and his son, Sir Anthony Woodville, were two of those who looked at her askance and she was aware, also, that her little son no longer exercised that charm which had once been among her most valuable assets.

Edward, Prince of Wales, had lived the seven short years of his life in his mother's warring shadow and, turning in contempt from her weak husband, Margaret had saddled him too early with the burden of being the family's man. Brought up to consider hatred a more worthy emotion than love, he was rapidly growing into an unhappy and belligerent boy. After St. Albans, the Queen had made the mistake of asking his advice on what should be done to the captive Lord Bonvile and Sir Thomas Kyrielle. His vehement demands, in spite of his father's feeble protests, that the two men should be beheaded had nauseated even Lord Clifford, Edmund's murderer. Too late, Margaret realised the damage she had caused by bringing Edward into the affair. Many men had rallied to her side because they saw in her vigorous little son a likeness to his grandfather, Henry the fifth. He might have been Monmouth Harry, himself, in his cold determination to have the two men's heads, but there were limits beyond which a child was not expected to step. By this act, the Queen had lessened, not strengthened, the loyalty of her supporters and, in some cases, she had shaken it loose once and for all.

She realised, too, that the Londoners did not like her. Although she would never admit that popularity with the common people was of the slightest importance, she knew, none the less, that the support of the capital city, controlling as it did two-thirds of the country's trade and wealth, was vital to her cause. Whatever her captains might urge, she must enter London peaceably or not at all. With a few more days' grace she could have achieved this object, but Warwick had recovered too fast. Coppini, writing to Francesco Sforza that 'affairs in England have had their ups and downs, but Lord Warwick has come off best in the end by making a new King out of York's eldest son,' summed up Margaret's feelings. It was ironic that the thing she had most dreaded during York's lifetime should finally have come to pass after his death, just when she had thought herself safe. She had seen the Duke as a contender for the crown but had not reckoned with his son. The news that Warwick had proclaimed his cousin King and that the people were already referring to King Edward the fourth, had cost Margaret her nerve. She remembered Mortimer's Cross and, in blind panic, ordered a retreat.

By the time she reached Yorkshire, however, the Queen had recovered her courage and leaving a detachment of troops, commanded by Lord Clifford, to destroy the bridge over the Aire, she and the rest of her host moved a few miles further north to strike camp and fortify the ground for battle.

Warwick, together with Lord Fitzwalter and the advance guard of the new King's army, arrived at Ferrybridge on Friday, the twenty-seventh of March. Huddled into their miniver-lined cloaks for protection against the icy wind, the two commanders gloomily surveyed the bridge.

'Margaret's work,' Warwick said bitterly. 'There's nothing for it but to build another. That bitch will be back in Scotland before we can catch her.'

He stared across the swollen river. Somewhere to the north the woman he so detested was eluding him, taking with her her prisoner, Lord Montagu. Once Margaret crossed the

Border, Warwick feared for his brother's life; although Somerset's brother should go straight to the block in Calais should anything happen to John. Fitzwalter was ordering the building of the temporary bridge. Neither man suspected that the Queen was preparing to fight: neither man saw one of Clifford's scouts as he wriggled clear of a clump of bushes, growing near the opposite bank.

By nightfall, a rough wooden structure had been erected across the Aire. Three men had been drowned, six others severely injured, but as far as Warwick was concerned, it was a small enough price to pay for tomorrow's renewed pursuit of the enemy. It irked him that he could not set out at once, but to get more than a minimum force across the bridge during the hours of darkness was to ask for trouble. He sent over a party of scouts, blissfully unaware that each man fell straight into the murdering hands of the waiting Lancastrians.

Warwick lay in his tent lazily contemplating the future. It was too cold to sleep, but he was not sorry. Gazing into the years ahead had lately become one of his favourite occupations. Life was at last opening up to him in a way totally impossible before York's death. He saw his self-appointed destiny within his reach; saw himself King

135

in everything but name; saw himself ordering the government of the realm while Edward indulged his endless capacity for pleasure. And there would be no fear now that the King would be wrested from his grasp; lost in a moment's ill-luck in battle. Moreover, King Edward, unlike King Henry, would be Warwick's devoted slave, bound to him for ever by ties of gratitude and affection.

The Earl's reverie was rudely interrupted by a muffled scream, followed by the clashing of swords. He lay still for a second, thinking it nothing but two of his men having a quarrel. But the noise increased, augmented by terrified shouts and the crash of steel upon steel. Lord Fitzwalter burst into Warwick's tent, his eyes frightened and staring.

'We are surrounded,' he shouted. 'The Queen's men are everywhere!'

Warwick leapt to his feet, yelling for his squire to bring him his armour.

'There's no time for that,' Fitzwalter said, his voice shaking. 'They are coming at us in their hundreds.'

'Impossible! And you know it!' snapped the Earl. 'If they are using our bridge, as they must be, they can only be coming at us in very small numbers.'

But even as he spoke, he knew what havoc and devastation could be caused by even the smallest number of men using the cover of night to fall upon a sleeping enemy. His troops, drowsy and totally unprepared for battle, would be overwhelmed in minutes. There was nothing for it but flight. He waved away his armour and ordered his horse to be saddled. Already drifts of smoke were curling through the opening of his tent and the smell of burning filled the air. As Warwick emerged, sword in hand, Fitzwalter's tent went up in a sheet of flame. It was as he had expected: his own men, although greatly superior in numbers, had been completely crushed. Rallying such troops as he was able, the Earl fled to rejoin Edward and the main Yorkist army.

The night was abnormally cold and a few flakes of snow swirled down from the heavens, but Warwick was unconscious of anything except a burning sense of shame and frustration. To have suffered two defeats was humiliating in the extreme. He pictured to himself Edward's face when he heard the news and in doing so, became aware for the first time of the slightly mocking smile that played about the King's mouth when he looked at his cousin. An unnerving thought came to Warwick. Was it conceivable that Edward, instead of being humbly grateful as he ought to be, felt some contempt for the man who had given him a crown?

Such disturbing reflections had their effect and made Warwick determined to re-establish his reputation in the eyes not just of Edward, but of everyone present. As he approached the King's encampment in the chill of a grey dawn, he sent his squires ahead to apprise Edward of his coming. As the King emerged, shivering, from his tent, his friends and captains joined him. The men, also, roused from far less comfortable quarters, crept from under hedges, out of ditches or from anywhere that afforded some shelter from the bitter weather.

Into their midst rode the Earl of Warwick. Leaping from his horse, he drew his sword and, before anyone could stop him, cut the unfortunate animal's throat. Then, holding the dripping blade, he advanced the hilt to within an inch of Edward's astonished face.

'By this Cross,' he shouted, 'I swear that I shall not fly another step.'

8

By ten o'clock on Saturday morning, the Yorkist forces were once more approaching Ferrybridge. Scouts reported that Warwick's temporary structure had been damaged, but not demolished, and that Lord Clifford was still keeping watch on the other side of the river. One of the scouts, more daring than the others, had managed to swim across and penetrate the enemy's defence post.

'It's my opinion, Your Grace,' he told Edward, 'that they have no idea Your Highness is so close. They think that they only have to deal with Lord Warwick and the advance party.'

Edward looked thoughtful, then sent more scouts to inspect the crossing at Castleford, three miles further up river. Their reports were favourable; it seemed that the floods had receded somewhat and the ford was no longer impassable. Turning to Fauconberg, Edward said: 'Uncle, I want you to take your men and cross with them there. A surprise flank attack might well rid us of Clifford and his troops and allow the bulk of our army to get over the river in safety.'

139

Before Fauconberg could reply, his other nephew pushed angrily forward.

'I shall go,' Warwick said. His face was suffused with a dull red. He had much to avenge; his honour, his defeat, his humiliation; but more than this, he resented the way in which Edward had assumed command. This was not what the Earl had envisaged when he had obtained the crown for his cousin. When Warwick was present, he presumed that Edward would still defer to him as he had done in the past.

Fauconberg glanced uncertainly from one to the other and Edward felt his temper rising. It was one of his chief attributes, however, that he could dissemble his feelings, so he merely raised his eyebrows. He disliked life to be made unpleasant by wrangling. He had long ago learned that there were easier and more comfortable methods of getting his own way than by open conflict.

To his uncle he said: 'That is my order . . . as King,' and he emphasised the last word. Then, turning to Warwick, he laid his hand affectionately on the Earl's arm.

'I understand how you feel cousin, but you are too valuable to me. I cannot risk losing you in an unimportant skirmish.'

Warwick was mollified at once. He did

not notice, would not have recognised even if he had done so, the conspiratorial smile that passed between Edward and William Hastings. His self-confidence soared as quickly as it had fallen and he began to see both the second battle of St. Albans and last night's affray as nothing more than the ill-luck that afflicted most commanders from time to time. As for Edward, it was natural that he should assert himself a little in the first flush of his newly-acquired sovereignty. When they had defeated Margaret and Henry and assured their overthrow, then he had no doubt that Edward would settle down to the sybaritic life, while he, Warwick, ruled the country.

Fauconberg, meanwhile, had mustered his followers and by midday reached Castleford. It was indeed as the scouts had said and the Aire had returned to its course. Patches of grey slime bordered the river and made it treacherous to heavily shod feet, but Fauconberg was, if not a brilliant, then a competent commander and had his men across in under an hour. It was bitterly cold still and an east wind whipped the wet clothes about the archers' shivering bodies, but the little Earl urged them on. He had the deaths of a brother, two nephews, and a brother-in-law to avenge and, furthermore, it was Lord Clifford who had murdered Edmund.

A messenger galloped towards them, his teeth chattering in spite of the sweat on his face.

'My lord!' He controlled his voice with an effort. 'Our plans are known! Lord Clifford is withdrawing.'

'Hell and damnation!' said Fauconberg, and let it go at that. He had no time to waste even in giving vent to his feelings and ordered the march to be speeded up, praying fervently that he might intercept his enemies before they got too far. His prayer was answered and within a short time, his advance forces reported Clifford and his men to be near Dintingdale. Fauconberg quickened the pace and his mounted troops fell upon the enemy flank a little before two o'clock.

The Lancastrians turned and fought bravely, but as the Yorkists had found to their cost some hours previously, the element of surprise was worth more than courage. Clifford had not thought himself to be so closely pursued, but, more than that, the realisation that it was Fauconberg and not Warwick who was his opponent unnerved him. This meant that the main Yorkist army had caught up with its advance guard and his one thought was that Margaret must be warned.

Turning to a messenger, Clifford tried to push up the visor of his helmet, only to discover that it had jammed. Furiously he tore at the buckle and straps which fastened his helmet to his breastplate, frantically motioning to his squire to do the same at the back. Finally it was loose and lifted from his head. For a brief second he stretched his neck to ease the soreness where the helmet had chafed it . . . and fell dead with an arrow in his throat.

The death of their leader demoralised the Lancastrians. They fled towards Towton, where Margaret was encamped, leaving Fauconberg triumphant in the field. And by nightfall, using both the ford and the bridge, which had been repaired, the entire Yorkist army was safely across the Aire.

★ ★ ★

Warwick awoke on the morning of the twenty-ninth of March to the distant pealing of bells and remembered with surprise that it was Palm Sunday. Then he realised that the sound was muffled and that the roof of the tent sagged under a heavy weight. Such light as he could see had a brilliant quality which could mean only one thing. Wrapped in his cloak, he stepped outside.

Every undulation, every contour of ground had vanished under a thick pall of snow. It lay, inches deep, in pure, dazzling drifts, stained here and there with lingering shadows the colour of bilberry juice. Against the overcast sky, the branches of the trees rose in a froth of white lace and over all was that peculiar soundlessness which he could remember on winter mornings in the Yorkshire dales. He felt again the insensate longing of his youth to stamp down the snow, mile after mile after mile; felt the same animal urge to spoil the pristine freshness. It was as though such unadulterated beauty was an insult to the eye; challenging, begging for destruction.

But he had little time for these reflections. The camp was already in a bustle and, calling for his squires, Warwick began the slow process of getting into his armour. He ate standing up, a hasty breakfast of bread and salted fish, flavoured with a little oatmeal and saffron. He made his confession and received absolution, tucking the small cross of dried palm leaf into his left gauntlet. He was not a deeply religious man. The teaching of the Church was as much a part of his life as eating and sleeping and as little thought about and as little questioned. Its symbols were, to him, more in the nature of talismans than reminders of Christ's Life and Passion. By ten o'clock, together with Edward, he was in his place at the centre of the Yorkist army. Norfolk commanded the right wing; Fauconberg the left.

The Lancastrians were drawn up a few miles south of Tadcaster, between Saxton and Towton. Their right flank lay against the Cock beck, a tributary of the river Ouse. This had been fortified with stakes, their wickedly sharpened heads now prettily capped with snow. Margaret had been persuaded to take refuge at York with Henry and their son and it was in vain that Warwick searched for the familiar and hated figure on the rising ground behind the Lancastrian army. The enemy banners indicated the presence of Somerset and Edward's brother-in-law, the Duke of Exeter; the Earl of Devon, Lord Dacre and, in the centre, Henry Percy, Earl of Northumberland.

Among the many banners floating above the Yorkist host were Warwick's own Bear and Ragged Staff; the Falcon of the Plantagenets; the Fetterlock and White Rose of York; and a White Rose-en-Soleil, used by the King since his victory at Mortimer's Cross. In the ranks were to be seen the standards of nearly every city in England, Warwick's prediction that people would flock to join him having been overwhelmingly justified. Never before, never afterwards, did the commoners embrace either side as they did the Yorkist cause at Towton. In the past, in the future, battles had been, and were to be, regarded by the majority of people as a struggle for power; the rending fury of family strife. But today, it was different. Margaret had outraged an entire population and she would pay for it very dearly.

It began to snow again. A wind sprang up, increasing in velocity so that the air was a mass of whirling, dancing flakes, biting and stinging every exposed portion of the body until the skin burned under its touch. Within minutes, it was almost impossible to see the Lancastrian lines, but — and Warwick noted this with a great upsurge of spirits — the wind was blowing in a northerly direction and the snow was blinding the enemy.

In the Lancastrian ranks, Anthony Woodville waited, but his heart was not in the coming fight. He had remained loyal to Henry because he was sorry for him; because, as she constantly reminded her family, his mother was aunt-by-marriage to the King; because, above all, he had sworn fealty and Anthony was not the man to make or break an oath lightly. But the atrocities he had seen during the past few weeks, commanded or tolerated by the Queen, had sickened him. He could no longer bind himself to such a cause. If he survived the battle, he must break his oath. That God would one day punish him for doing so, he accepted with resignation. He would have prayed for death today, except that such a course was wrong.

Beside him, his father also stood ready. Lord Rivers wondered what Anthony was thinking; whether, if events went against them, his son would be prepared to see reason and abandon Henry and the Queen. Now that there was a new King, matters had changed. Richard Woodville foresaw golden opportunities awaiting the right man at Edward's court. It would no longer be necessary to hide one's interest in hunting, in dancing or in the more concupiscent delights. He had taken Edward's measure at Calais; had recognised, in spite of his anger, a kindred spirit, devoted to the pleasures of life. Existence could be good for such as Lord Rivers in a Yorkist world. If he escaped today, he would pay homage to Edward the fourth. An idea came to him: he would invite Edward to stay at his home at Grafton before the King returned south to London. He would wine and dine him. Richard Woodville would show Edward Plantagenet that he was a fitting companion for his leisure hours; deserving of a place at court.

It was so cold that men's teeth chattered in their heads. It was nearly April and yesterday the woods and fields had been starred with early spring flowers; now they had disappeared, hidden under their white canopy. Snow lodged in armour joints; bowstrings needed tightening; breath froze on the air. Warwick, in a sudden panic, felt unable to move, convinced that he had been turned into a pillar of ice, a sensation shared by nearly everyone on that bitter plain.

Then, Edward's trumpets sounded. There was a roar from the Yorkist ranks. The Lancastrians began to move and the two armies met with a deafening crash.

★ ★ ★

In the house in Southwark, William Paston took up his pen to write to his brother, John. The house was very quiet since the departure of little George and Richard for Burgundy, but in view of the good tidings received that morning, no doubt they would soon be returning to London.

The intense cold had passed, but the

148

fire crackling on the hearth was more than welcome on this Good Friday morning. The watery sunlight was without warmth and the servants blew upon their fingers as they crossed the yard. William sniffed, noting as he did so that the rushes needed changing; such stale odours would never do for his distinguished guest. He started to write.

'You will be glad to know that My Lady of York has today received a letter from King Edward, sent with his note of credence and his token. She showed it to me and graciously permitted me to read it.

'Our Sovereign Lord has won the battle at Towton —'

And a very nasty affair it had been by the messenger's account. It had lasted until well after dark and the snow had been sodden with blood all the way to Tadcaster. In some places it had been impossible to cut a path through the heaps of dead bodies, so high had they been piled, and the Cock beck had been choked with the slain and wounded. The Lancastrians had fought hard and, on more than one occasion, had seemed likely to carry the day. But the generalship of the King and the Earl of Warwick had eventually defeated them.

William Paston continued: ' — and last Monday he entered York where he was

149

greeted by the Mayor and citizens. His kinsman, Lord Montagu, was also there.'

And very lucky John Neville had been to escape with his life, William thought. The Queen might well have taken him with her when she fled from York; a hostage to trade for Somerset's brother.

The pen scratched again. 'Lords Fitzwalter and Scrope are dead; also John Stafford and Horne of Kent. Humphrey Neville and William Hastings have been knighted. Amongst the enemy dead are the Lords Welles and Willoughby and Andrew Trollope.'

William Paston smiled grimly to himself. Warwick would be pleased at the death of the man who had betrayed him. He went on: 'About twenty thousand were killed altogether.

'The Queen, together with the Prince and King Henry, the Dukes of Somerset and Exeter, has escaped to Scotland.'

William laid down his pen and threw another log on the fire. He could hear Cicely's voice upraised in peremptory command as she ordered the horses to be harnessed to her carriage. She would be going to Westminster and William's chest swelled with pride to think that a Paston roof sheltered the mother of the undisputed King of England.

★ ★ ★

Lord Rivers was trembling with suppressed excitement. True to his promise to himself, he had made his peace with Edward at York and now the King, returning to London for the coronation, was to break his journey and spend a night at Grafton.

Rather to Rivers' surprise, Anthony had proved obedient in renouncing his former allegiance, but it did not occur to Richard Woodville that his son might be prompted by motives other than his own. He therefore found it difficult to reconcile Anthony's dejected appearance with his apparently willing rejection of Henry. But Lord Rivers had other, more important things to worry about and he hoped that Jacquetta, warned of the turn of events by advance messenger, would not prove recalcitrant or rude.

He need not have worried, however, for the Duchess had also been doing some thinking of late. Being astute and worldly-wise, she had come to the same conclusion as her husband: namely, that she could not go on supporting an obviously losing cause. If Henry were beaten, she had no intention of going into exile or retirement; she had too many children to whose future advancement she was dedicated, to do that.

Moreover, Edward was young and extremely good-looking — already someone had called him 'the handsomest man in Europe' — and what woman could resist that? She therefore appeared on the steps of her home wreathed in smiles and dressed in green, the colour of sexual passion.

'Welcome, Your Grace!' She sank into a deep curtsey from which Edward raised her and, because she was still an attractive woman, kissed her resoundingly on both cheeks.

'I am delighted to be here,' Edward replied with truth, as he allowed himself to be escorted indoors. At this moment, the doubt and uncertainty passed, he was in love with all the world and ready to be friends with anyone who swore him allegiance. He was even ready to forgive Somerset, himself, should the occasion arise.

'The Earl of Warwick is not with you.' Jacquetta's words were more statement than question, but Edward answered her, nevertheless.

'He stays in the north to settle matters there. Margaret may be beaten but I doubt that we have heard the last of her.'

The Duchess smiled. 'Indeed, no! She is a most . . . masculine woman.' She trilled with laughter and shot Edward a coquettish glance from beneath her lashes. He responded at once, kissing her hand gracefully and managing to imply that if she were not a lady of exalted rank, he would be more familiar than that. Such a mixture of daring and deference was irresistible and Jacquetta was more than content with her change of sovereigns.

'Lord Warwick does not attend the coronation?' she asked and smiled when Edward shook his head. A look of understanding flashed between them as each unerringly divined the reason for the Earl's absence. The Duchess guessed as well as Edward that Warwick would not wish to be present at an event where he must inevitably take second place. He would remain in the north, busy about the King's affairs so that everyone would see how indispensable he was.

Dinner was superb and no expense had been spared to make it a memorable meal. The almond soup was delicious, with just the right flavouring of beef; the pork had been pulped with pine-cones; the roast capon had been stuffed with a special mixture of Jacquetta's own devising, which included saffron, suet and eggs.

During the meal, Edward made the acquaintance of the large Woodville family, five sons and eight daughters, although only seven of the girls were present.

'My eldest daughter, Lady Grey, is in mourning,' Jacquetta explained. 'Her husband was recently killed at . . . ' She paused, coughing delicately, then finished: 'He was killed at St. Albans.'

Edward inclined his head. 'I should like to meet her, nevertheless,' he said courteously. 'Allow me to compliment you on your very fine family, Duchess.'

She beamed. 'Your Highness is very gracious. Large families can be a little overwhelming to the outsider, but I know that Your Grace is accustomed to it. I know that your mother's family of Neville is equally large and equally devoted.'

Edward smiled as he bit into a cheese tart. 'True,' he answered, 'and by the look of it, the Woodvilles may one day rival the Nevilles in numbers.'

It was an idle remark, idly spoken, but it sank into Edward's mind and stayed there, like a stone at the bottom of a pool.

After dinner, he was taken to a small ante-room where, in accordance with his wishes, the Lady Elizabeth Grey was waiting to greet him.

Edward's first thought as he lifted her from her knees, was that, with the exception of his

154

mother, he had rarely seen a woman who looked so well in mourning. Black was a trying colour and in Edward's experience, a difficult one for any woman to support. If she could do so without looking pale and wan, then she was worth a second glance.

He took a second glance . . . and a third . . . and a fourth. The lady was certainly very lovely, with periwinkle-blue eyes, a short, straight nose and a small, delicately curved mouth. Had he not been so deeply enamoured of Eleanor Butler, and had Elizabeth Grey not been so recently widowed, he believed that he must have pursued the acquaintance.

Standing at one side, the Duchess missed nothing. Her shrewd eyes watched the flicker of emotion on Edward's face and knew that he was smitten with her eldest daughter's undeniable charms. It was something she had not foreseen when she had welcomed the King into her house, but now that it had happened, it might very well be turned to good account.

9

It was a quiet morning of muted greens and mud-browns. Here and there grew a patch of early primroses whose pale gold only served to accentuate the drabness of the scene. Warwick longed for something, anything — a scarlet flower, a pink and gold cloud, the flash of a kingfisher's brilliant sheen — that would put life and colour back into the greyness of the day.

Three years had passed since Towton; three years filled with activity for the man whom most foreigners regarded as the master of England. The Lancastrians had not submitted tamely to Edward's seizure of the crown and the years 1462 and 1463 had seen many attempts by Margaret and her friends to regain all that they had lost. With Scottish aid, they had raided over the Border, keeping Warwick and his brother, John constantly in the north. At last, however, ten months ago, in the July of 1463, Warwick had won a decisive victory at Norham Castle and Margaret, leaving Henry in Scotland, had fled to France to beg help from her cousin, King Louis — that same devious young man whom Warwick had once met in Burgundy and who had ascended the French throne three months after Edward's coronation.

Louis, however, was playing for time. He wanted English help to crush Burgundy. All his predatory instincts had been aroused during his years of exile in the duchy. He had already taken advantage of Duke Philip's failing health, forcing him to sell the Somme towns, thereby reducing his frontiers; but, for Louis, that was not enough. He wanted to crush his mighty vassal's power once and for all and so he was disinclined to help the exiled Margaret. Instead, he sent the Seigneur de Lannoy to negotiate with Edward.

Unfortunately for Louis, his one great failing was his inability to keep his mouth closed. He loved to talk and it was only a matter of time before a certain remark of his was wafted across the Channel to the palace at Westminster.

'I hear,' Louis had told a friend in the strictest confidence, 'that there are two rulers in England; the Earl of Warwick and — ah — another man, whose name I can't remember.'

The smile on his face had been echoed on Warwick's when the remark had been repeated to the Earl, but there had been no answering gleam of amusement in Edward's eyes. And when Jean de Lannoy landed in England in the spring of 1464, he found himself subjected to some very rough treatment at the hands of the English officials. Warwick, appalled, hastened to Dover and personally escorted the French embassy to London. But as they rode through the countryside on this cold spring morning, Warwick could not rid himself of an uneasy feeling that Edward might have been behind the insults offered to Louis' envoy.

Lannoy, however, appeared to have no such suspicion. To him, it was natural that the English, children of the Devil who hid tails beneath their doublets, should have been so uncivilised and brutish. He talked gaily to the Earl of Warwick, whom his master was so eager to woo.

'King Louis,' he confided, 'is anxious to conclude terms for the marriage treaty as soon as possible. There is no objection, I take it, on the part of the King of England?'

The Earl smiled. 'The King usually does as I suggest. I assume that the Lady Bona of Savoy is as attractive as reports make her out to be?'

'King Louis' sister-in-law is an extremely beautiful woman,' Lannoy replied stiffly.

'Beautiful enough for a man twice as — er — fussy as King Edward.'

It was a thrust which annoyed Warwick and he said sharply: 'Rumour has it that one of your King's men, Guillaume de Cousinot, has recently landed in the north and is with Henry in Bamburgh Castle. There are also reports that your countrymen are planning to attack Calais. However lovely the Lady Bona may be, you can hardly expect King Edward to make terms under such conditions.'

Lannoy realised that he had angered the Earl and forbore to point out that the English occupation of Calais was a perpetual affront to every right-minded Frenchman. He promised, instead, to look into the matters which Warwick had raised and had the satisfaction of seeing his companion grow more mellow towards him. That very night, from his sumptuous lodgings in the House of the Preaching Friars, near Ludgate, Lannoy dispatched a message to King Louis and, a week later, received from his master a rather startling reply.

That same evening, he and Warwick met at a banquet given by Edward at Ely House in the city. In Lannoy's experience, such public functions were ideal for confidential discussions. In the privacy of his lodgings, there was always the danger of prying eyes

159

or ears at the key-hole, but in the middle of a chattering crowd, he felt safe. As he sat by Warwick's side, waiting for the arrival of the King, he muttered in the Earl's receptive ear. Warwick's startled gaze met his.

'You mean . . . ?' The Earl's eyes blazed in sudden excitement. 'Louis is offering . . . ?'

Lannoy spread his hands expressively. 'Why not?' he asked. 'There must come a day when King Edward is safe upon his throne. A day when there is nothing more for you to do.' He saw the Earl's brows snap together and added hastily: 'In the *distant* future, of course! And even then His Grace will want you near at hand to consult and to give him advice. But you would not be too far away . . . in Normandy!'

Warwick tried to speak, but failed. Lannoy smiled understandingly. 'King Louis feels that nothing could be more fitting than for Normandy to become the apanage of one of Duke William's descendants. And who more suitable than the one who has been described as being everything in this kingdom? In short, yourself!'

Warwick stared into a future suddenly brilliant beyond even his imaginings.

Lannoy continued: 'You would, of course, hold the duchy in fief from my master and King Louis would expect some little — ah — service

160

in return.' The envoy flung up a bejewelled hand. 'Nothing that would conflict with your natural loyalties, you understand. Just the safeguarding of French interests in England. English help against his enemies.'

Warwick felt dizzy with happiness. Already, in his mind's eye, he saw himself Duke of Normandy; a palatinate where he could truly be master. Now, indeed, he must work unceasingly to ally England with France against Burgundy.

Watching the Earl's face, Lannoy's admiration for his sovereign knew no bounds. What a team-master Louis made; how exactly he gauged the size and juiciness of the carrots which he dangled before his donkeys.

There was a sudden diversion. A loud voice demanded: 'I want my rightful place. This is an insult to the whole of London.'

In splendour of scarlet and ermine, the Mayor, Matthew Phillip, had arrived, only to find the seat of honour already occupied. The newly knighted Hastings, in his capacity as Lord Chamberlain, hurried forward, an anxious frown creasing his face. He bent and whispered something, but the occupant of the chair merely shrugged, turning his rather prominent eyes upon the Mayor with a look of disdain.

His Worship's response was swift and

161

dramatic. With a nod to his friends, he turned on his heel and strode from the hall, his aldermen rising and following in his wake.

Lannoy was horrified. 'They dare to leave before His Highness arrives? Don't they fear his anger?'

Warwick shook his head. 'It will be Edward who is worried, believe me. There is an old saying which it is always wise to remember: 'The Londoners shall have no King but their Mayor' and you could apply that maxim to every town in England. Within a city's limits, the Mayor is its most important personage.'

'Who is the gentleman who refused to move?' the envoy wanted to know and Warwick sneered.

'That, my dear Seigneur, is the Earl of Worcester, Constable of England and one of the most erudite men this country has ever produced; but in his dealings with his fellow beings, an absolute fool.'

'He looks to me as though he doesn't like people,' Lannoy said astutely, but his observation was lost in the blare of trumpets as Edward made his appearance.

Hastings hurried to his side. As he spoke, the King became agitated; then, commanding silence, said in a loud voice: 'I wish my profoundest apologies conveyed to His Worship, the Mayor. And I want something of every course served here tonight to be carried immediately to his house.'

Edward took his place, frowning angrily at the Earl of Worcester, but he said nothing because he had no wish to quarrel with so useful a man. There were many unpleasant tasks in the course of government with which Edward preferred not to be associated and John Tiptoft was not only able, but willing to perform these duties for his master.

From the kitchens, scullions and sewers hurried into the night, bearing covered dishes to the house of the Mayor. Half an hour later, they returned still carrying the food, untasted.

The Mayor willingly accepted the King's apology but had no need of his victuals. The red-faced messengers were forced to admit that His Worship was entertaining his fellow councillors to a better meal than that which even the King could provide.

★ ★ ★

It was a beautiful morning, as clear and transparent as a bubble. The sunlight filtered through the trees, filling them with its radiance, turning each leaf into a quivering pendant of gold. Even the flowers had a crystalline quality and the distant hills looked as brittle and shining as glass.

Warwick, riding slowly towards Middleham, felt serene and full of confidence on this late summer's day. To begin with, he was going to spend a week in his favourite castle in the company of his family, a rare treat for him nowadays. Secondly, the country was at peace after the Lancastrian uprisings in the spring.

Shortly after the banquet at Ely House, word had reached London of unrest throughout the midlands and the north. Warwick had hurriedly left the capital, to be followed, a week later, by Edward. But by the time the Earl and King had been reunited at the end of May, the Lancastrians had been crushed by John Neville in two brilliant engagements, one at Hedgeley Moor and the other at Hexham. And at York, Warwick had had the pleasure of seeing John made Earl of Northumberland, a title forfeited by the Percy family after Towton. Henry Percy, himself, was now in the Tower.

Other Lancastrian supporters had not fared so well. Sir Ralph Percy had been killed at Hedgeley Moor; the lords Hungerford and Roos and the Duke of Somerset beheaded on the orders of John Tiptoft after Hexham. King Henry, who had been present at the second battle, had escaped, but Warwick felt that it was only a matter of time before he was taken.

As the Earl rode up the steep slope of Middleham town, his trumpeters sounded warning of his approach. The drawbridge was lowered and he clattered into the courtyard at the head of his attendants. His heart soared, as always, at the sight of the massive keep, the bakehouse, the smithy and the mill, for this, to him, meant home. He loved this place as he did no other and he was always glad when he knew that his family was in residence here, on the edge of the windswept Yorkshire moors.

The inner ward filled with servants, hurrying to hold his horse, assisting him to alight. His wife came sedately down the steps to greet him, but decorum was thrown to the winds by the two little girls who appeared in the doorway of the great hall. Isabel and Anne came running to throw themselves into his arms and cover him with kisses.

'Why aren't you at your lessons?' he asked with mock severity, but his eyes twinkled lovingly. He still mourned the son he would never have now, but he did so in secret. To his wife he said, smiling: 'These two, my dear, are worth a whole pack of lubberly boys.'

At the mention of the magic word 'boys', seven-years-old Anne pulled at her father's sleeve.

'Father, let the boys off their lessons today. It's so nice. We could ride to Nappa Hall and James Metcalfe could tell us about the things he did at Agincourt.'

Her mother laughed. 'If you're not tired of those stories by now, you never will be.'

Warwick gave an answering grin. 'Stories greatly exaggerated, too, if I know Metcalfe.' He pinched Anne's cheek. 'I'll see what I can do about the boys.'

He found his apprentice-knights debating an obscure point of law with their tutor and more than ready for their unexpected holiday. Dismissing them with a smile, the Earl detained the youngest and smallest of them, carrying him off to the privacy of the family solar.

'I was very proud of you last spring, Diccon,' he said approvingly. 'You did extremely well.'

Little Richard Plantagenet, now Duke of Gloucester and apprentice-knight in Warwick's household for the past two and a half years, glowed at his cousin's praise. He was in his twelfth year and had been commissioned during the spring uprisings to array the entire south-west of England, which he had done with a competence beyond his years. A shy child, he had not found it easy, but to have won his cousin's approbation made up for everything.

Anne ran to meet them, throwing her arms affectionately about Richard's neck. Warwick watched them thoughtfully and that night, in the intimacy of their huge, canopied bed, he remarked to his wife: 'It is high time, my dear, that we made plans for our girls.'

The Countess placidly agreed, snuggling into her goosefeather mattress with a sigh of contentment. 'What had you in mind, my love?'

'The Dukes of Clarence and Gloucester; George for Isabel; Richard for Anne.' And that, he thought, would bring both the King's brothers safely within the sphere of Neville influence; the final step in ensuring his position as the most powerful magnate in the kingdom.

'Richard tells me,' said the Countess, 'that Lord Rivers and his son, Sir Anthony Woodville, were with Edward in the spring. I thought, sweetheart, that you had committed them to the Tower.'

Warwick snorted and reached for his 'all-night', a jug of ale and a loaf of bread which stood on a table near the bed. Tearing a piece from the loaf and cramming it into his mouth, he answered thickly: 'So I did, but Edward had them released. It's nothing to worry about! He takes the bit between his teeth on occasions, but he finds out that I'm right in the end.' He gulped some ale noisily. 'Just as he did with Somerset.'

In spite of all warnings, Edward had insisted on making his peace with the Duke of Somerset. He had befriended Henry Beaufort to the extent of having him to sleep in the royal bed; heaping him with gifts and defending him against attacks by outraged, loyal citizens. But, after all, Somerset had been unable to turn his coat, unlike so many others. He had abandoned Edward and returned to his former allegiance, finally being captured and executed after Hexham. The title had now passed to his younger brother, Edmund.

'Yes, Edward will find out I'm right about the Woodvilles,' Warwick said confidently, wiping his mouth on the back of his hand.

'Must you leave at the end of the week?' asked his wife, but without much hope of receiving a negative answer.

'I must,' Warwick replied, lying down beside her. 'There's a Council meeting at Reading. Edward wants to discuss reforming the coinage — the people will never stand for it, you know. I've told him so — and the final terms of the marriage settlements must be thrashed out. It's high time that Edward was married, and Bona of Savoy has waited long enough.'

The Earl turned on his side and closed his eyes. Life was very good and would be even better when Queen Bona shared the throne. Sleep engulfed him and he drifted into a world of dreams — dreams in which the pleasant land of Normandy played a prominent part.

★ ★ ★

The Earl looked round the Council table, a slight frown on his face. Not only were both Lord Rivers and his son present, but also that little, insignificant, middle-aged prelate, Robert Stillington. When such as he were allowed into the King's innermost councils, it demeaned the position held by others, Warwick thought, and he turned a cold shoulder upon the obsequiously smiling priest.

Edward entered the Council Chamber and took his place at the head of the table. The Councillors seated themselves and sewers passed round a very cool, light wine, most acceptable on this close, mid-September day. There was some general chatter and Warwick noted uneasily the familiarity which Edward employed towards the Woodvilles.

The servants withdrew and the Council settled itself to the business in hand. Warwick waited impatiently while minor matters were dealt with; the forfeiting of certain estates by rebel lords; Edward's pet scheme for a revised monetary system; the sending of loyal greetings to the new Pope, Paul the second. Finally, the Earl could contain himself no longer and, rising to his feet, said briskly: 'The marriage settlements must be fixed. Your Highness' — he bowed perfunctorily to Edward — 'knows that King Louis is expecting me soon in France with definite demands and proposals. The Lady Bona, herself, is growing impatient at the delay. My lords, I beg you to consider this matter next.'

There was a murmur of agreement from the rest of the Council, with the exception of the King and the two Woodvilles. Edward glanced briefly at Rivers, who, in turn, got up.

'My Lord Warwick, is this marriage such a desirable thing?' he asked. 'We all know that Margaret's friend, Piers de Brézé, is now in good standing at the French court. This does not suggest to me that King Louis is of good faith in his protestations of friendship.'

170

'Suggest to you!' shouted the Earl. 'And what is your opinion worth, my lord? It's not so many years since you were my prisoner at Calais and even less since you fought for King Henry.'

He was shaking with rage. That this upstart, this time-server, should dare to query the wisdom of the great Warwick was not to be borne. But was the pretentious fool depressed by the mighty Earl's displeasure? He was not and immediately started burbling again.

'Does Your Lordship know that a certain Pierre Puissant, who was captured recently during a French raid on the fortress of Hammes, declares that King Louis is plotting against both England and Burgundy?'

'Pierre Puissant!' Warwick spat the name back into Rivers' face. 'Return him to his King and see if he repeats such stories then. Let Louis deny them for himself.'

Anthony Woodville looked up and said in his quiet way: 'King Louis is not a man whose word can be entirely trusted, my lord. Prince Phillip of Savoy entered France under Louis' safe-conduct and now rots in the Château of Loches.'

Warwick turned furiously to the King who still lounged in his chair at the head of the table, listening to this exchange without a

171

word. His lids were half-lowered and there was an enigmatic smile on his lips.

'Your Grace!' the Earl exclaimed, hotly. 'I appeal to you!'

'And not before time,' Edward said smoothly. 'I do feel, my lords, that my marriage *has* something to do with me.'

He looked blandly round the table and there was a moment's uncomfortable silence. The Duke of Norfolk wiped his nose uneasily on his sleeve; the Duke of Suffolk, husband of the King's sister, Elizabeth, shifted in his chair; Stillington started to sweat; the other Councillors coughed or shuffled their feet. Warwick, himself, was seized with a sudden fear.

'The fact is, my lords,' Edward continued, 'that I cannot, in any case, marry the Lady Bona of Savoy.'

'Why not?' demanded Warwick in a harsh, strained voice which he hardly recognised as his own.

'Because,' Edward replied, 'I am already married. The Lady Elizabeth Grey did me the honour of becoming my wife last May.'

Part Two

... AND PULLER-DOWN OF KINGS.'

1464 – 1471

10

'You have married that . . . that . . . '

Cicely Neville looked into her eldest son's blue eyes and decided to moderate the guard-room expression which was hovering on the tip of her tongue. It showed, however, the measure of her agitation that she had been ready to indulge in the vulgarity of a male word which she would normally have deplored.

She continued: 'You have married that creature! A woman five years older than yourself! A woman with two grown children, one of whom is nearly as old as your youngest brother.'

'As to that,' Edward said, smiling, 'I also have a couple of children of my own.'

Cicely was too much a woman of her age to be shocked by such an admission, but she snorted, nevertheless. 'You, who could have married any princess in Europe, to choose a nobody like that!'

Edward, lounging in a chair in his private apartments at Westminster, watched his mother as she paced to and fro about the room like an angry tigress. He was uncomfortably aware of the penetrating quality of Cicely's voice and could guess only too well how many straining ears were listening in the ante-room. The obvious course was to end the interview, but the habit of deference to parental authority was strong in every one of Cicely's children. He might not like what his mother had to say; it might be reported by gossiping tongues throughout his kingdom and beyond; but Edward would no more have dismissed Cicely from his presence than he would have walked naked through the streets. Besides, as he reflected with a grin, she would not have gone.

He said, placatingly: 'Hardly a nobody! Elizabeth's mother is Jacquetta of Luxembourg; a descendant of Charlemagne and considered a fit wife for John of Bedford. Moreover — '

'Moreover, her father was a common squire,' spat Cicely, whirling round in a flurry of black draperies, 'before he made himself by his marriage. Lord Rivers, indeed!'

Edward's eyes hardened again. 'I was going to say,' he went on, 'that her uncle is the Seigneur de Richebourg and a friend of Duke Philip.'

'Is that what you want? Closer alliance with Burgundy?' His mother looked at him shrewdly. 'Why? Because Warwick wants confederation with France? If that's the case, there were easier ways of cutting your leading strings than marrying . . . Elizabeth Woodville!'

The contemptuous way in which she spoke his wife's name brought Edward to his feet with a crashing oath, all circumspection, all thought of his unseen audience banished from his mind.

'God's Belly! Do you think I married Elizabeth because I saw her as a political pawn?'

'And didn't you?' Cicely's temper matched his own and they were both now shouting with rage. 'Didn't you?' his mother repeated. 'Aren't all her brothers and sisters arriving at court by the carriage-load? And isn't she planning rich marriages for each and every one of them?' Cicely's hand flashed out and dealt her son a resounding slap, her rings biting into his flesh. 'How dare you set up the Woodvilles against the Nevilles?'

Edward stepped back, nursing his swollen cheek. 'And how dare you touch me? Don't you know that anyone else could lose her hand, if not her life, for such an act?'

Even as he said it, trembling with fury as he was, a small part of the King's mind admired his mother's acumen. How quickly she discerned motives of which he, himself, was only just aware. It was true

177

that Elizabeth's large family had been one of the factors in his decision to marry her. The Woodvilles, dependent upon Edward's generosity for everything they were to become, were his answer to the growing power and domination of the Nevilles.

Cicely hooted in derision. 'Are you threatening me?' she demanded with a laugh. 'Why, I've a good mind to go before a commission of enquiry and tell them that you are a bastard.'

Edward went white with anger. 'Archer Blackburn being my father, no doubt!'

'Who else?' There was a note of bitterness in Cicely's voice.

For a moment they faced each other across the room, breasts heaving, eyes cold with dislike. Then, suddenly, Edward began to grin and, throwing himself back into his chair, poured out wine with an unsteady hand.

'I should like to see you do it,' he jibed, 'if only to watch you deal the death-blow to Neville pride.'

His mother regarded him straitly; then, reluctantly, smiled.

'Well, perhaps I wouldn't go that far,' she admitted, coming to sit opposite him. 'But as to dealing the death-blow . . . I should think that my nephew, Warwick, did that when he agreed to escort your . . . your wife into Reading Abbey for the ceremony of homage.'

Edward drank deeply from the mazer and looked thoughtfully at the little verse carved into its wooden base.

Let your fellows live at ease,
Do this if you would them please.

A worthy sentiment, thought Edward, but not one from which he was likely to benefit.

Replying to his mother, he said: 'That was George's doing,' and encountered a look of enquiry from the Duchess. 'George Neville, I mean. My own dear brother, George, is as much enraged at my marriage as you are, only he sulks instead of spits.' Cicely's head reared up and Edward patted her hand soothingly. 'I'd rather have your anger than George's sullens any day, my dear. He is becoming an extremely difficult young man.'

'Your own fault entirely,' was his mother's spirited retort. 'He has been pampered by your lady-friends — especially Elizabeth Lucy, who, I take it is the mother of your children — and utterly spoilt.'

'I know! I know!' agreed Edward with a sigh. 'I should have sent him to Warwick with Richard.'

'And where is Warwick now?' enquired Cicely. She felt disturbed. Her nephew was not the man to submit tamely to such humiliation as he had recently endured.

Edward shrugged, the blue velvet — the colour of marital fidelity, his mother noted with an incredulous smile — rippling over his shoulders.

'On his way to Middleham, I should imagine.'

* * *

Warwick was indeed on his way to Middleham, like an animal going to earth to lick its wounds, but, on his way, he remained for a night or two at Warwick Castle.

He still found it hard to believe that Edward's marriage was not part of some hideous dream. He had been humiliated not only in his own eyes, but in the eyes of the world; scorned and rejected by the one person from whom he had reason to expect most gratitude. He felt as though the eyes of Europe were upon him, laughing at, and mocking him. Worse than that, was the knowledge that his plans lay ruined, in the dust. Without the French marriage there would be no apanage of Normandy; without Edward, no shadow-crown for Warwick. It

180

did not need his brother, George, to tell him that Edward was lost to him. Such a dramatic and defiant gesture as the King had just made, could not be misinterpreted, even by the Earl. He felt duped; he would never be able to see that the deception had been in his own mind and not in any of Edward's past actions. But of one thing he was certain: he would allow no upstart Woodvilles to elbow him from his place. He was Warwick! Nothing could alter that!

The future, until a few weeks ago so rosy, was now dark and uncertain. He was unsure of his ground, but, before leaving Reading, he had listened to some sound advice from the astute George Neville.

'Don't,' the Chancellor had urged him, 'do anything drastic for the present. We are not lost yet and it will be a bad day when the Nevilles cannot outpoint the Woodvilles. We must go cautiously, but, at the same time, if there are any little ways in which we can . . . express our displeasure, shall we say? then let us not leave them undone.'

'Pinpricks,' Warwick had said and George had laughed delightedly.

'Precisely, my dear Richard! The day will undoubtedly come when we can inflict greater injury, but for now . . . Let us remember that a sufficient number of pinpricks can prove extremely painful. Let us not miss any small opportunity.'

And the Earl rode into Warwick Castle on a blustery October day to find just such an opportunity awaiting him in the persons of three Coventry men.

The deputation from the nearby town was on behalf of a certain Will Huet, whom his friends felt to have been shabbily used by the Mayor and the King.

'Tell me the whole story,' Warwick invited when he had changed his travel-stained clothing and the men had been ushered into his presence-chamber. 'What is the complaint?'

There was a good deal of shuffling and coughing before the tallest of the group, a big man with a flea-bitten nose, finally plucked up courage to speak.

'It's like this, Your Honour,' he said and Warwick noted with distaste that the fellow's breath stank of garlic. 'Our friend, Will Huet, had a quarrel with William Bedon over some woman. Bedon is the — '

'Yes, yes!' Warwick exclaimed testily. 'Leave the details.'

The man nodded; wiped his nose in his fingers; glanced imploringly at his companions, who stared woodenly before them; then continued: 'Very good, Your

Honour. Well, the quarrel got worse. It was causing a lot of upset in the city and at last His Worship decided to take a hand. He put the case to the King and His Grace ruled that the Mayor should give judgement.'

A shrewd decision, Warwick thought, not without a touch of pride in his former protégé. 'So?' he prompted.

One of the others decided to take a hand. His voice was sharp and shrill, in direct contrast to the first speaker's gruff tones.

'The Mayor decided in favour of William Bedon, my lord. Not only was Will Huet told to ask Bedon's forgiveness, but he was made to pay forty shillings towards Bedon's costs and expenses.'

'And that's not all.' The third man found his voice, made bold by anger. 'Huet was told that there would be an increase of ten marks if he objected to the judgement.'

'And did he?' Warwick enquired.

'Well . . . yes.' The three men looked at one another, suddenly uncomfortable.

The Earl smiled. 'In fact, your friend was offensive.'

'And so would you have been, Your Honour,' the first man burst out, scratching his nose and stamping his feet with indignation. He stopped and coloured. 'What I mean is . . . anyone . . . '

'I quite understand,' Warwick said. 'What happened?'

'He was sent to prison, my lord, and is still there.'

'Haven't you appealed to the King?'

'It wouldn't do any good,' the third man muttered truculently, afraid that Warwick was not going to help Huet, either. 'The Mayor told His Grace what he had done and His Grace wrote that he was very pleased. It was unfitting, he said, for vulgar language to be used in the courts.'

The flea-bitten man spat in the rushes, which was as near as he dared go towards expressing his contempt for the King's opinion in particular and the law in general.

'Very well! I shall see what can be done.' Warwick got to his feet, dismissing them and, when they had gone, stared unseeingly into the fire. He knew that to overset the judgement of the Mayor could cost him Coventry's good-will. Had he not told Lannoy, earlier that same year, that it was wise always to remember the importance of the Mayor? Any insult to His Worship was an insult to the dignity of his city and the Earl knew his fellow-countrymen to be extremely touchy on that score. But against that consideration was to be weighed the chance of thwarting Edward; the first of those pinpricks which were to convey to the King the displeasure of his Neville kinsmen.

After a brief struggle, animosity, the thirst for revenge, triumphed over common sense. Within the month, Huet was freed and Bedon was forced to refund him a third of the additional ten marks.

★ ★ ★

Warwick had not expected Edward to accept meekly this challenge to his authority, but neither had he anticipated the nature of the King's reprisal. In the early spring of the following year, Edward removed his youngest brother from Warwick's care and brought Richard back to Westminster.

It was now more necessary than ever to the Earl's plans that he should exert as much influence as possible over the Dukes of Gloucester and Clarence and this action of Edward's seriously perturbed him. He said as much to George, but the Chancellor merely shrugged his shoulders.

'Don't trouble your head about it,' he advised. 'As Edward doubtless knows by now, the precaution was pointless.'

'Why?' demanded Warwick.

'Because, my dear Richard, you would have

found it impossible, in any case, to wean your young namesake from his allegiance to the King. He wears his devotion to Edward like a cloak.'

'Pooh!' said Warwick, scornfully. 'Richard is extraordinarily fond of me.'

'Richard is fond of us all,' George answered with weary patience. 'A little less of me, perhaps, than of you and John, but he loves Edward more. Concentrate your energies on my namesake. He loves nobody but himself.'

In this, George Neville did George Plantagenet an injustice. The fifteen-years-old Duke of Clarence was fonder of his family than he appeared to be, particularly of his two brothers. Unfortunately for George, his chief vice, conceit, had been aggravated by his chief attribute, charm. He had early discovered how to ingratiate himself with all manner of people and was his mother's favourite son, his sisters' favourite brother. On his return from Burgundy, Cicely, whose partiality did not blind her to his faults, had tried to remove George from a court which abounded with easy living and his eldest brother's lights-o'-love. Edward, recognising a convivial and kindred spirit, had protested as vehemently as George, himself, against his mother's decision, with the result that the Duke of Clarence had remained to become the indulged and petted darling of a lax and immoral court. In these circumstances, together with the fact that he was heir-presumptive to the throne, it would have taken an older and wiser man than Clarence to have kept his head or a sense of proportion.

Edward's marriage had come as a serious blow to the Duke, not because he had expected his brother to remain celibate, but because he had more than his fair share of Plantagenet and Neville pride. To have been second in importance only to the King and now to find himself expected to make way for a family with no great pretensions to nobility; a family, moreover, who had always fought for Lancaster, was more than George could stomach. Within a few months of Edward's marriage, a passionate hatred for the Woodvilles had supplanted all other emotions in his heart. He was willing to befriend anyone who said or did anything likely to embarrass the detested parvenus. And it was for this reason that he welcomed with such enthusiasm the Earl of Desmond, who had come to England from Ireland in this April of 1465 for Elizabeth's coronation.

They were among the glittering crowds of courtiers who were thronging the Queen's garden, most important of whom was Elizabeth's maternal uncle, Jacques de Luxembourg, Seigneur de Richebourg, who had come to grace the festivities and impress the English with his niece's noble connections. It was not, however, in the islanders' nature to take kindly to foreigners and the Londoners had been extremely rude.

'Did you hear what the people called him, yesterday?' George asked Desmond and Thomas Fitzgerald's honest eyes sparkled in return.

'While we were riding to the picnic? Yes, I heard. I think it was 'Lord Jakes'.'

George nodded, gleefully. 'The Woodvilles all looked as sour as could be. And then, your remark to Edward! I was never more delighted about anything in my life.'

The Earl seemed a little puzzled. 'But His Grace asked me for my honest opinion of his marriage,' he said. 'I simply told him what I truly believe: that while the Queen is a charming and attractive woman, the King would have done better to have married some foreign princess who could have brought him all the advantages of a military alliance.'

George looked into the smiling face before him. The Earl of Desmond was such a frank and open character, that the Duke felt ashamed of having, even secretly, attributed to him a wish to discomfort the Woodvilles. He laid a hand on Fitzgerald's arm.

'Whatever your motive was, take care!' he warned. 'The Queen's family are unlikely to forget such a slight.'

They were joined by George's sister and brother-in-law, the Duke and Duchess of Suffolk. Elizabeth nodded towards the scented and fashionably dressed figure of the Seigneur de Richebourg as he bent solicitously over his niece.

'This is another blow aimed at Warwick,' the Duchess said. 'Luxembourg is an ally of Burgundy. Edward obviously hopes to strengthen the ties.'

Her husband, John de la Pole, a florid faced man, stopped picking his nose and grunted: 'He'll have a hard job bringing about that alliance now. There have been violent anti-Burgundian demonstrations ever since Duke Philip banned the importation of English cloth, last October.'

'Hasn't your Parliament since forbidden imports of goods from Burgundy?' Desmond enquired, laughing, and Suffolk nodded complacently. He was a simple man and he liked simple politics; if an insult was offered to his country, he liked to see it neatly avenged in the same manner. Not that he meddled personally, if he could help it. His father had been that first Duke of Suffolk who had been murdered by Channel pirates. His great-grandfather, Michael de la Pole, had been raised to high places by Richard the second, only to find all men's hands turned against him. His mother's grandfather, the poet, Geoffrey Chaucer, had slaved for little reward in the service of John of Gaunt. No; the present Duke of Suffolk would take as small a part in politics as his high rank and his ties with the crown would allow.

He sat down on a rustic bench, mopping his face. His feet were hurting him badly. Usually disinterested in clothes, he had been inveigled by his wife into trying a pair of the modish leather boots with toe-pieces so long that they had to be fastened to the knees with ornamental chains. The Pope had been so horrified at this fashion, that he had forbidden the making of toe-pieces more than an inch or two in length, the penalty for disobedience being a papal curse. The English cordwainers, however, with customary indifference, had promptly declared that the Pope's curse would not hurt a fly and had continued to make shoe-pikes as long as before. The King, not to be outdone, had given them his patronage. The long English 'pikes' were so renowned, that a foreigner, when writing his account of the battle of Towton, had declared that Edward and his army had been forced to cut off the toes of their shoes before they could fight — a story which had kept the King and his court amused for months.

A bevy of the Queen's ladies-in-waiting entered the garden, among them Margaret of York, who grimaced at her brother and sister as she went by. A pert twenty-one-years-old, she resented Edward's marriage as strongly as did the rest of her family and she stayed now on the fringe of the group, determined to remain as aloof from the proceedings as possible.

The ladies, with high-pitched giggles and much fluttering of gauzes, advanced on Anthony Woodville, who knelt before his sister, deep in conversation. One produced from behind her back a garter of gold and pearls, which she fastened round Anthony's thigh. Another leaned over and dropped a roll of parchment, tied with gold thread, into his hat which lay on the ground beside him.

The Queen clapped her hands in delight and the courtiers gathered around, jostling and craning their necks; exclaiming and demanding to know what was written on the parchment.

Anthony unrolled and read it, then smiled, rising to his feet. 'I am to challenge to a joust a nobleman of my own choosing, provided he is of noble lineage and above reproach.'

'And whom do you choose, nephew?' the Seigneur de Richebourg cried in excitement.

Anthony hesitated for a moment, then he said: 'Herald, Nucelles Pursuivant, shall carry my challenge to Antoine, the Grand Bastard of Burgundy.'

'Bravo! Bravo!' shouted his uncle. 'A truly worthy opponent,' and the Queen smiled her approval.

There was a good deal of excited laughter and comment from the courtiers. Life was very pleasant since their handsome young King had come to the throne. It was, thought some of those present, even better since his marriage. The Woodvilles were beginning to attract a following of their own.

11

The news of Anthony Woodville's challenge to the Grand Bastard was brought to Warwick at Calais and he laughed.

'Edward and his new family are determined to strengthen ties with Burgundy,' he remarked to Wenlock, 'but we shall see. Duke Philip and his son are none too popular in England at the moment.'

There was, generally, quite a lot of unrest in the country, as Warwick well knew. The farmers were annoyed about the importation of cheap grain from abroad; the ship-owners complained that their freight charges were being undercut by foreigners; cordwainers and weavers were facing growing competition from Burgundy and the Netherlands; and the introduction of seven new coins into the currency, had upset a highly conservative nation to whom any sort of change was anathema.

But however much information such as this cheered Warwick's heart, news of the honours and titles being heaped upon the Woodvilles certainly did not. Lord Rivers was now Earl Rivers and Anthony had become Lord Scales.

Lionel Woodville was rising rapidly in the Church; Richard and Edward Woodville had been made Knights of the Bath at their sister's coronation; whilst John Woodville, a boy not yet twenty, had created a scandal by marrying the Dowager Duchess of Norfolk, a very wealthy lady, old enough to be not merely his mother, but his grandmother.

As for the Queen's sisters, rich and advantageous marriages were being arranged for each and every one of them and Elizabeth had obtained for her eldest son, Sir Thomas Grey, Edward's niece, the heiress of the exiled Duke of Exeter. Anne Holland had been promised to her cousin, John Neville's son, and it was, therefore, a double triumph for the Woodvilles and an affront to every member of the Neville family.

Not that the Nevilles, themselves, were doing too badly in the matter of matrimonial alliances. One of Warwick's sisters had married the powerful Lord Stanley and another, the King's closest friend and confidant, William Hastings. Furthermore, in this late May of 1465, the Nevilles' power, outwardly, at least, seemed to have strengthened and Warwick was in Calais armed with all the authority of the crown, to observe and report on a France hovering on the brink of civil war.

* * *

Nucelles Pursuivant rode through the streets of Brussels to Duke Philip's estate on the outskirts of the Forest of Soignes, where the Burgundian court was in residence. The château was surrounded by a vast parkland, ornamented with shining lakes and shimmering fountains. Thousands of birds flew among the branches of the trees and deer roamed the woodlands in their hundreds. The herald would dearly have loved to look around him, but on this ceremonial occasion he dared not do more than catch what glimpses he could from the corners of his eyes.

Inside the castle, he was dazzled by the kaleidoscope of colour; the shifting patterns of red, blue and orange, tawny, green and scarlet. Diamonds and pearls, rubies, sapphires and emeralds adorned every person. Cabinets full of gold and silver chalices glimmered from each corner; rich tapestries warmed the grey walls; aromatic flowers were strewn in profusion amongst the rushes on the floor. Here and there was the almost unheard-of luxury of a carpet. At the far end of the hall stood Antoine, the Grand Bastard of Burgundy, eldest of Duke Philip's thirteen love-children, and, beside him, his half-brother, Charles of Charolais, Regent now that his father's failing health was rapidly turning to senile decay.

At the blast of trumpets which announced his arrival, Nucelles Pursuivant moved forward, counting the number of paces with agonised concentration. Here in this court, where protocol was more inflexible than the laws of the Medes and Persians, a major scandal could ensue by the taking of one step too many.

After twenty-four strides, the herald came to a halt. The trumpets sounded again: the Grand Bastard advanced five paces and stopped. Nucelles Pursuivant raised the velvet cushion on which lay the gold and pearl garter and Antoine extended a beringed hand to touch it in token of his acceptance of Anthony Woodville's challenge. There was a final fanfare and the herald thankfully withdrew, grateful to a benevolent Providence that all had gone smoothly.

Later, when he returned to his inn after an invigorating climb to the top of the Hotel de Ville — from where he had obtained an unparalleled view of the whole city — he found one of the Bastard's servants awaiting him.

'You have done well for yourself,' the man told him and indicated, draped over the table, a black velvet doublet, decorated with golden clasps, and the sable-lined gown which Antoine had worn during the afternoon's ceremony.

'For me?' the herald enquired, but he was already caressing the fur with an eager and shaking hand.

'For you! Also this money. Also, my friend, a word to your Lord Scales. The Lord Antoine will honour his commitment as soon as he can, but it may not be for some time. At present, his sword is pledged in the service of his brother.'

And Charles of Charolais, that young man known as both 'The Bold' and 'The Rash', was enlisting other swords besides the Bastard's into his service. The French King's brother, the Duc de Berri, and Louis' discontented vassals, the Dukes of Brittany and Bourbon, were all intriguing with Burgundy to overthrow their sovereign. Charles, who had never forgiven Louis for persuading his father to sell back the Somme towns, dreamed night and day of bringing about his cousin's downfall. And he had little doubt that he could do it.

A self-opinionated young man, Charles was an ardent admirer of the ancient heroes and saw himself as another Hannibal or Alexander. Every night before going to bed, he listened while his librarian read to him from the histories of Rome. His father's Chamberlain, Phillipe de Commynes, had once remarked sapiently to a friend: 'He will make war, that one, just for the glory of it. He wants, more than anything, to be like some prince of antiquity; to be talked about after he is dead.'

But at present, Charles was very much alive and busy; much too busy to visit Calais and treat with the Earl of Warwick. The most he was prepared to do was to send his envoys, and them no further than Boulogne. Contrary to his friends' expectations, this pleased Richard Neville rather than otherwise, confirming him in his opinion that the future Duke of Burgundy was a somewhat oafish young man and blighting Edward's hopes of a Burgundian alliance. The Earl had no difficulty whatever in reporting unfavourably to Westminster on his meeting with Charles' ambassadors, particularly when he learned from one of them that the new Duke of Somerset was with Charles at Brussels and apparently high in his favour.

The Burgundians, however, were not the only envoys in Boulogne enjoying the fine June weather. Louis, more anxious than ever now for England's support, had sent his own extremely special messenger, Olivier le Daim.

As they sat together in Warwick's inn, the quondam barber took the Earl's arm and shook it with a familiarity which would have greatly amused his master had he seen it.

'King Louis,' he whispered hoarsely, 'has a special message for your ears alone. You understand?' A greasy finger stroked his dirty nose and the fawning smile on the thin lips was not reflected in the eyes, which were as cold and as hard as agate. Warwick could well understand why this man was the most feared and hated in France. The rasping voice continued: 'He has not forgotten . . . Normandy!'

Warwick's heart gave a great leap. He had thought that particular dream, like so many others, to have faded with Edward's marriage, but it seemed that he was mistaken. The French King was still dangling the golden bait and Warwick still leapt as eagerly to swallow it.

'Assure your master,' he told le Daim, 'that he shall have nothing to fear from England while I am in — ' he broke off suddenly, the colour flooding his cheeks. He had been about to say 'in command' but was he? Could he any longer be sure of that fact?

'As long as I have King Edward's ear,' he finished and saw a gleam of amusement in the eyes watching him with such cruel understanding. His temper flared. 'And as long as King Louis can keep his throne,' he snapped out and had the satisfaction of seeing the amusement fade abruptly.

'King Louis,' le Daim assured him angrily, 'has nothing to fear from the so-called League of Public Weal.' He spat out the words as though they would choke him. 'Rebel lords, all, and the wicked, my lord, shall not flourish.'

But his words proved to have been over optimistic. A few weeks later, on July the sixteenth, Charles of Charolais gained the victory over King Louis at Monthléry and turned to threaten Paris. At the same time as this inauspicious news reached Warwick at Calais, a messenger arrived from England with more joyful tidings.

'My lord,' he said, producing Edward's token, a glove, and his letter of credence, 'Henry Plantagenet has been captured in the north and is being brought prisoner to London. His Grace requests your immediate return so that you may be the one to lead the captive into London. King Edward particularly wishes that you, as the greatest magnate in the realm, as his chief minister of state, should have this honour.'

Warwick took a deep breath and then

smiled. Perhaps life had not changed, after all. Perhaps Edward had already seen the error of his ways. Perhaps the Earl of Warwick was again 'everything in this kingdom' as before.

★ ★ ★

George Neville was far less sanguine than his brother. As the splendid cavalcade rode towards Islington, where Henry the sixth was being held pending his formal arrest by Warwick, the Earl had confided to the Chancellor his resurgent hopes for the future, but George was difficult to convince.

'If you think that Edward is repenting his marriage, you are wrong,' he said moodily. 'You have only to look around you at Westminister. The Woodvilles are everywhere; not merely the brothers and sisters of our gracious Queen' — he sneered — 'but cousins, uncles and in-laws as well. Now that Fauconberg is dead, his earldom of Kent has been given to Lord Grey of Ruthyn, Elizabeth's cousin-by-marriage.'

Warwick swore and lashed out with his whip at the foxgloves which stood in tall, ragged clumps, bordering the track; pink sentinels guarding their lesser brethren, the heartsease and the daisy. Tansy and

201

celandine, trefoil and buttercup grew in golden abundance and loosestrife and willow-herb spread themselves in purple profusion. At any other time Warwick might have had eyes for the beauty around him, for he was not totally insensitive to the glories of an English summer, but his brother's words depressed him, awakening fears which had been lulled by his absence from court.

It was these new misgivings which caused him to treat Henry with needless severity when the former King was brought before him at Islington. The world, or the London world, at least, should see that the Earl of Warwick was still all-powerful; should remember who had delivered them from the misrule of this enfeebled man and given them his own good government. He ordered that the King should be tied to his horse and the reins held in Warwick's own hand. They would ride through the London streets side-by-side, the dispossessed and his supplanter.

Henry made no demur. His thoughts would not behave themselves today. They wandered off on their own, twisting down dark by-ways, where half-forgotten terrors of the past lurked around hidden corners, waiting to rear their ugly heads and scare him until he shook from head to foot. Then, suddenly, his reason would escape into the daylight, giving him a moment of lucidity and everyone else a surprise; just as when he turned to Warwick and pointed with a quivering hand to some boys playing football on the green.

'Forbidden by law! Forbidden by law!' he muttered. 'Archery's the thing.'

Warwick, experiencing a sensation of shock, turned to peer more closely at his prisoner, but encountered only the blank stare of a man whose understanding had already receded. Nevertheless, he enquired in an undertone of George: 'Might he ever recover his reason? Oh, not completely! I realise he will never do that. But in part; sufficiently, shall I say, to be a . . . figurehead?'

It was the Chancellor's turn to look sharply at his brother. 'Perhaps,' he answered warily. 'Why?'

But his agile mind was already in tune with the Earl's. Edward had once been Warwick's alternative to ruling through Henry. In that case, might not Henry be the alternative to ruling through Edward?

It was a process of thought too elementary to have been conceived in George's devious brain, but once the idea had been implanted in his thoughts, he was enchanted by the sheer simplicity of the plan. He felt, however, that the fortunes of the Nevilles were too deeply involved with those of the House of

York to abandon Edward lightly. He would have to be utterly convinced that there was no other way before committing himself to the Lancastrian cause. All the same, it was a course of action which could always be held in mind; an idea to be tucked away carefully, but brought out and given an airing once in a while; to be considered with caution until finally embraced or dismissed.

The London streets were packed to see them go by, but the people were strangely quiet. It was hot, sultry weather; one of those days when everything had an edge to it and the distant trees and rooftops were cut from thunder-clouds, paper shapes against a primrose sky. Clearly it would rain before evening and the heavy, windless air may have accounted for the silence of the crowds, but with the English it was difficult to say. The deposed King obviously evoked some sympathy and Warwick was conscious of the fact. A little while ago it would have worried him, but now, with new thoughts clamouring in his brain, it gave him a sense of power. If the people could still feel affection for the poor, weak creature beside him, how easy it would be to unmake one King and remake the other. The Earl smiled to himself: the English were invariably sorry for the underdog. They might hate a man while he held power, but once he was down . . . That was another matter. Richard the second bore ample witness to that fact as did Edward the second before him.

But, as always, Warwick's assessment of the situation was incomplete. While his eager imagination made pictures of his cousin defeated; the Woodvilles crushed; while his busy mind made splendid visions of himself triumphant and Henry restored — dependent upon Warwick as the present King would never be — the Earl failed to see that by such an action he would have put Edward in the underdog's place.

As they neared the Tower, the Earl of Worcester, its Constable, rode out to meet them and Warwick dragged himself reluctantly from the world of daydreams to the world of reality. He did not like this cold, clever man whose translations of Scipio and Flamenius and Cicero's Essays on Friendship had earned him the praise of scholars all over the world. Like his fellow countrymen, the Earl had a profound distrust of true erudition.

When they had formally handed over their prisoner, to be installed in a not uncomfortable room in the Lantern Tower, Warwick and his brother returned to Westminster. As always, the roads were jammed with traffic; carts, drays and carriages being forced between wandering pedestrians, itinerant friars, piemen, sailors and messenger-boys. The noise was even more deafening than usual; people cursing and yelling; cries of 'Beefribs! Steaming hot!' 'Clean rushes!' 'Good sheep's brains!' 'Strawberries and cherries! Every one ripe!'; political agitators haranguing the crowds; boatmen, the roughest and toughest of all Londoners, brawling with one another over prospective clients; and the continuous jangling of the bells.

By the time they reached the palace, George's head was aching and Warwick's nerves were strained to breaking point. One misplaced look, one awkward word could have precipitated a crisis there and then, but Edward was at his most urbane. He expressed his thanks with deference and gratitude, then clapped George Neville on the shoulder.

'There are rumours,' he said with a broad wink, giving his Chancellor a friendly hug, 'that our cousin here is soon to be elevated to the Archbishopric of York.' And he smiled at George with the utmost affection and goodwill.

* * *

The Nevilles held high court in Middleham Castle. The year of 1465 was drawing to its close and the Christmas festivities were a double celebration. Warwick, supported by his two brothers, had completed a truce with the Scots which would last, all being well, until the autumn of 1519. It was a notable achievement and as Warwick walked from the chapel, having heard the Boy-Bishop preach his Christmas morning sermon, he felt at peace with the world at last.

He had forgotten his plans of the summer. Henry was just another prisoner locked in the safety of the Tower. He was quite well treated, clothed and fed and he could receive visitors, but the Earl of Warwick was not among them. With the promotion of George Neville to the See of York, the successful conclusion of the Scottish peace negotiations and the brilliant, strategic recovery of his friend, King Louis, in France, Warwick's confidence had reasserted itself. He felt that the Woodvilles were no longer a threat. How could they ever really hope to compete against the power of the Nevilles? Why had he ever imagined that they could?

The coming year would be a good one. When George was enthroned, the family would give a banquet, the like of which had never been seen before. Warwick was determined on it. It would be more magnificent than anything that either Edward or the Woodvilles could produce and, as guests of honour, he would have the two brothers of the King. It was time to put into action that other plan; the marriage of Isabel and Anne to Clarence and Gloucester. Once George and Richard were firmly bound to his cause by the ties of matrimony, he could feel that his ascendancy over the Queen's family was complete.

The procession made its way to the great hall. A powdering of early snow crunched under their feet and the voices of the chapel-children rang out, round and clear in the frosty air. Warwick paused before entering the castle, savouring the crisp, invigorating tang of the moors; looking towards the distant hills, etched sharply black and white against the fragile egg-shell pink of the sky. How he loved this country!

But even as he took his place at the high table, an uneasy thought crossed his mind. If the Scots ceased to trouble the north and with the Lancastrian power at its nadir, what was the mighty Warwick to do? He could not sit at Westminster with the Woodvilles; the intrigues of court life he could safely leave to George. His brother, John, would be satisfied to administer his estates, vast territories since

208

he had become Earl of Northumberland. But Warwick was not content to do the same. He craved the action by which he had lived for so many years. The answer, it seemed to him, was still France and King Louis.

That wily monarch had again snatched victory from the jaws of defeat. Just as it had appeared that the League of Public Weal must triumph, Louis, not by any military feat, but by a stroke of the purest political genius, had won over the Duke of Brittany, placated his brother and set the rebellious pair squabbling with each other. Charles of Charolais had found himself alone.

As the boar's head, traditional fare for Christmas Day, was set on the table amidst cheers and singing, Warwick smiled to himself. With his capacity for action and Louis' flare for politics, what could they not accomplish between them? Undoubtedly he must still work unceasingly for the French alliance.

12

January and early February of the year
1466 were very cold. The covered boats,
which cost twopence instead of the usual
penny, were much in demand and the
boatmen could congratulate themselves on
a successful winter season. People kept within
doors whenever possible and in Westminster
Palace the Queen thanked Heaven for the
icy weather. Her first royal pregnancy was
almost at an end and as she withdrew into
the all-female world of the lying-in chamber,
every door and window was shut against the
air and a fire kindled on the hearth. In
the depths of winter such a ritual was not
unpleasant, but in the stifling heat of summer
it could become an unendurable ordeal.

Elizabeth was naturally anxious for a boy,
but she had proved her ability to bear sons
and if this were to be a daughter, she
knew herself to be a healthy and prolific
woman who had children easily. She had
been assured, however, on the authority of
the King's physician, Master Dominic, that
she was carrying a male child.

'Obviously! Obviously!' the little man had

cried, viewing the Queen's thickening body from all angles. 'Undoubtedly a boy!'

'You think so?' Edward had enquired, laughing, while the rest of the courtiers present had gathered round with sly grins and bawdy jokes.

'But of course!' The physician had spread plump hands. 'See how Her Grace carries the child to the back. The sure sign of a boy.' And he had spun round excitedly on his heels, clapping the young Duke of Gloucester on the shoulder. But the King's brother had given him no answering smile.

The pains began and Elizabeth began to pace the chamber floor, supported by two of her ladies, and her thoughts accelerated with the movement. What a puritanical youth her youngest brother-in-law was! She had no particular feeling for him; she neither liked nor disliked him. There was only one deep emotion in Elizabeth's life and that was love for her family. Her attitude to other people was governed entirely by their reaction to the Woodvilles. Apart from a mutual physical attraction, she had seen her marriage to Edward as a chance to advance the fortunes of her beloved brothers and sisters; as a chance, also, to realise the long cherished ambition of establishing herself as the most important of their number. A close-knit, devoted and talented family, there had always been rivalry among the older members of the Woodvilles for its leadership. Now, Elizabeth held undisputed sway and her love brimmed and spilt over, so that there was little to spare for anyone else, except her children.

Her growing hatred for Warwick and Clarence was rooted in their open contempt for her family. Nor had she forgotten the Earl of Desmond and his insults to herself last year. One day, she would show him what the power of the Woodvilles meant. As for the Duke of Gloucester, he displayed no overt hostility, although Elizabeth was not such a fool as to imagine that he liked her. She knew that Anthony respected him and wished for his friendship, but found the boy cold and unapproachable. But Richard showed no outward disrespect. He loved his brother and accepted the Woodvilles for Edward's sake. Elizabeth, therefore, beyond considering him something of a prig, was indifferent to him.

The pains grew worse and Elizabeth took to her bed. The midwives were called and, through a red haze, the Queen's feverish thoughts continued to mull around in her head. How she hated the arrogant Nevilles! How she loathed her self-opinionated eldest brother-in-law, the Duke of Clarence!

'God,' she prayed, 'let it be a boy.'

A boy! A boy who would oust George of Clarence from his position as heir-presumptive to the throne.

There came the cry of a newly-born baby. Outside, Master Dominic removed his ear from the keyhole and knocked gently on the door. A brawny midwife answered the summons.

'Well?' she asked, arms akimbo.

'What is it?' the physician enquired anxiously.

The midwife spat. 'Oho!' she said. 'I thought you knew, Master Know-it-all!'

'What is it?' he repeated, breaking into a sweat, and the woman eyed him with scorn.

'I'll tell you this,' she replied insolently. 'If it's a boy that Her Grace has in there, it's an idiot that's standing out there!' And she slammed the door in his face.

★ ★ ★

The Lord of Rozmital, brother of the Queen of Bohemia, was a gentleman who liked to travel and, with a party of similarly disposed friends, had arrived in London a few days before the christening of the little Princess.

Edward had hastened to accommodate

such distinguished guests in the city's largest inn and to ensure that every attention was paid to their comfort. He personally presented the Bohemians with collars of gold or silver — depending upon each man's rank — and the visitors were delighted with the custom which brought all the local ladies to their hostelry, carrying gifts of fresh flowers. They were even more enchanted to discover that English women never shook hands, but kissed everyone they met, friend and stranger alike. Rozmital recorded, with pleasure: 'This country produces women of outstanding beauty.'

He was unable, however, to enthuse about the rest of the islanders.

'The English are treacherous and sly,' he wrote home. 'The lives of foreigners are unsafe in their midst and no matter how much they may fawn on you, they are not to be trusted.'

This outburst was sparked off by the offensive behaviour of the Londoners, who were tired of paying court to visiting foreign dignitaries. They chose to make the Bohemians' curling, waist-length hair an object of derision and, as soon as one of the visitors appeared in the streets, he was surrounded by a crowd.

'Is it real?' some wag would ask, giving

the long, blond tresses a tug.

'No!' would come back the answer. 'They've stuck it on with tar.'

Their reception at court, however, amply recompensed Rozmital and his friends for their treatment at the hands of the commoners. They did attempt a protest to the King, but Edward only smiled.

'My people,' he explained, apologetically, 'are not overfond of foreigners. It comes, I think, from living on an island, cut off from the rest of Europe by the sea.'

'But cannot Your Grace control them?' suggested Rozmital, as he followed Edward into his private treasury. The King, signing for a cupboard to be unlocked, looked startled.

'I do control them,' he answered gently, 'but . . . subtly! Not by force! The various peoples of this island are very independent. There are areas of life where even I, as King, would not dare to trespass.' He smiled again and made an airy gesture. 'Enough of that! Here are the relics you wanted to see. The ring and girdle of Our Lady! One of the jars in which the water was turned to wine! And one of the stones from the Mount of Olives, bearing the imprint of Our Lord's foot.'

The vagaries of the English nation were forgotten before such sacred mementos and in the ensuing two days, the Bohemians walked happily around London visiting Becket's birthplace; praying at the tombs of his mother and sister; exclaiming over the golden, gem-encrusted splendour of the Confessor's shrine in Westminster Abbey.

'Glorious!' breathed Rozmital, looking with awe at the delicacy of Cavalini's carving. He added, to the supreme satisfaction of the Abbot: 'Not even St. Martin's tomb at Tours can compare with it.'

The climax of the Bohemians' London visit came with the churching of the Queen on the eleventh of February, a day or so after George Neville had christened the little Princess Elizabeth. As etiquette forbade the King's presence at the ceremony, Rozmital, as guest-of-honour, was escorted by Edward's deputy, the Earl of Warwick.

And it was a wrathful Warwick who watched the magnificent procession in Westminster Abbey; whose eyes were dazzled by the innumerable candles, crosses and reliquaries; whose unmusical ears were assaulted by the singing of the Queen's ladies and the playing of pipes, trumpets and strings; and whose every nerve was stretched in anger at the pomp and homage accorded to this former lady-in-waiting to Margaret of Anjou.

But worse was to come. At the banquet which followed the churching, Elizabeth sat alone on a golden throne, speaking to no one. All her women had to kneel throughout the forty-course meal and even the Duchess of Bedford had to go down on her knees when addressing her daughter. Warwick, leading Rozmital through four huge rooms packed with guests, to view this outrageous display, found himself trembling with suppressed passion. His cousin, Margaret of York, who was dancing, had to curtsey each time she turned in her sister-in-law's direction. She saw Warwick standing in the doorway and winked, pulling down the corners of her mouth in a disdainful grimace. Warwick raised his hand in affectionate greeting, then swung on his heel, Rozmital hurrying after him.

'What an impressive sight,' the Bohemian breathed reverently as they resumed their seats in the first of the four chambers, but Warwick's only response was a snort. Rozmital, however, made nothing of this: he had already noted the peculiar habit of silence which the English observed at mealtimes.

From his position at the high table, Warwick looked for Clarence and Gloucester. Their young heads were inclined towards each other and George was talking earnestly into his brother's ear. Warwick nodded in satisfaction. If the elder boy were following instructions, he was busy implanting in Richard's mind the idea of a marriage with his cousin, Anne Neville.

★ ★ ★

The Duke of Clarence reported failure. In his opinion, Richard, at thirteen, was not ready for marriage, but Warwick was indifferent to George's opinion.

'Leave it to me,' he ordered and went off to beg an audience of the King. When it was over, he had ensured that Edward would send his youngest brother to Cawood Castle in Yorkshire for George Neville's enthronement as Archbishop of York.

In the circumstances, he decided that Clarence should not be present as he had formerly planned, so that Richard would be the King's sole representative at the feast. Nothing that could be done should be omitted to make the young Duke aware of the regard and esteem in which his Neville cousins held him.

George of Clarence agreed, a little ill-naturedly, it was true, to absent himself from the glittering occasion, but he was

218

very fond of his younger brother. That apart, he was willing to make a sacrifice in any scheme which might lessen the power of the Woodvilles.

As Warwick had promised himself, the banquet which followed the religious ceremony was one to outdo every effort of Plantagenet and Woodville, alike. Six thousand guests had been assembled to honour the new Archbishop and to prove to the world that the Nevilles were still the most powerful family in the land. Warwick, himself, performed the office of Steward; John Neville was the Treasurer; and Hastings had agreed to act as Comptroller, and, no doubt, would also act as spy on the proceedings for Edward. Warwick smiled to himself. The King should have something worth listening to; something to make him think.

Four hundred swans, five hundred stags, a hundred oxen and four thousand calves, sheep and pigs, together with thirteen thousand sweet dishes and subtleties had been laboriously prepared by sixty-two overworked cooks, to press home the fact that Warwick and his brothers could still live more luxuriously than the King.

While the guests got steadily drunk on three hundred tuns of ale, a hundred tuns of wine and a pipe of hippocras, Warwick kept his eye on his young cousin, whom he had placed near his wife and daughters.

Anne was now almost ten years old; a pretty, fragile child, with fair hair and eyes whose colour was reflected by the matching blue of her dress. It was a shade which suited her, but the Earl wished that his youngest daughter could have worn white on this occasion. Blue was fast falling into disrepute. Originally the colour of marital fidelity, such were the conditions of the times that throughout Europe, it was becoming the colour of the cuckold and the adulteress.

It was unlikely, however, that young Richard would entertain any such thoughts about his little cousin, whose freshness and innocence shone brightly in her face. As he watched their heads draw close together in friendly conversation and the smiles which passed between them during their equally companionable silences, Warwick felt elated. Richard and Anne had been fond of each other when the Duke had lived in the Earl's household and now Warwick was convinced that, with very little prompting, this affection could be made to burgeon into a desire for marriage.

The day drew to its close and torches were lit, licking the darkness with bright tongues of flame. Warwick glanced around him and noted his cousin, Elizabeth, now the mother of two sons, snapping some remark to her husband, which Suffolk, in surly mood, pretended not to hear; his other cousin, Anne, Duchess of the exiled Exeter, uneasily twisting a black and gold cramp ring on her finger; and yet another of his relations, the eleven-years-old Duke of Buckingham, sullenly submitting to the caresses of his wife, Catherine Woodville. No one, Warwick reflected sourly, was safe nowadays from being commanded to take a Woodville for a wife.

The debris of the banquet stretched before him and the servants began collecting the left-over food into the wooden alms dishes. The poor would feast well tonight. The Earl yawned contentedly. George Neville was now the second most important cleric in the country. Their brother-in-law, Hastings, would carry details of the banquet to Edward, and if he magnified them in the telling, so much the better. Richard and Anne were holding hands and laughing. Altogether, a most satisfactory day.

★ ★ ★

The Lord of Rozmital and his companions went to Windsor as guests of the King.

They rode into the castle watched by the masons whom Edward had recruited from all over the country to make the castle the most beautiful in the land. The interest of these men, however, was brief. Princes might come and go; rule all England one day, be incarcerated in the Tower the next; but they were the kings of the professional world whose services would always be in demand. They had been too often on the fringe of great events not to have more than their share of the Englishman's contempt for his betters; not to know how infinitely superior they were to the men who ruled over them. And their indifference to these outlandish foreigners bordered on the insolent. The Bohemians, in their turn, eyed the masons with dislike.

Edward, as usual, was forced to atone for his subjects' lack of warmth. He came to meet his visitors with a brilliant retinue; a cavalcade dressed in scarlet and purple, rich blue and vivid green, gold and silver ornaments gleaming against the luxury of sable and ermine, miniver and budge. But while he entertained his guests with lavish hospitality; while he showed them, with pride, the holy relics of St. George (the saint's heart, arm and a part of his skull, brought to England fifty years before by the

Emperor Sigismund); while they hunted the black, white and dappled deer with which the park abounded, the King's thoughts were elsewhere. His spies had brought him word concerning Warwick's plans for his brothers.

'Would it be such a bad thing for Richard and George to marry Anne and Isabel?' Hastings demanded as they emerged from early morning Mass, ready for the day's sport. 'It would keep Warwick wedded — and I use the word advisedly — to your interests.'

The King mounted his horse, his cross-bow slung across his back, and signalled for the hunt to begin.

'You think so?' He laughed, sourly. 'I'm fond of my brothers, William, but I don't trust George. He was born discontented with his lot and my marriage has affronted his pride. In conjunction with Warwick — '

He broke off to take aim and bring down a fine dappled buck. Then, shrugging aside the congratulations of Rozmital, he continued in a low voice to his friend: 'My cousin is ambitious. He thought to rule England through me. He still hopes to do so. But when he finds that he can't, he'll look for someone else and the obvious choice, particularly if he is married to Warwick's daughter, is my heir-male.'

Hastings was horrified. 'You believe that Warwick and Clarence would overthrow you? Perhaps kill you? And what of Richard?'

The King winced. In the turmoil of his mind, it was this, the fear that his cousin and George had suborned his youngest brother, that so embittered him. He had for Richard a love so strong that it surmounted the natural incompatibility of their temperaments; a love which overcame the antipathy of the immoral for the moral, the lecher for the puritan. He had believed this affection returned and now to find that the boy was apparently intriguing with his enemies, hurt him more than he cared to admit, even to himself.

'I don't know,' he said, briefly. Then: 'In any case,' he added, 'it behoves me to take precautions. If George is prevented from marrying Isabel Neville, temptation is removed a little further from Warwick's grasp. I doubt if he will back George unless his daughter can be Queen.'

For once, however, Edward, normally a very percipient young man, had read into Warwick's actions a motive of which the Earl was, as yet, unaware. The Earl's ardent desire for the alliance of his daughters to the Dukes of Clarence and Gloucester was governed by nothing more than a wish to extend his influence over the King and to build up at court a counterparty to the Woodvilles. No other idea had so far entered his head and Edward's adamant refusal to allow the marriages came as a blow to his understanding as well as his pride.

In late March, he went to Salisbury, where George of Clarence was entertaining the ubiquitous Bohemians at his palace of Clarendon. As they rode out for the Palm Sunday procession, depicting Christ's entry into Jerusalem, Warwick did his best to soothe and placate George's furious resentment and bolster his hopes for the future.

'Nothing is lost yet,' he assured his young cousin. 'George,' he continued, referring to his brother, the Archbishop, 'will use all his influence at the papal court to secure a dispensation. Once we have cleared that hurdle . . . ' He paused, giving the Duke a significant look and Clarence grunted.

'Edward's agents will work against us in Rome,' the Duke replied, pessimistically, but his despondency was already lifting. Turning to Rozmital, he cried: 'I hope you will walk in the procession with me, my lord. And afterwards, you shall dine on one of our rarest delicacies; a fish that lays eggs like a bird.' (Such was the wondering Bohemians' introduction to a creature which later generations were to know as barnacle-goose.)

Rozmital was delighted to accept both invitations and Warwick nodded approvingly. His cousin's spirits were as mercurial as his own and, for the moment, he saw nothing in the future to depress them unduly. He believed that once the dispensation was theirs and the marriage achieved, Edward would bow to the inevitable. And in the secret places of his mind, put away like some precious jewel, only to be brought out and looked at on special occasions, was the thought of the dukedom of Normandy. But his efforts to bring about an English alliance with France were soon to receive a serious setback.

Charles of Charolais, frightened by Louis' startling recovery, was indicating his willingness to consider marriage with Margaret of York. On his return to Westminster, Warwick found himself, together with Hastings, deputed to lead the embassy which Edward was sending to Boulogne. A matrimonial alliance with Burgundy was just what the King and Queen most desired.

★ ★ ★

The two men faced each other across the council table. Hatred was in the air. It hung so depressingly over the negotiations that Hastings, seated at Warwick's right hand, could feel it, almost like a living force within the stifling room.

'You ask the impossible,' Warwick snapped, rearing his head and looking at Charles of Charolais in the same arrogant way in which he might have regarded a pot-boy. 'You ask for our unconditional support against France and this King Edward is not prepared to give.'

The future Duke of Burgundy gave him back look for look, curling his rather thick lips in disdain.

'Either you wilfully misunderstand me, my lord Warwick, or your intellect is poor.'

Hastings hurriedly recruited his strength with a sip of wine as he waited for the explosion of Warwick's wrath.

Charolais continued: 'I am not demanding *unconditional* support, as I have made abundantly clear. I am offering myself as husband to the Lady Margaret of York.'

His haughty way of speaking, his over-bearing manners, had the effect of making the proposed bargain appear grossly unequal. What, his contemptuous eyes seemed to ask, was a little matter of English assistance for Burgundy when he was offering that most sought-after, that most glittering of all European prizes, himself?

Warwick rose in an uprush of velvets and furs, his face contorted with rage.

'I shall report to King Edward,' he shouted, 'that the failure of these talks are entirely due to your overweening pride.'

'This, from you, my lord!' But Charolais' words fell upon empty air. Warwick had swept from the chamber, followed, in agitated procession, by Hastings and the rest of the English delegation.

The Earl returned in a fever of anger to Calais, a circumstance not long in reaching the ears of the ever vigilant Louis. Rubbing his hands in glee, the French King sent his own embassy to the little staple town with some of the most tempting offers he had yet made.

'King Louis offers a truce by both sea and land until March of 1468.'

'King Louis wishes to hold a conference of enduring peace this coming October.'

'King Louis will give no aid of any kind to Queen Margaret or to any of her followers, if King Edward gives none to Brittany or Burgundy.'

Warwick listened rapturously and the envoys burbled happily on.

'Our master will find a husband for the Lady Margaret and provide the dowry from his own pocket.'

'Our master will pay his cousin of England forty thousand crowns a year.'

Warwick was enchanted. Surely, even Edward could not be so foolish or stubborn as to refuse such offers. He signed a provisional agreement and crossed to England late in May.

Edward's congratulations were formal in the extreme and his manner so reserved that Warwick shook the dust of Westminster from his feet in a flurry of justifiable rage. He had secured peace with France on the most favourable terms of the century; he had extricated his King from what could only have proved a most disastrous alliance with Burgundy and yet all he had received for his pains was the minimal display of gratitude.

He departed in a huff to Oxford, where the Archbishop of York awaited him. In the cool cloisters of the University, the two brothers walked and talked.

'How is our little matter going in Rome?' Warwick wanted to know and George spread his soft, expressive hands, his many rings catching and reflecting the light in shimmering pools of blue and red. The great diamond at his throat sent diffused rainbows of colour trembling across his thin, clever face.

'So-so,' he murmured cautiously. 'But His Holiness, Pope Paul the second, is not proving as malleable as many of us . . . as many of his cardinals had hoped.'

'Was that the reason for his election?' Warwick asked with a grin, but George clucked disparagingly with his tongue.

'It does not behove me to criticise Vatican politics,' he answered repressively and Warwick realised that his brother's hopes were centred on a cardinal's hat; perhaps on the triple tiara itself. No English pontiff had worn it since Nicholas Breakspear had become Adrian the fourth in the twelfth century, but for a Neville all things were possible.

'The dispensation may be forthcoming,' George continued, 'but it will take a little time. My agents, however, report a modicum of success.'

'Sufficient success,' Warwick asked, 'for me to proceed with my plans?'

The Archbishop inclined his head and his brother smiled. After his cool reception at Westminster, he longed heart and soul to do anything which would flout Edward's authority. He sent at once for the Dukes of Clarence and Gloucester to join him.

George set out immediately, taking Richard with him, but they did not arrive in Oxford. As they reached the outskirts of the city, they were arrested on the orders of the King and taken back to Westminster under guard.

A week later, Warwick heard that a reconciliation had taken place between the three royal brothers on the strict understanding that neither George nor Richard would seek marriage with either of their Neville cousins, Isabel and Anne.

Warwick's place in the world, which he had so laboriously rebuilt after Edward's marriage, seemed to be crumbling about him once more.

13

The papal envoy and his companions struggled along the winter roads.

In this January of 1467, hard frosts were turning the furrowed tracks into pitfalls for the unwary horseman. The bare branches of the trees snaked into the air, weird, contorted shapes that spoke to the superstitious of hobgoblins and the Devil. The Italians crossed themselves, shuddering. The rivers and streams lay like sheets of black glass and the moorlands stretched, bleak and dun-colorado, into the distance, where a leaden sky merged into the horizon. Never before had they seen such a dismal landscape; a countryside so bereft of sunlight and colour.

The little party plunged into the shelter of some woods, thankful for any alleviation from the icy wind, which cut across their faces and deadened their hands. Drifts of last year's leaves lay in piles, heaped against sodden, greying tree-trunks, or masking the ruts in the highway, making it even more treacherous than before. Moreover, the Italians could only pray that they were on the right road, for there were no signposts to direct them and they had been unable to ask for details of their route at court — for the simple reason that they had not passed through Westminster nor paid their respects to England's King. They were on a secret mission to the Archbishop of York.

They came out once more on to the open heathland and breasted a rise, to see before them, at last, the great house, 'The Moor', as it was called, which was now one of George Neville's many possessions.

The emissaries were welcomed in and made much of: so much so, that at dinner, they were given new bread, a privilege normally reserved for the master of the house. George was out to impress. His butler and sewer went through the rites of assay, tasting each dish before it was brought to the table and sipping the wine before it was poured into the cup; a ritual only accorded to those of royal blood. The Pope's representative should not go unreminded that the Archbishop was a descendant of kings.

After the meal, the chief envoy was shown George's library, which contained an impressive number of manuscripts, and where a Greek clerk spent his days translating his country's masterpieces. Copies of the Archbishop's correspondence with many of the world's leading scholars were kept in velvet-bound folios, ornamented with tassels of gold and silver. By the end of his conducted tour, the envoy was willing to agree with Chastellain that George was an eloquent and erudite prelate, but was less inclined to the Burgundian's view that his host was retiring and modest.

Ensconced, finally, before a blazing fire of logs and peat in his private solar, the Archbishop touched upon the reason for the envoy's visit.

'How are my affairs in Rome?' he asked tentatively and the envoy smiled with some encouragement.

'They go slowly, my lord, but that, as you know, is the way in St. Peter's. The granting of dispensations and the disposal of cardinals' hats are not matters to be decided in a moment.'

The Archbishop made an impatient gesture. 'I should hardly call twelve months a moment. I refer to the permission for the Duke of Clarence to marry my niece, Isabel. If it's a question of money . . . '

The Italian pursed his lips and shook his head, an indication that such plain speaking was unappreciated by one versed in the subtler and more diplomatic ways of the Vatican.

'These things must go through channels,' he murmured. 'One cannot approach the Holy Father direct. A most courteous man, as was his uncle, Eugenius the fourth, but he likes his cardinals to know their place. However, I am not unhopeful of either issue being brought to a satisfactory conclusion. But I was led to understand that two dispensations were required.'

'They were,' George answered, tersely, then added: 'Since the King refused his sanction to the marriages, the Duke of Gloucester has evinced no further interest in the matter.'

The Italian raised mobile brows. 'Indeed! It seems that we have an extremely loyal young man.'

'It seems that we have a fool who will cut off his nose to spite his face,' George snapped. 'His loyalty to his brother will cost my cousin the affection of his friends and land him on the side of his enemies. No! One dispensation is all we need.' The Archbishop shook his head regretfully 'Now! About that other matter!'

★ ★ ★

The palace of Westminster was as full of foreigners in this chill spring of 1467 as it

235

was of Woodvilles. An embassy from King Louis jostled cheek by jowl in the draughty corridors with the ambassadors of Burgundy, and Edward suddenly found himself the most courted of European princes.

In the struggle for power between France and her mightiest vassal, England's support was of the utmost importance to each of the protagonists. And as both sides made claims and counterclaims and outbid the other's offers, the court split into its two inevitable factions. Warwick, Clarence and all opponents of the Woodvilles pressed upon Edward the necessity of making terms with the French, while the Queen and her family insisted that their kinship with Burgundy be recognised by a treaty with Duke Philip.

As he strolled with his cousin to the tennis courts, Warwick, who had hastened south from Yorkshire in the bitter winter weather to be present at this crucial time, urged upon Edward the rewards to be gained from the French alliance.

'As I told you last summer,' he said in reproof, 'the Burgundians have been unpopular in this country since Philip's embargo on English cloth.'

'The French,' Edward responded, drily, 'have been unpopular in this country since the Conquest.'

'Pooh!' said Warwick, airily. 'Just because the Agincourt song is still sung in a few of the taverns . . .'

Edward turned on his cousin in exasperation. They had reached the courts and the King threw off his cloak and doublet. Standing there in shirt and hose, swinging his parchment-covered racket impatiently against his legs, he looked like some golden Colossus. Warwick was not a small man, but at this moment he was uncomfortably aware of the disproportionate advantage which Edward's six feet, four inches gave him.

'I cannot believe,' the King said, angrily, 'that you believe in what you say. Amongst our countrymen there is an inherent antipathy towards France which nothing will ever dispel.' He flung up a ball and lobbed it over the silken net. 'On the other hand, their dislike of Burgundy is unlikely to survive next month's tournament when the Grand Bastard meets my brother-in-law at Smithfield.'

'You cannot mean to marry Margaret to Charles of Charolais,' Warwick protested, shocked. 'And that is a part of Burgundy's terms.'

'Why not?' the King replied, casually, but there was a faint flush on his cheeks.

'A man twice a widower, with a daughter almost as old as herself.' The Earl was

237

outraged. His affection for his young cousin was as strong as his hatred for Charolais and his concern was completely genuine. It showed in his face and made Edward angrier than before.

'Few princesses can choose where they marry,' the King answered, roughly, adding: 'Very few women of any sort, if it comes to that, including your own two girls. Did they have any choice when you tried to push them into marriage with my two brothers?'

Warwick flushed in his turn, but before he could justify his action, the King went on: 'Which reminds me! I've had word of a certain papal embassy which visited our worthy Archbishop earlier this year. Did you know of it?'

Warwick shrugged, insolently. The King's two stepsons, Thomas and Richard Grey, had entered the courts and he had no mind to continue this conversation in front of them. Edward swung round, catching his arm.

'Tell this to George,' he whispered, fiercely. 'I'll have no interference in my affairs. I have forbidden these marriages and that is my final word.'

'You are unreasonable,' Warwick hissed, one wary eye on the two interested young Greys.

'Unreasonable!' Edward was breathing hard and his eyes had a red glow in their depths. 'I tell you this, Richard! You'll not get a crown for either of your daughters while I have the means to prevent it.' He was too furious to notice the arrested look on Warwick's face. 'And you may warn your brother that on the next occasion that he offers me any affront, there will be consequences which he has not foreseen.'

But for Edward, this conversation was to have consequences for himself which he had not foreseen. His judgement had been seriously at fault and his words, far from having the deterrent effect which he had intended, had implanted in Warwick's mind a new idea that he was not long in communicating to his brother.

At the Archbishop's sumptuous home near Charing Cross, Warwick paced the newly rushed floors, excitement in his eyes.

'Why not?' he demanded. 'Edward has no male heirs as yet and George is his next in blood. The Woodvilles are badly spoken of everywhere you go. The people would welcome their removal.'

George Neville looked at his brother with annoyance, tempered with affection. There were times when the Earl reminded him forcibly of their father and in the Archbishop's eyes, the comparison was not a happy one.

'Richard! Richard!' he sighed. 'You have too many irons in the fire and it's making you indecisive. One day, Edward; now it's Clarence; sometimes Henry. Hold these other ideas in readiness, by all means, but for God's sake pursue one course of action through to the end. Unpopular the Woodvilles may be, but Edward most certainly is not! Our chief hope for the present lies in him. Until we have proved beyond all shadow of a doubt that we cannot win back our power by using Edward, we shall do well to put aside all thoughts of Henry or of George.'

Warwick seemed inclined to demur and the Archbishop caught him by the arm, the black velvet of the Earl's sleeve turning silver-grey under the pressure of his brother's fingers.

'We helped to put Edward on the throne,' George Neville said, 'and consider your two alternatives. Give the crown to Clarence and he could be as awkward as the King — and without his brother's wisdom! As for Henry! Oh, docile enough, I grant you, but take Henry and you have to take Margaret.' He saw Warwick's face change at that and nodded triumphantly. 'A very different kettle of fish, that!'

'What do you suggest?' Warwick asked,

with unwonted humility, as George turned to pour wine from a silver ewer which had been set, together with goblets of the finest Venetian glass, on a side table.

'Go to France when the French embassy returns. Meet Louis. Assure him of Edward's goodwill. Extract even better terms from him — if you can. Once we secure the French alliance, we are back in our old position. We have proved our ability to sway the King to our way of thinking and we have thumbed our noses at the Woodvilles.'

And so it was, that when the French envoys left Billingsgate on the twenty-seventh of May, they were accompanied by a fleet of ships bearing the Earl, his household, knights, attendants and archers. As the painted sails lifted to the wind, Warwick knew a moment's uneasiness. Why, he wondered, had Edward given his permission for this visit with such alacrity? And why had he given his sanction to the Earl's proposed negotiations gaily, almost as though it were no longer of any importance what his cousin did?

It was as well for the Earl's peace of mind that he could not see the equally jocund, arras-hung ships which sailed up the Thames three days after his departure, bringing not only the Grand Bastard of Burgundy and all his chivalry for the tournament, but also

241

more of Charolais' envoys; quiet, serious men with a look of purpose in their eyes.

★ ★ ★

Some miles from Rouen, on the banks of the Seine, amongst the tossing apple-orchards of Normandy, lay the village of La Bouille and it was here, to his surprise, that Warwick found Louis waiting to greet him.

The King hurried to the water's edge, his protuberant eyes alight with joy, his enormous nose quivering with pleasure. He refused to allow the Earl to kneel to him, throwing his arms about his neck and calling him 'Friend!' It was a welcome at once more flattering and more touching than even Warwick had anticipated and he felt that here, at last, was a man who recognised his true greatness, his real worth. Behind his master's back, Olivier le Daim smiled. One of Louis' many talents was his genius for making people feel that they had not, after all, over-valued themselves.

'I couldn't wait to meet you,' the King explained as they walked by the bank and watched the Earl's ships bobbing like a string of gaudy beads beyond the clumps of willow. 'Oh, I know we are to meet in Rouen the day after tomorrow, but it will be an official welcome, all pomp and show and not a word shall we be able to say to each other without a score of people within ear-shot.'

It was fortunate for Warwick that his French was good, for the King spoke fast, the words bubbling over his lips in a froth of excitement. Looking at him in his coarse frieze tunic, at startling variance with his guest's silken magnificence, it was difficult to imagine that behind his spate of words and the unceasing movements of his hands, the King's brain was working with a calm and precision which most statesmen would have envied.

When Warwick would have talked politics, Louis silenced him with a gesture.

'This is a meeting between friends,' he said, taking the Earl's arm in a familiar embrace. 'The serious talk, that is for the days to come. I have lodged you in the Dominican Friary in Rouen. You will find nothing lacking for your comfort. Myself, I am in the next house.' He broke off to chuckle delightedly. 'It has a connecting corridor with the Friary and we can meet in secret whenever we wish.'

(Warwick was to learn that, for all his sophistication, Louis took a childish pleasure in small subterfuges such as this.)

The Earl expected that the King would

accompany him to Rouen by water, but Louis was adamant.

'No, no!' he exclaimed. 'You must travel in state! Alone and in splendour! I shall travel by land and be there to welcome you.'

He was as good as his word, for when the walls and towers of the city were sighted by Warwick's fleet, the bells pealing out their greetings, cannons firing and flags flying from every turret, Louis stood at the main gates surrounded by his knights, magistrates and city fathers, the chief burgesses and the clergy. He went impatiently through the formal greetings, then: 'Come in! Come in!' he cried. 'Enter the city which was captured and held by your Monmouth Hal.'

As they proceeded on foot, the priests singing and chanting, the Englishmen staggering a little, still feeling the heave of the ships under their feet, Louis whispered incessantly in Warwick's ear, pointing to places of interest.

'Here,' he said, 'is the market-place where our Maid was burnt — your father-in-law presiding, I believe.'

His large eyes twinkled as he relished his little jibe and he glanced sideways to see if it had struck home. He could never resist taunting even the people he most wished to please and it was a habit which had caused

244

him trouble on more than one occasion in the past. But not this time. The Earl wore his complacency like an armour, too strong to be pierced by Louis' darts. A typical Englishman, the King reflected with a sly grin.

'There is the castle where your Edward was born,' he reminded Warwick, 'when his father was Lieutenant-General of the English in France. I have often heard Edward called the 'White Rose of Rouen'.'

This time his guest did flush, a tell-tale tide of colour which informed Louis that his spies had spoken correctly when they reported a rift between Warwick and his King.

Louis added, gleefully: 'And then, of course, I have heard him referred to as 'Son of the archer'. Eh? What?' And he dug Warwick in the ribs, shaking with suppressed mirth. The dozen or so lucky charms suspended from the brim of his hat shook and tinkled with him.

The Earl smiled in return, but abstractedly. With the passing years, he had almost forgotten the rumours about his aunt and the archer, Blackburn, but Louis' words brought a forceful reminder. It was a story which, however unbelievable, might very well be used against Edward in the future.

He was thankful when they at last reached the precincts of the Friary. It was a close day and the French crowds which packed the streets were depressingly hostile and silent. Also, there was a wind; a hot, summer gale that whipped the dry earth into clouds and sent the dust particles whirling dementedly in and out of the sunbeams. It bellied the men's cloaks like sails before a breeze, spreading them on the bright air in patches of scarlet and tawny, azure, orange and green. Against the Friary wall, setting the grey aflame, a mass of roses tossed their fiery heads, their petals flying upwards like sparks on the wind.

'Alas, we couldn't manage a white rose,' Louis murmured, spreading deprecating hands.

During the next twelve days the French and English diplomats conferred in public; Warwick and Louis in private. At night, the King would come scurrying along the corridor from his own lodgings to the Earl's, flapping his grey tunic; his resemblance to some overgrown bird emphasised still more by the huge, beak-like nose. The envoys might discuss the terms of the treaty; the amount to be paid by Louis to Edward for England's support against Burgundy; the provision of a suitable husband for Margaret of York; the partitioning of Burgundy when she was conquered and the division of her trade. But Louis and Warwick whispered together of other things.

'Normandy? A dukedom? Phoo!' said Louis, waving aside his former proposition as one throwing aside a broken toy. 'Why not a principality? Why not Prince of Holland and Zealand? When Burgundy is mine, of course!'

The wavering light of the candles flickered over a face no longer bird-like, but vulpine in its cunning. The Earl trembled in excitement. Prince Richard! Why not, indeed! He was a great-grandson of John of Gaunt and descendant of the Kings of England. No man deserved such a title more. Only one thing gave him pause. He hated Charles of Charolais and longed for his overthrow, but he held no real grudge against Duke Philip.

This problem was suddenly resolved for him when, on June the sixteenth, on a cloudless day of brilliant sunshine, messengers arrived from Bruges with the news that Duke Philip had died the previous day. They gave to Louis a graphic and moving account of the new Duke's grief at his father's death.

'He screamed and wept, Your Grace, and fell on the floor, wringing his hands in anguish.'

If this description of his behaviour earned Charles the further contempt of the Earl of Warwick, Louis seemed to see nothing amiss in it and clucked and nodded understandingly. But even while his messengers sped on their way to Burgundy, carrying his formal expressions of sympathy and sorrow, the King of France was rubbing his hands in delight. Charles was not so popular as his father had been and it might be possible for Louis, with the aid of his agents and a little money judiciously spent, to arrange for his assassination. Charles' sole heir was a daughter, Mary, and what could a woman do against the might of France?

'We are almost there,' Louis chuckled to Warwick as they sat in splendour at the Earl's farewell banquet. 'It will not be long now before I hail my friend, the Prince of Holland and Zealand.'

Warwick was like a man in a dream, but it was a dream from which he knew that he could be rudely awakened. His whole dazzling future rested, as always, on his ability to make Edward accept the French alliance.

On June the twenty-third, he sailed from Honfleur, taking with him yet another embassy from Louis. He left France the most courted and honoured of guests; a man of limitless importance; close friend of a King. He arrived in England to discover that his brother, George, had been deprived of the Chancellorship and that a treaty would soon be completed between England and Burgundy, pledging Margaret of York to Duke Charles in marriage.

14

The stifling summer heat hung over London like a shroud and with the noisome vapours from the river there mingled another smell, the sickly-sweet smell of death.

As Warwick and the French envoys sped up river to Westminster, the Earl could already see a rash of crosses appearing on the doors of houses lining the river banks. The cranes upon the wharves lay ominously still and fewer boatmen plied their trade across the Thames. The bodies of executed pirates, left to hang upon the gibbets until three tides had washed over them, danced their macabre dance and added the stench of rotting flesh to the fetid, fly-infested atmosphere. It was one of the worst outbreaks of plague within living memory and Parliament had adjourned in panic to the fresher air of Windsor.

Since the Earl's return to London two days earlier, he had been lodging with the Frenchmen in the Bishop of Salisbury's palace, a building not long vacated by the Bastard of Burgundy, whose days of jousting with Anthony Woodville had been so tragically interrupted by the news of his father's death and his immediate recall home.

Warwick had not as yet shown Edward any of his anger over his brother's dismissal from office, an event brought about by George Neville's refusal to attend the opening session of Parliament.

'What would you have had me do?' the Archbishop had demanded when Warwick had reproached him for being so rash. 'Edward was intriguing with Charles as soon as you were out of the country. He is as good as committed to Burgundy. We've been duped and made to look fools. The Queen and her relations are cock-a-hoop and I warn you! Whatever extra inducements Louis is prepared to offer, it will make no difference.'

Warwick soon found that his brother was right. He had already had two interviews with Edward, but while the King was his usual pleasant self and listened courteously to everything which the ambassadors proposed, it was obvious to the meanest intelligence that he was disinterested. Today's interview at Westminster was Warwick's last bid to bring to fruition the all important French alliance.

At the landing-stage, Hastings, Anthony Woodville and George of Clarence waited to greet them, but it was only the Duke who hastened forward down the steps and showed that flattering attention which the envoys felt to be their due.

As soon as they entered the Council Chamber, Warwick was aware of the Burgundian ambassador, the Seigneur de la Gruthuyse, hovering at Edward's elbow, while behind him, all the Queen's male relatives, both those of blood and those of marriage, stood in serried ranks.

Jehan de Popincourt, Louis' chief envoy, stepped forward with a nervous cough, conscious of the antipathy all around him. Gruthuyse's presence cramped his style; he could not speak freely of the partitioning of Burgundy and the sharing of her trading rights within the hearing of Charles' representative. He spoke instead of Philip of Bresse as a suitable husband for the King's sister; of French trade concessions; and of that subject dear to every Englishman's heart, the rightful ownership of Normandy and Guienne.

'My master,' he said, 'is willing to have this matter put to papal arbitration.'

Even so, without the inducement of territorial gains in the Low Countries, de Popincourt's words sounded lame, and he was hardly surprised when, after a brief consultation with his advisers, Edward replied evasively that he would consider the proffered terms.

The whole proceedings were a farce and the traditional spiced wine, the drinking of which closed all such diplomatic occasions, nearly caused Warwick to choke. As the gilded barge returned the way it had come, the grey and muddied waters frothing about its sides, he said in a low, furious voice to de Popincourt: 'Did you see that nest of vipers round the King?'

The Frenchman was startled. He had no doubt to whom the Earl was referring, but such plain speaking argued the kind of breach between Warwick and Edward not soon to be bridged. He nodded, storing up these tit-bits of information for transmission to his master.

'They are the people responsible for my brother's dismissal from office,' Warwick went on, too angry to think carefully of what he said.

'The Archbishop is no longer Chancellor?' one of the other envoys enquired.

Warwick shook his head. 'The King has taken the Great Seal from him and given it to Bishop Stillington.' He hissed the name between clenched teeth, so that the Frenchman found the outlandish name impossible to catch.

Popincourt laid his hand on Warwick's arm. 'Never mind, my lord,' he soothed. 'A man such as yourself will most certainly know how to avenge himself.'

★ ★ ★

Christmas had come and gone. The Lord of Misrule had put away his cap and bells for another year and the Boy-Bishop had doffed his borrowed mitre. In Middleham, Plough Monday was being celebrated with the usual festivities as the men and boys, in fancy dress, pulled the plough through the village, churning up the land of anyone who refused to put money in their greasy hats.

When in residence at the castle, Warwick rarely missed the local celebrations, but this bleak January day was an exception. As he stood with his back to the fire in the great hall, his thoughts were far removed from the revelries of his tenants. Of the three men who watched him, only his brother, the Earl of Northumberland, regarded him with inimical gaze.

John Neville was the quietest of his family; an able soldier in war; a man content to mind his own affairs in peace. He had had more in common with Thomas, who had died with their father at Wakefield, than with either of his two remaining brothers. George he found entirely alien; subtle, devious, clever, an intricate character whose mind traversed tortuous paths unknown to the direct and simple John. While as for Richard, the hero of his youth, the easy, unaspiring elder brother, he had become a man consumed by the flame of ambition; a man ready to betray his King; to sacrifice his home, wife and family to the pursuit of his own aggrandisement. What had caused it? John looked at the familiar face with its drawn brows and the thin, uncompromising set of the lips. Was it Edward's ingratitude? Or wounded pride? Or was it that Richard truly believed himself to be the only person capable of ruling England? John shivered. In the old Greek plays such hubris had led to tragedy and Nemesis had stalked in its wake.

He got to his feet, making lame excuses. 'I must return home tomorrow. I must see that all is ready.'

He saw George's sneering smile and flinched from it as he had done when a boy, but he would not change his mind. Treason was in the air and he wanted nothing to do with their plotting.

Warwick laughed and stepped forward, gripping his brother's arm. 'Very well!' he said. 'Go home! But one day, my lad, you will find out what Edward is really like and then you'll whistle another tune. When you've felt the full weight of his ingratitude, come back to us.'

'If I ever do,' John answered, breathing rather fast, 'I'll do just that.'

When the door had slammed behind him, George gave a sigh of relief and a more relaxed atmosphere pervaded the room. The other man, Warwick's cousin-by-marriage, Sir John Conyers, drew nearer to the fire and smiled.

'Now,' he said, stretching his feet to the blaze, 'what do you want me to do?'

'Nothing, as yet,' Warwick responded. 'But hold yourself and your men in readiness for the time when I give the word.'

Sir John was disappointed. On a recent visit to London, he had been snubbed by Anthony Woodville and he was thirsting for revenge.

'Why not now?' he asked. 'No one will connect me with you. I shall call myself Robin of Redesdale. How do you like that?'

'Unoriginal, but no doubt effective,' murmured George, helping himself liberally to sugared violets from a flat, wooden dish. 'Shades of Robin Hood, outlaws and so forth. But the point is, armed rebellion is not our intention . . . yet!'

Sir John resented the Archbishop's tone of voice. 'I hear,' he said, nastily, 'that your kinsman, Archbishop Bourchier, has obtained a cardinal's hat. I had thought that you would beat him to it, George.'

The Archbishop flushed and rose to his feet, but before he could think of a suitable retort, Warwick said: 'And that reminds me! What of the dispensation?'

'The matter progresses,' his brother replied, pleased to turn the subject. 'I think that I have enlisted James Goldwell to work on our behalf.'

'Edward's own Vatican representative?' Warwick was incredulous and George inclined his head triumphantly. Even Sir John Conyers forgot their momentary unpleasantness and began to laugh.

'That would be a feather in your cap,' he said. Then, reverting to more serious matters, he asked: 'The Burgundian agreement is certain, I suppose?'

Warwick nodded, glumly. 'Margaret of York appeared before the Council last September and agreed to the marriage.'

The short day was closing in and the sky showed in slits of dark, moth-wing blue. A page entered, carrying candles, whose flame flickered in pale competition with the deep-orange glow of the fire.

'There's a messenger, my lord,' he said, 'from the King.'

The three men glanced quickly, almost furtively at each other, before Warwick ordered curtly: 'Bring him in.'

The message was brief and to the point. The King demanded the Earl's presence at Coventry, where he had been keeping Christmas. The Duke of Clarence was with him.

Warwick, caught unawares by this peremptory summons, hesitated, looking speculatively at Conyers, but George swung his brother round, away from the messenger.

'For God's sake, go!' he muttered. 'We are not ready for . . . anything else.'

Loth as he was to submit, Warwick knew this to be true, but still he wavered.

The messenger said in a flat, toneless voice: 'The Queen also bade me give you a message, my lord.' His face was as expressionless as his voice.

'Well?' Warwick raised imperious eyebrows.

'The Earl of Desmond, my lord, has been executed at Drogheda.'

The implied threat was crystal clear.

★ ★ ★

258

A cold spring blossomed into early summer. The speedwell and pimpernel — the 'poor man's weather vanes' — opened their delicate petals to the sun. Snowdrop gave place to violet and vetch; cowslip and buttercup dusted the fields with gold and the hedges were thick with dog-rose. Butterflies peacocked from flower to flower, their wings jewel bright under the shining heavens. Minstrels and mummers, jugglers and dancers from the great houses took to the road to entertain the villagers. The Christian services of Easter were followed by the pagan rites of bringing in the may, while the festival of Corpus Christi was shared by thousands who were equally familiar with the ancient mystique of dancing round the maypole.

In London, preparations went apace for the bridal journey of Margaret of York from Westminster to Burgundy. As far as Margate, she was to be squired by the Earl of Warwick. Furthermore, to demonstrate his renewed faith in the Earl's loyalty, Edward had appointed him, together with Clarence, to head the treason trials taking place in London.

To the world at large, the reconciliation which had taken place at Coventry in January, had apparently healed the breach in the two men's friendship. Only the King and the

Earl and a few of those close to each, knew how tenuous were the threads which bound them.

It had taken all George Neville's diplomacy to put an end to the estrangement. Better than Warwick, he realised the disaster which would follow if they sprang to arms too soon. Promises of men, given by many Yorkshire lords, was one thing; levying the troops before the King got word of it was another. Time was the Nevilles' ally and they must use it to the full.

The execution of Desmond had aroused much bad feeling among people who remembered his courtesy and charm. Ostensibly put to death for treason on the orders of the present Lord-Lieutenant of Ireland, the hated Earl of Worcester, it was felt, nevertheless, that the Queen had been the architect of the tragedy and there were rumours that she had stolen Edward's signet ring to seal the death warrant. Certainly, the King's distress on hearing the news had lent colour to the suspicion that he had previously known nothing of the matter.

But it was the subsequent murder of two of Desmond's children that had roused public animosity to the full. With the exception of Anthony Woodville, however, the Queen's family seemed impervious to the feelings they

260

aroused. Some months before, Sir Thomas Cooke, a former Mayor of London, had refused to sell his tapestries depicting the Siege of Jerusalem to the Duchess of Bedford. Now, Jacquetta was rubbing her hands in glee, for Cooke was one of the men accused of treasonable correspondence with Margaret of Anjou and was at present standing his trial in Westminster Hall.

The hall was crowded and stuffy. One of the exiled Queen's captured spies, a man broken by torture, unable to walk because of the hot irons which had been applied to his feet, had just been dragged away, having given his evidence. He was replaced at the bar by the man who was his accomplice; one, Hawkins, a servant of Warwick's friend, Lord Wenlock. Warwick leaned forward.

'You say that these letters were given to you by your master?'

'Indeed, my lord, they were.' The man was shaking all over. His one hope now, he felt, was to enlist the Woodvilles' protection by implicating their enemies. 'Everyone knows, my lord, that he fought for King Henry at St. Albans.'

'And that is our only evidence? Your word and the fact that Lord Wenlock once fought for Lancaster?' Warwick was scathing, angry that his personal friend should be involved.

'If it comes to that,' he went on, 'then Earl Rivers and his sons should be indicted. They fought for Henry as lately as the battle of Towton.'

There was a ripple of mirth, hastily suppressed by those who realised that Earl Rivers sat at the back of the hall, or swollen into a belly-laugh by those who, like the Duke of Clarence, wished to enjoy a jibe at the Woodvilles' expense.

The hot afternoon wore on. Testimony was taken from Lord Wenlock and Sir Thomas Cooke and both were released on bail.

'You, Sir Thomas,' Warwick told the latter with his warmest smile, 'are released at the personal request of my cousin, the Lady Margaret of York, because you arranged the bond which guaranteed her dowry.'

A sudden noise claimed everyone's attention; a soft snort as of a pig rooting in its trough. People turned, searching for the source of this familiar sound and tracking it unerringly to the Mayor, Thomas Owlgrave, a plump, stocky man, who, in the warmth of his scarlet robes, had dozed off, mouth agape, and was gently snoring.

There was a moment's silence. Then, as people discreetly averted their eyes, a laugh rang out.

'Do speak softly,' the Duke of Clarence

begged his startled cousin. 'The Mayor is asleep.'

He rocked to and fro in one of those uncontrollable paroxysms of laughter which, on occasions, afflict the very young, egged on by his friends and encouraged by the sniggers of Alderman Derby, who had recently been fined by the Mayor for refusing to remove a dead dog from his doorstep.

Warwick smiled thinly, but, underneath, he was seething. He could see the angry faces of the rest of the Corporation and had no doubt that the majority of Londoners would, when apprised of the story, react in just the same way. A time might come when Warwick would need the support of the capital city and it would be unfortunate for him if his future son-in-law were to be remembered as the man who had made fun of the Mayor.

★ ★ ★

At the Priory of Stratford Langthorne, in Essex, three whole days and most of the nights were given over to feasting, dancing and general celebration, before Margaret of York embarked at Margate in the *New Ellen*. Everyone of note was there; her three brothers and two sisters; the Queen and

263

her family; the Archbishops of Canterbury and York; Chancellor Stillington and John Neville, Earl of Northumberland; Warwick, his wife and two daughters.

On the surface all was friendliness and jollity, but to the more perceptive it was apparent that Warwick, Clarence and the Archbishop of York formed an enclave of their own. They walked, talked and whispered together and at the banquet-table, in the dance, or during the hunt, their eyes would meet and they would exchange small, significant smiles.

Warwick looked with regret upon the young Duke of Gloucester, now almost sixteen years of age, still steadfastly loyal to his eldest brother and lost to him, Warwick felt, for ever. The boy had not only taken a mistress, but had recently become a father, with another child already on the way. In any other man at Edward's court this would have meant nothing, but the Earl knew his strait-laced young relative well enough to realise that had the Duke even still hoped for marriage with Anne, nothing would have induced him to live with another woman.

George of Clarence confirmed this view. 'Diccon's a fool,' he remarked to Warwick as they strolled in the Priory gardens, the smell of herbs heavy and aromatic in their nostrils. 'He hates the Woodvilles — more than ever since Desmond's execution — and yet he will not abandon Edward.' George added, with a sudden rush of sentiment and self-pity: 'I miss Edmund.'

It was a lovely morning of warm sunshine and quivering shadows. Warwick had breakfasted well and the odd little pains which frequently teased his body in this, his fortieth year, were dormant today. It was one of those rare moments of happiness when the desire to share his contentment surged up in him, spilling over into unguarded words and dangerous confidences.

'You shouldn't regret Edmund too much,' he said. The distant sound of the hunting-horns proclaimed that the morning's chase had begun. 'Edmund, had he lived, might have stood between you and a throne.'

George of Clarence gave him a quick glance and the Earl felt the sudden tension in the arm under his hand.

'You mean — ?'

Warwick raised his eyebrows and nodded. 'Have you never wondered,' he asked, 'why your father showed such a marked preference for Edmund? It's not usual for the second son to receive such preferential treatment — unless, that is, there has been an open breach between the father and his heir. But

York liked Edmund best from birth.'

George was puzzled. 'I don't quite see — '

Warwick pinched his arm. 'Oh, come now!' He turned to look his cousin full in the eyes. 'You have heard the story of Archer Blackburn, surely.'

George digested this. After a while, he said, slowly: 'Edward is a Plantagenet in looks.' But there was an eager look in his face, not lost on Warwick. What a pleasant feeling it gave him to make his cousin happy.

'As to that,' he scoffed, 'why not? Cicely is half-Plantagenet.'

'But my mother! An archer! No . . . It's impossible!'

'Didn't she offer to adduce Edward's bastardy at the time of his marriage?'

'But she didn't! She didn't!'

Warwick realised that he had not, after all, shared happiness; only created doubt and perhaps misery. His elation was pricked like an exploded bubble. To make matters worse, his brother, the Archbishop, was suddenly beside him, padding softly over the loose stone path, his velvet cloak brushing the thyme and rosemary; alert, suspicious, his eyes searching the two faces turned so guiltily towards him.

Later that same day, as Warwick dressed for the final banquet of this three day

266

saturnalia, his brother was admitted, demanding a word in private. When they were alone, except for the Countess, he said, urgently: 'Richard! I beg of you to be more circumspect in what you say to Clarence. He has just come to me, asking my opinion of Edward's parentage. Do you want us clapped in the Tower on a charge of high treason?'

Warwick resented the reprimand in his brother's tone and saw the frightened glance which his wife sent in his direction. He went to her, patting her hand, comfortingly.

'I told George nothing which is not common knowledge,' he answered, curtly. 'Nor, I think, did I put ideas into his head which were not already there.'

'That's as maybe,' the Archbishop replied. 'But take care! Edward is still our hope, not George.'

Margaret Paston sat in the garden of her Southwark home and read her son's letter.

'The Lady Margaret was married at Damme, last Sunday at five o'clock in the morning, then taken to Bruges. We had the best pageants I've ever seen and the Lord Bastard Antoine jousted with twenty-four knights during the eight days of feasting. There is plenty of everything here. As for the court, itself, there can never have been anything like it anywhere, unless it was the court of King Arthur.

'We are leaving sooner than expected because Duke Charles believes that King Louis intends to invade him . . . '

Margaret Paston sighed and laid the sheet of paper in her lap, resting her head against the tree trunk at her back. The world, she felt, was in a sorry state, particularly here, in England. However loud her John might sing Burgundy's praises, there were many who did not, and over London, at least, there hung an air of intrigue and treachery.

In June, Jasper Tudor had landed in Wales from France, burning Denbigh. He had been driven back by the Herberts, but it showed that Lancastrian hopes were not yet dead. And that, to Margaret Paston, as to all women, meant more fighting, more killing.

In London, Sir Thomas Cooke had been thrown into prison and his house ransacked by Earl Rivers. The Duchess of Bedford now possessed the Jerusalem tapestries and her husband most of Cooke's other belongings. When Chief Justice Markham had found the former Mayor guilty of misprision of treason only, he had been deprived of office, and Margaret Paston felt a deep sense of foreboding that such things could happen.

As the year wore on, her sense of misgiving deepened. There were riots against the

Flemish weavers and, only just in time, the Mayor, on the last night of August, forestalled a plan of the apprentices to cut off the hands of any Flemings they could find. The Steelyard was closed and the Hanseatic merchants thrown into prison in retaliation for the seizure of English ships. The Earl of Warwick took to the sea again in an effort to repeat his naval victories of ten years earlier. The Pastons prayed for his safety, for the Nevilles backed them in their quarrel with the Duke of Norfolk over the possession of Caister Castle.

Later that autumn, another Lancastrian plot was uncovered and its instigator, the Earl of Oxford, saved his head by betraying his accomplices. He was released from prison . . . and promptly married Warwick's sister, Katherine Neville.

In France, Louis had again been trapped by Charles of Burgundy and again escaped, while in England, Edward held a precarious balance between Woodvilles and Nevilles. But as winter came in with flurries of snow and the lash of sleet on the panes; as the Steelyard remained silent and empty; and as the foreigners hurried back across the Channel to escape the persecutions of the xenophobic English, the Pastons were not the only family to wonder how long the uneasy peace would last.

In the Yorkshire home of Sir John Conyers messengers came and went and as the year 1468 faded into history, the name of Robin of Redesdale began to be heard in the north.

15

Warwick glanced at the man before him and asked: 'Do you speak English well?'

He was treated to a surprised stare. 'I'm a Devonshire man, my lord,' John Boon replied, 'not Cornish. I'm from Dartmouth.'

Warwick shrugged. The wild south-western tip of England was all one to him and the niceties of country distinction something which he found difficult to grasp. Beyond Exeter, except for the little sea-port town of Plymouth, all was wilderness where, so far as he knew, all men spoke the old, lost tongue of the Celtic tribes.

'The King is sending you to the Count of Armagnac, promising him aid against King Louis?'

Boon nodded and Warwick continued: 'I want you to delay that journey until I can send word to France of Armagnac's proposed rebellion.' He pushed the heavy purse towards the man, who reached out for it with a large hand, none too clean. 'After that, you know what to do. But don't wait here in London.'

Boon, playing a double game and knowing

the hideous penalty for treason, was only too willing to obey his patron's behest and in the bitter cold of mid-winter, went back to his native county. Then, in the early days of the new year, 1469, he received his orders from the Earl and, sailing from Fowey, crossed the sea to France.

The Count of Armagnac, believing, as he had been meant to believe, that it was Edward who had betrayed him to Louis, refused to see the King of England's emissary and Boon, smiling inwardly, went on to Amboise.

Had this tough, swarthy man been asked why he was risking his neck by betraying his King, he would have found it hard to say. The money which Warwick paid him was partly the answer, but it was not altogether this that fashioned Boon's devotion to the Earl. Throughout Warwick's political career, he had taken upon himself the mantle of popular hero; the champion of the people against oppression, both domestic and foreign. It was not an assumed role, for Warwick, never probing far beneath the surface of ambition, shared this vision of himself with a people who had been starved of a folk-hero for too long. Edward, with his magnificent physique and handsome face, might have stepped into that place left vacant by the long-dead Harry of Monmouth, but his marriage had alienated much of his support. The Londoners might love him and tolerate the Woodvilles for his sake, but in the remoter parts of the country, it was felt that the King had demeaned himself, and, therefore, his people, by marrying a woman who was not of royal birth.

Boon, having made himself known, was admitted to Amboise Castle, but kept cooling his heels all day until, in the lengthening shadows of the January evening, he was conducted to a small room, sparsely furnished, where a man in a crimson velvet robe sat on a bench by the wall.

'Kneel! That's the King,' whispered his guide, as Boon glanced contemptuously about him. The man in crimson, whose face was shadowed by a large black hat, motioned his guest to a seat on the bed and when he had heard Boon's story and looked at Edward's letters, which should have been delivered to Armagnac, waved his hand in dismissal.

Bewildered, Boon returned to his quarters, and throughout the following day, wasted his time in fruitless speculation about his mission. Had he walked into a trap? At night, torches and cressets spluttering on the walls and casting eerie shadows over floor and face, he was again taken to the same room, where a taller man, this time in a robe of yellow silk, an orange hat on his head, was introduced to Boon as the King.

'Tell me your story once more,' said this person, taking his arm. 'I was ill last night and could not properly understand it.'

Confused almost to the point of incoherence, Boon, after a struggle, managed to comply. His listener was evidently satisfied, for he squeezed the Englishman's shoulder and waved him away in a friendly fashion.

Somewhat relieved, Boon spent another idle day until, in the evening, he was taken yet again to the same room. On this occasion, three men were present and it was the shortest of the three, an ugly man with popping eyes and a huge nose, who raised Boon from his knees.

'Welcome! Welcome!' he cried. 'I am now satisfied that you are indeed from my friend, the Earl of Warwick. I could not see you myself, until I was sure. Meet my other selves! Monsieur Jean du Lude, your 'King' of the first night! And my loyal Tanguy du Chastel, your 'King' of last night! Now, before anything else, something to drink.'

Louis clapped his hands and a servant came in, carrying a ewer of wine. Behind him, another man, holding the mazers, glanced curiously at Boon. As the Devonshire man moved into the candlelight, a look of recognition flickered on the other's face; then was gone.

But in the small hours of the morning, the spy wrote steadily and at length, in cipher, to his master, King Edward, informing him that John Boon was in the pay of the Earl of Warwick, who was treating secretly with King Louis.

* * *

Unfortunately for Edward, the information supplied him by his agent only served to confirm him in his opinion that Warwick's dealings with France were merely designed to undermine the Burgundian alliance. Consequently, instead of putting him on his guard, it lulled him into a sense of false security.

'Let him dabble in France,' the King said to his brother, Richard. 'It can do no harm. He'll not achieve his object and while he's meddling there, he will be too occupied to busy himself elsewhere.'

The Duke of Gloucester, who was extremely fond of his past mentor and cousin, and whom he was reluctant to suspect of treachery, was content to agree. His mistress had just died, following the death of their

275

second child, and he was preoccupied with his grief and his own affairs.

Neither man suspected that the recent disturbances in Yorkshire, led by a certain Robin of Redesdale, had any connection with Warwick. The Earl had been in Burgundy, visiting the Duke and his new Duchess and paying court to their visitor, the Archduke Sigismund of Austria. This circumstance, together with the news that the revolt had been suppressed by the Earl of Northumberland, argued the Nevilles' innocence in the matter. The fact that Robin of Redesdale had escaped John Neville's vengeance, aroused no suspicions.

What was aroused, however, was Warwick's wrath. Returning to London in early May, he went immediately to his brother's palace at Charing Cross.

'John! The traitor!' he fumed, rejecting all offers of refreshment. 'If he cannot be for us, he need not be against us. And Conyers! After all our careful preparations, to be defeated so ignominiously. It was lucky for him that John was his opponent or he would have lost his head by now.'

As always, when agitated, he paced to and fro, his cloak whispering amongst the rushes like the hushing of sea on sand. Beyond the windows, with their panes of blown glass, the spring rain poured steadily down, curtaining river and houses and trees in a shimmering, silvery, veil.

George shrugged his shoulders in resignation. 'Of course, it was too soon,' he said. 'If Conyers had waited for his orders as arranged . . . ' He broke off, staring unseeingly before him. Then, giving himself a shake: 'However,' he continued, 'all is not lost, by any means. As you say, it could have been worse. What we need now is a diversion of some sort to hold Edward's attention while Conyers' army has time to re-form.' He raised his eyes to his brother's restless figure and smiled; a smug little simper that made him appear almost feline. 'You haven't asked me your usual question,' he murmured. 'About the dispensation.'

Warwick stopped, his attention caught and held. In his eyes there glowed a sudden excitement. 'You mean . . . ?'

George smirked even more and drew towards him a box, which his brother had idly noted, standing on a table beside him. George unlocked it and took out a rolled parchment.

'Ours! At last! And obtained, as I told you, through the good offices of James Goldwell, Edward's own Vatican agent. Let's look on the bright side of things. We have had one piece of luck. Why should we not have another?'

There was no reason at all, as Fate seemed bent on proving to him. The diversion which the Archbishop so craved, was unexpectedly provided towards the end of the mouth by a Robin of Holderness. ('A positive rash of would-be Robin Hoods', as George derisively remarked to Warwick.) A protest about the corn taxation levied by St. Leonard's Hospital at York, this particular disturbance was the perfect decoy for any suspicions which Edward might have entertained and was again efficiently put down by the Earl of Northumberland. This time, however, the leader was not allowed to escape and Robin of Holderness, unlike his namesake of Redesdale, was executed with ruthless speed. The fact that, among other grievances, he had demanded the restoration of the imprisoned Henry Percy to the earldom of his ancestors, had prompted John Neville to swift and expedient revenge.

★ ★ ★

June arrived in a blaze of heat. Yellow spears of agrimony thrust between the fading speedwell and cowslips. Honeysuckle and meadowsweet scented the air and, in the

278

woods, betony raised purple spikes. Pilgrims were thick upon the road to Canterbury, Holywell or Walsingham; whilst, for the more venturesome, lured by the tomb of St. James of Compostella, Edward's clerks worked night and day, issuing licences, authorising ships' Masters to transport the faithful to Spain. And the warm weather also brought out the bagpipers and bearleaders; dancers, wrestlers and mendicant friars with their potions and pills.

The Archbishop had retired to 'The Moor' in Hertfordshire; Warwick to Sandwich, ostensibly to review the fleet. The news that Edward had decided to go north, himself, did not disturb the Earl. The King, far from realising how serious the opposition really was; how well organised were Robin of Redesdale and his men, planned to make his journey something of a royal progress. Warwick, who had spent a few days with him at Windsor, knew that Edward intended visiting the shrines of St. Edmund and Our Lady of Walsingham, as well as the cities of Norwich and Lynn, before finally joining the Queen at Fotheringay. In fact, nothing could have been more propitious for the Earl than Edward's absence from the south at this particular moment. The information that the Duke of Gloucester had, at the last minute, accompanied his brother, set the final seal upon Warwick's resolution to effect Isabel's marriage without delay.

His messengers went galloping through the dusty countryside and, on the eighth of June, George of Clarence arrived in Sandwich. He was followed, the next day, by the Archbishop of York.

In the inn which had once housed Anthony Woodville and his parents, the Earl greeted his brother and cousin.

'My wife and the two girls crossed to Calais last week,' he told them. 'Has there been any trouble?'

The Archbishop smiled his slow smile. 'Edward and Richard called at 'The Moor' and it was suggested that I travel north with them. As the recent troubles have been in my diocese, Edward felt that I should . . . take an interest, shall I say?'

George of Clarence laughed. 'Little knowing how deep your interest goes! What did you answer?'

'I said that I had some pressing business and that I would join them as soon as I could. Now, what is your news?'

'Conyers is marching south with a sizeable army,' Warwick answered, 'and Edward is still moving north. I've had this prepared' — he pushed a paper towards them — 'and

280

I shall despatch it to Sir John tonight.'

The two Georges bent their heads over a document which accused the King of neglecting the lords of his own blood for his favourites, the Woodvilles and the Herberts, who had given him evil counsel. Let him remember Edward the second, Richard the second and Henry the sixth.

George of Clarence looked up uneasily. 'Why the last sentence?' he demanded.

'Just a reminder that kings can be deposed,' Warwick said, nonchalantly; but his cousin was still not satisfied.

'The first two were also murdered, as well as deposed,' he replied. 'I'll have no part in harming Edward.'

'No harm is intended,' Warwick assured him and the Archbishop patted his hand.

'This proclamation is intended simply to frighten the King. Nothing more! Indeed, all our plans are centred upon keeping Edward on his throne. The Woodvilles are the ones we wish to displace.'

Three days later, the Archbishop dazzled the people of Sandwich in his episcopal robes as he blessed Warwick's newly-refitted ship, *The Trinity*.

'Now everything is ready for our trip to Calais,' Clarence remarked, delightedly, but he had reckoned without his mother. That redoubtable woman arrived from Canterbury and treated her son and two nephews to some uncomfortably plain speaking.

'I don't know what you're planning here,' she said, repressively, 'but I know all of you well enough to guess that there is something afoot. Don't be fools and try conclusions with Edward. I know him better than any of you and I'll tell you all this: you may worst him for a while, but he will be the winner in the end.' She raised a gnarled forefinger, whose joints had thickened with the passing years. 'Edward has a knack of absorbing misfortune and turning it to his own advantage. He always has: he always will. I repeat: don't try conclusions with him.'

She looked at the politely attentive faces before her and saw disbelief in every line of them.

'Very well!' she said, briskly. 'I must prevent you in spite of yourselves. If this little . . . family party doesn't disband, I shall feel it my duty to write and tell Edward of my suspicions. And I may say that he has a greater faith in my judgements than you have.'

When she had gone, George Neville, as ever, counselled caution.

'She will do as she threatened,' he warned.

'I don't really need to tell you both that. Fortunately, she suspects only a part of the truth. But the marriage must be postponed. If we all go about our normal business for a while, she will think that we have taken her advice and she will do nothing.'

Accordingly, the party dispersed. Warwick went back to London and spent this enforced delay in the writing and sending of messages. To Sir John Conyers, still making good progress south in the orderly manner which was so essential to their cause — Warwick had never forgotten the consequences to Margaret of Anjou of that terrible march of ten years ago — he sent yet more advice.

'Try,' he wrote, 'to get between the King and the capital.'

To the city of Coventry, he announced his intention of joining the King — which, after all, was no more than the truth — and demanded an armed force. But the citizens of Coventry still remembered his slight to their Mayor and rudely refused this request. By the time that their curt reply was received, however, Warwick was once more at Sandwich and, on July the sixth, in the company of his brother, the Archbishop, George of Clarence and his sister and brother-in-law, the Earl and Countess of Oxford, he crossed to Calais.

And on July the eleventh, he saw the dream of many years come true, when Isabel, now a young woman of sixteen, was married by her uncle to her cousin, the Duke of Clarence.

★ ★ ★

The Earl of Warwick and his new son-in-law returned to the capital from Calais, rallying the ever loyal Kentishmen as they went. The Londoners looked askance at the bands of armed men in the bright red jackets, blazoned with the insignia of the Bear and Ragged Staff. But to the Mayor, sent by an anxious populace to question him, the Earl replied that he was on his way to help the King.

'These risings, as Your Worship knows, must be put down.'

The Mayor looked doubtfully out of the window at the courtyard of the Archbishop's palace, teeming with men-at-arms and awash with the swift ebb and flow of messengers. Even as he watched, one of these latter swung to the ground from his sweating horse and pushed out of sight towards a side door. And as His Worship was ushered out, he passed the man in his stained leather jacket, hurrying in.

The news which the messenger brought was that Edward, after a week spent at Fotheringay with his wife and three little daughters, had proceeded north against the rebels. At Newark, however, one of Warwick's proclamations had come into his hands, together with information of Robin of Redesdale's true identity. Suddenly realising the true nature of the uprising and that, far from being merely a rebellion of malcontents, it had behind it the full weight of Neville power, he had fled for the safety of Nottingham Castle, taking his brother, Richard, Lord Hastings and his other army captains with him.

'And the Woodvilles?' Warwick asked eagerly, as no mention of them was made.

'They were given permission, my lord, to leave His Grace and make for the shelter of their own estates. Earl Rivers and his son, John, were last reported heading westwards.'

'And Lord Scales?'

But Anthony Woodville, it seemed, had managed to disappear. 'He has not been seen since, my lord, but in response to a summons from the King, the Herberts are advancing from Wales and the Earl of Devon from the south.'

Warwick bit his lip. If these men and their forces were able to reach the King,

Edward would have an army far larger than Conyers' and the whole rebellion would be in jeopardy. After a brief consultation with Clarence and George Neville, it was decided that the time had come to declare themselves openly and that they must take to the field without delay.

* * *

In the little town of Banbury, William Herbert, now Earl of Pembroke in place of the exiled Jasper Tudor, and his troops converged with the Earl of Devon and his levies, approaching from the south-west.

This Sunday of July the twenty-fifth was a cold one and a thin drizzle turned the roads to mud. A wind, bitter for the time of year, rippled trees whose leaves were already going brown at the edges, whilst no hint of sun shone from a sky as flat and grey as pewter. Nothing, thought Devon with a shiver, was as miserable and depressing as a cold English summer's day. As Banbury came into view, he thought with pleasure of a fire and a cup of warm ale.

Banbury, however, was already full, every cottage and barn packed with Pembroke's Welshmen and the inn occupied by the Earl and his captains. Not an inch of room was to be had for Devon and his men.

Cursing at the top of his voice, Devon strode into the inn and confronted Pembroke, demanding that quarters be found immediately for himself and his troops. William Herbert, who had just begun to feel the benefit of a roof over his head and the warmth of a meal in his stomach, had no intention of so doing.

'First come, first served,' he said, truculently. 'You and your men must camp in the fields. No doubt, your wild westcountrymen are used to that.'

'Not nearly so much as your heathen Welshmen,' Devon shouted, stung on the raw by the other's smug grin. 'Get some of them out of their quarters and let my soldiers in.'

'Soldiers?' Pembroke sounded amused. 'I've heard that some of those Somerset men can't tell one end of a pike from the other.'

His captains guffawed delightedly and Devon went white about the mouth.

'For the last time, will you move your men?'

'For the last time, no!'

'Very well!' Devon glared round the room and snapped his fingers in the faces which laughed back at him from the wreathing smoke of the fire. 'My men and I will go elsewhere and I pray that before long you'll have cause to regret the loss of my archers.'

Within twenty-four hours, Devon's wish, no more than the parting shot of an angry man, was disastrously granted. As Pembroke and his men approached Edgecote on the following morning, across the flat stretch of ground known as Danesmoor, the Earl became aware that the surrounding hills were alive with red-coated men. He had walked straight into an ambush. Sending a scout to scour the surrounding countryside for Devon, he hastily deployed for battle.

At first, all seemed to be going his way. His brother, Sir Richard Herbert, led the charge which took the most westerly of the three hills and Pembroke ordered an attack on the one to the east, at Culworth, whose capture would give them access to the Thorpe-Mandeville road.

Sir John Conyers, from his position on the crest, let them come on; then, just as success seemed within the Welshmen's grasp, he ordered up his reserve, hidden below the brow of the hill. Pembroke's men, disheartened by the appearance of fresh and vigorous troops, and badly handicapped by their lack of bowmen, broke and ran. At once, Sir John began a flanking movement and, within half an hour, had regained the hill previously lost.

The men on the southern hill now began to move, streaming down the slopes with shouts of 'A Warwick! A Warwick!' In vain did the two Herberts try to shore up their battle-line and stem the tide of flight until Devon should arrive. The men surged past them, throwing down their arms, and Pembroke and his brother were surrounded and captured.

They were taken to Northampton, where Warwick and George of Clarence had made their headquarters, and the next day, they were both beheaded in the market-place; a fate soon to be shared by another of their family, Thomas Herbert, at Bristol, and by the Earl of Devon, who was captured at Bridgwater.

As he returned to his inn, after watching the executions, Warwick was met by one of his scouts who reported that the King was at Olney. His army had fled on hearing the news of the Edgecote defeat and he had dismissed his captains and friends. Only the Duke of Gloucester remained with him.

George Neville smiled at his brother. 'I told you that Edward was still our best hope. Everything has worked out as planned. Now!

Who will fetch him from Olney and what is to be done with him?'

George of Clarence refused point-blank to go. He could see that his cousins thought him afraid and, to a large extent, fear of his brother's anger prompted his refusal. But George, beneath the layers of envy and resentment, still retained for Edward an affection rooted deep in the hero-worship of childhood; whilst for Richard, his love was the deepest emotion ever to touch his rather shallow nature. Warwick had already proved himself in an avenging and blood-thirsty mood, and if violence was to be offered to his brothers, Clarence preferred to have no hand in it.

'You must go then,' Warwick said to his brother and the Archbishop nodded. 'Clarence and I will go on to Coventry. There are rumours of trouble there.'

Coventry, he reflected with a sigh, had certainly never forgiven him for his affront to the Mayor all those years ago. Well, he had known the risk at the time and must not whine now over the consequences.

The forces dispersed, the triumphant Conyers riding north with Warwick and Clarence to Coventry and George Neville setting out with an armed force for Olney. And on August the second, he brought the unresisting King and his youngest brother to Coventry, where, for the first time, they learned of George's marriage to Isabel.

Edward was surprisingly docile, a fact which should have put Warwick on his guard, but the Earl had never really understood his wily cousin.

'He has at long last seen the error of his marriage,' he told the Archbishop happily, but George was sceptical.

'If you believe that, then you are a very great fool,' he answered, not mincing his words. 'We've regained our power in the kingdom, but take my advice and keep Edward closely guarded. Send him to Warwick or Middleham, but don't let him out of your men's sight for an instant.'

16

On August the twelfth, Earl Rivers and his son, Sir John Woodville, who had been captured in the Forest of Dean and taken to Kenilworth Castle, were executed outside Coventry. In his prison at Warwick Castle, the King received the news with a stoic calm which, Warwick felt, bordered almost upon indifference. True, Edward did request that he be allowed to wear mourning, but other than that, he expressed no regrets whatsoever. The Earl wondered how deeply attached the King had ever really been to any of his wife's family.

There was no doubt, however, about Elizabeth's feelings. At her apartments in the Tower, which the Earl had instructed she be permitted to keep, she gave vent to such a paroxysm of grief that her women feared for her reason; but Elizabeth was made of sterner stuff. Once she had shed her tears, she turned dry-eyed and tight-lipped to thoughts of revenge.

Sitting by her window, she could see the river, thick with refuse. It was so humid that rivulets of sweat ran down her body inside the loose gown she wore and the stench and noises of the city rose together, battering at her senses. She should have been at Windsor instead of London during the heat and stink of August. She closed her eyes, moving her eyeballs so that she could see their impressions, black against the oranges and reds of her lids. How short a time — a few weeks only — since they had all been at Fotheringay. Now, Edward was Warwick's prisoner; her father and brother, John, dead.

She lived in terror that news would reach her of Anthony's capture and execution. Of all her brothers, he was the favourite and Elizabeth was astute enough to know that it was because he was somewhat different from the rest of them. Of all her numerous family, he was the only one in whom she recognised a force for good.

The Queen stirred and opened her eyes. Her ladies came fussing, but she waved them away. It was said that the Duke of Clarence had signed her father's and brother's death warrants. If that were so, she would never forgive him. She would wait years if necessary, to bring about her brother-in-law's own death, for she believed implicitly in Old Testament justice; an eye for an eye, a tooth for a tooth.

It would be no good demanding retribution of Edward. Elizabeth had long ago learned that she could no more influence her husband against any member of his family than he could influence her against hers. Her triumphs came through patient waiting; waiting for those opportunities when her desires and Edward's inclinations walked hand-in-hand.

She got up, wandering about the room, looking into a future suddenly bleak. Surely this situation, so unreal, could never last. Edward must make some move to regain his freedom before long. He had Richard with him, and, although Elizabeth was indifferent to the Duke of Gloucester, she would be the first to designate him a young man of strength and resource, devoted to his brother. Moreover, William Hastings and all the rest of the King's supporters were still at large and the Londoners had always been his friends.

And the Londoners remained Edward's friends now. They cheered a letter, handed to the Mayor by the Burgundian ambassador, and read to them at Paul's Cross, promising Duke Charles' vengeance if any harm should come to his brother-in-law. Normally, any such threats from a foreign power would have caused riots of anger and disapproval, but now they were greeted with delight. The merchants, of whom Edward was an excellent customer and to whom he owed money, were more than anxious for his restoration to full authority; whilst their wives, desiring their sovereign's return for totally different, but none the less compelling reasons, all became Lysistratas overnight and forswore their husbands' beds until the King should be once again at Westminster.

In the rest of the country, it was the same. Just as, eight years previously, the people had prayed for the Duke of York's return to reform the government, but not to usurp it totally, so they had hoped for Warwick to overthrow the Woodvilles, but had never expected him to imprison the King in the process.

A wave of lawlessness swept the country. The Bristol pirates seized the opportunity to ravage the coast of Greenland and rape all the women they could find — which brought a fury of protest down on Warwick's head from the Danish ambassador; the Duke of Norfolk pressed the siege of Caister Castle which, without the help of the Nevilles, who were much occupied elsewhere, John Paston was forced to surrender; the Berkeleys called on the men of Bristol to aid them in making war on their ancient enemies, the Talbots;

and on the Border, there was a Lancastrian uprising led by Warwick's own Kinsman, Humphrey Neville of Brancepeth.

In the New Forest, robbers and outlaws increased their raids on the pack-horses carrying silk and velvet from Southampton to Bristol or woollen cloth from Bristol to Southampton. In Nottingham, the apprentices rioted and Channel Pirates waited in the Thames estuary for the Genoese ships which brought spices and oranges, or the French vessels with their cargoes of Normandy apples and fine Caen stone.

By the middle of August, it was obvious that Warwick's hard won victory was already slipping away from him. Edward might gaily agree to anything which his captor suggested, append his name to anything that he was requested to sign; but he had already realised, even in the fastness of Middleham Castle, to which he and Richard had been transferred, that without his physical presence, the Earl's authority was as nothing.

Warwick, himself, was bewildered. He had counted on his immense popularity, both in the south-east and the northern half of England, to tide him to victory. That the people, even his most loyal supporters, would clamour for the King's freedom, was something totally unexpected. He could not even raise his own tenants to put down the Lancastrian revolt without first producing a personal order from the King.

He summoned the Archbishop to Sheriff Hutton from London, only to learn that in the capital, things were nearing a state of anarchy.

'Why, George? Why?' he asked, pathetically.

The Archbishop shrugged. 'I can't tell you,' he said. 'If I could, I should become the most able and efficient ruler this country has ever had. But the English are completely unpredictable. We might have done this last year — next year — and had total success. As it is . . . ' He broke off, disconsolate. 'Well, one thing is certain,' he continued, 'we shall never get Edward in our power again. He'll see a Neville plot behind every apprentices' riot and will always be on his guard. What do you want me to do?'

Warwick grunted despairingly. 'Go to Middleham, I suppose, and release Edward. Humphrey Neville has been captured and Edward can go with you to York to watch the execution.'

The Archbishop nodded. 'And then I'll escort him to London. There will be no rest until he is back at Westminster, but, at least, I might be able to make it look as though he is there only with our permission.'

Warwick laughed, savagely. 'I doubt it,' he said. 'Well, Aunt Cicely warned us, didn't she? And for once in her life,' he added, disparagingly, 'she was right.'

★ ★ ★

Richard, Duke of Gloucester, Constable of England, President of the Courts of Chivalry and Courts Martial, overlord of the Manor of Sudely and Chief Steward, Approver and Surveyor of Wales, returned to the court at Westminster in time for Christmas.

He was greeted as a hero; as the man who had won back the castles of Cardigan and Carmarthen from the Welsh rebels and received the surrender of Morgan and Henry ap Thomas ap Griffith.

But this respite was slight, as Richard well knew. Wales was still seething with discontent. People refused to pay their taxes; the valleys echoed with the wild chanting of the bards as they urged their people to war; the Welsh lords were arming their servants.

The capture of the King the previous summer and the subsequent unrest in England, had been sufficient to stir old hopes and longings in the Celts; to set them once more remembering the glories of Arthur and Caradoc, Llewellyn and Glendower; to revive the ancient brotherhood of the Cymry and to evoke again the name of Uther Pendragon. And yet, as he rose from his knees to receive the King's embrace, Richard could wish himself back again in Wales, where the dangers were clear and recognisable. Already he could sense the intrigues and bitter hatreds that corroded life at Westminster.

Over his brother's shoulder, Richard saw the faces of Warwick and Clarence, come to bury past differences in a grave of Christmas cheer, the outward sign of which was to be the betrothal of Edward's eldest daughter, Elizabeth, to the loyal John Neville's eldest son. But on Edward's other side, stood the Queen with her mother and brother, Anthony, now Earl Rivers, dressed in the unrelieved black which denoted their continuing sorrow for the deaths of father and husband, brother and son. More than their clothes, their grief-ravaged faces told their own tale and the stirrings of pity had almost moved the young Duke to compassion, when he saw, at the Queen's elbow, the long face and protruding eyes of the Earl of Worcester, recently recalled from Ireland. And, as always, the ghosts of his friend, the Earl of Desmond, and Desmond's two children stood between him and those who had ordered their deaths.

The kiss which Richard offered the Queen was perfunctory and dry and he escaped as soon as possible to his own apartments and the solace of his two children.

Warwick and Clarence watched him go, each with different thoughts; George full of envy and jealousy for the great titles and honours which had been heaped upon Richard during these past few months, in recognition of his loyalty to Edward; Warwick with regret that he had never been able to enlist his one-time pupil and favourite cousin on his side.

The seasonal festivities, soon in full swing, were like a brilliant, many-coloured cloak, hiding the dismal rags beneath. The choir-children sang their songs of peace; the Boy-Bishop preached of love; the Lord of Misrule led the court in dancing and dicing, mummings and disguisings. The ladies displayed plucked eyebrows and shaven foreheads beneath the high, wired head-dresses of fluttering gauze, while the men vied for their attentions in parti-coloured hose and the new, excessively short doublets, which outraged, so delightfully, the proprieties. The King, supported by the Earl of Warwick and the Dukes of Clarence and Gloucester, dined in the Inns of Court and watched, amidst shouts of laughter and sweating excitement, the traditional chase of a cat and fox around the groaning tables. Gifts were exchanged and, on New Year's Day, the palace waits sang outside the bedchamber doors of Edward's guests.

But beneath the surface gaieties, the Nevilles and the Woodvilles, now utterly irreconcilable, worked for each other's downfall. To add fuel to the fire, the King and his brother, George, were now totally committed to opposite sides; Clarence to the Nevilles, by reason of his marriage to Isabel, and Edward to the Woodvilles, because he knew that in Warwick's future plans, his crown and, probably, his life, would be worth nothing at all.

In this, the King's instinct warned him correctly. It had been conclusively demonstrated to the Earl that his scheme to rule the country through Edward, was nothing more than a dream. The complete failure of the King's capture had, for a while, depressed him profoundly, but, with a resilience which the Archbishop deeply envied, he was already embroiled in new plans.

As he and the Queen regarded each other in sullen hatred across the festal boards, he contemplated those two alternatives which he had stored for so long in the back of his mind; Henry of Lancaster and George of Clarence.

Two reasons, both equally important, made him decide upon the latter. First, George was to hand, easily accessible as Henry, immured in the Tower, was not. Second, Isabel was five months pregnant and if George of Clarence became King, he Warwick, would hold undisputed sway as the grandfather of England's heir.

There were other considerations, also, which influenced Warwick in his choice: he would not have to face the stigma of having changed his coat from York to Lancaster, and the story of Edward's bastardy could be fashioned into a legal pretext for removing him in favour of his brother.

But it would need a deal of hard work, for, after the summer's fiasco, many of the northern lords would be chary of throwing in their lot again with Warwick. It needed some reason, some spark which would set alight a larger conflagration.

Fate once again showed herself the Nevilles' friend. As the short, cold days of January opened up, with tiny, flame-like crocuses and delicate tints of green to give the promise of an early spring, news reached Westminster of trouble in Lincolnshire.

George of Clarence sped hot-foot to

Warwick's lodgings in the Greyfriars'. 'Sir Thomas Burgh's mansion has been razed to the ground by Lord Welles and his son,' he informed his cousin, breathlessly. 'Burgh arrived last night to beg the King's protection. And as he is Edward's Master of the Horse — '

'Edward intends to give him satisfaction as well as protection,' Warwick interrupted, 'is that it?'

When his son-in-law nodded, he gave a smile. 'It so happens,' he went on, 'that Lord Welles is a cousin of mine — distant, it's true, but nevertheless we are related.' He rose from his chair and clapped Clarence on the back. 'I think, my dear George, that we should waste no time in assuring him of our strongest support.'

* * *

George of Clarence and his brother, the King, met in Baynard's Castle, Cicely's London home on the banks of the Thames, on the afternoon of Tuesday, March the sixth. If Edward suspected that the Duke had begged for this interview in order to delay the departure of himself and a substantial body of men for the wilds of Lincolnshire, he kept his thoughts to himself. Nothing could have exceeded the warmth and affability with which he greeted his brother.

'We see too little of each other, George,' he said, throwing his arm across the Duke's shoulders with one of his typical gestures. 'Especially since your marriage.'

'I'm on my way to visit Isabel, now,' his brother informed him; adding, with unnecessary emphasis: 'She's at Clarendon.' Did Edward know that for the lie it was? he wondered uneasily.

'Ah! I see! Your destination is westwards, not . . . northwards.' The King regarded his brother with a faint smile which became more pronounced at the Duke's next question.

'Is Richard still in Wales?'

'At Ludlow! Keeping the peace.' Edward's face softened for a minute, as it always did at any mention of his youngest brother. 'He's proving himself a very fine soldier; a remarkable achievement for one who was never strong as a child.'

'He's not joining you in Lincolnshire?' George's uneasiness was now obvious, but Edward seemed not to notice it.

'Is there any reason why he should? This is only a minor affray, surely?'

'Yes . . . yes . . . of course!' George forced himself to meet Edward's eyes and smile in return. 'Shall we,' he suggested, 'go to

St. Paul's together and hear Mass?'

Edward's eyes were hooded for a moment as he looked at his brother through half-closed lids.

'Atonement, George?' he muttered, but so low that the Duke did not hear him. Then his eyes flashed open again. 'By all means,' he answered pleasantly.

And so the Londoners were edified by the sight of their King and his estranged brother going to church together and parting in seeming amity; Edward to go north, twenty-four hours later than he had originally intended; George, ostensibly setting out westwards to join his wife at Salisbury.

In reality, however, George also went north, to Coventry, to join Warwick. He arrived on Friday, the ninth of March, at the same time as a messenger from Edward delivered to his father-in-law a commission to array troops in Warwickshire.

The Earl laughed. 'Edward is still so far from guessing the truth,' he said, 'that he instructs me to levy men on his behalf.'

The Earl had withdrawn from Coventry and its always hostile atmosphere, to Warwick Castle, to be with his wife and two daughters. George warmed himself gratefully before the fire in the great hall, for the weather was cold and the ride had been long. At the Earl's words, however, he turned away from the blaze.

'I suppose he is,' he said, 'and yet . . . He gave me the same impression when I saw him in London, but I've learned that you can't tell with Edward. He's cunning. He dissembles his feelings.' George stooped and threw some pine cones on the fire, watching them uncurl in the heat until they looked like brittle, golden roses, opening flame-edged petals to the sun. Their perfume, clean and heady, scented the draughty hall. 'What exactly *has* been happening?' he asked.

Warwick poured some wine and handed it to his son-in-law. 'Last Sunday, all the Lincolnshire churches published a call to arms in our name. Lord Scrope and Sir John Conyers have sent word that they have managed to gather another army. My brother-in-law, Lord Stanley, is hoping to join us with a force, at Manchester. And I have sent to all our friends, apprising them that they will shortly have a new King — Your Grace!' He bowed low, but not before he had seen the gleam of excitement in George's eyes.

'B — But, Edward?' the Duke stammered.

Warwick looked at him in assumed amazement. 'The son of an archer? King of England?'

This time they both smiled and Warwick took George's arm, giving it a squeeze. 'Now we must contain ourselves and wait for news.'

Four days later it came, on Tuesday the thirteenth, but it was as unpropitious as the date. The preceding day, Sir Robert Welles had been beaten at Stamford by the King's army in a rout so complete that it had already been dubbed 'Lose-coat Field', because the defeated rebels had not waited to get clear of the battlefield before throwing off their heavy brigandines, in order to run the faster. Sir Robert Welles and his father had both been executed.

An hour later, messengers arrived from Yorkshire with the tidings that, once again, John Neville, still loyal to his King, had put down the northern rising.

The messenger, who had asked to see Warwick in private, told him: 'My lord, it was an easy victory for your brother. Most of the army which Sir John Conyers had gathered together, refused to rally to King George.'

The day finished as it had begun, with yet more cheerless news. The Earl of Shrewsbury, rejecting utterly Warwick's call to arms on behalf of Clarence, had joined the King. But, for old friendship's sake, he sent to warn the

Earl that papers had been found on one of the dead of 'Lose-coat Field', revealing to Edward all his cousin's and his brother's plans. Warrants had been issued for their arrest on a charge of treason.

The Duke and the Earl fled towards Manchester, hoping to join up with Lord Stanley, but Stanley, too, had deserted them. His troops had been scattered by the Duke of Gloucester, advancing from Wales, and he had been forced, regretfully, of course, to make his peace with the King.

With sickening clarity, it was borne in upon both Warwick and Clarence that there was nothing left but flight. Returning to Warwick Castle, they collected the Countess, Isabel and Anne, and, with a hundred or so of the Earl's most loyal retainers, rode southwards through the night.

★ ★ ★

The wind lifted the sails of the painted ships and the little fleet moved slowly towards the river mouth. Warwick looked back at the receding village of Dartmouth, huddled against the rising cliffs, and sent up a silent prayer of thanks. After days of being a hunted fugitive, he was gaining the comparative safety of the Channel and would soon be in the total safety of Calais. He took a last look at the Devon coastline and shivered. How that county depressed him; the earth red as blood; the low-lying hills, crouched like animals about to spring. Dyvnaint, the old Celtic people had called it; the 'Land of the Dark Valleys' and so he had found it.

He hoped that he would be able to put in at Southampton and collect *The Trinity*, which was berthed there, but Anthony Woodville was waiting for him in the Solent and, had it not been for the Earl's skilful command of his fleet, they might well have been captured. As it was, they got safely away and, on April the sixteenth, sighted Calais, now under the command of Warwick's old friend, Lord Wenlock.

The necessity to land had become doubly urgent, for Isabel had started her labour. In the stuffy cabin, the Countess and Anne, a frightened fourteen-years-old, began to do what they could.

'It's all right,' the Countess assured her eldest daughter, 'we shall soon be ashore.'

Even as she spoke, the whine of a cannon-ball sounded in their ears, before the ball itself splashed into the sea, sending a spray of foam across the window.

As the Countess turned for the door in astounded disbelief, her son-in-law came in, sweat pouring down his face.

'Wenlock refuses to let us land, on the orders of the King.' He glanced in terror at his wife, now racked with pain and unable even to speak to him. 'We must go on to Honfleur.'

'For God's Sake, tell Richard to try again,' the Countess implored. 'Isabel must be got ashore.'

Warwick, as desperate as his wife, sent more messages, but Wenlock remained adamant. He dared not go against Edward's commands for fear of his life. He sent, however, some wine to ease Isabel's sufferings.

The ships lay anchored off Calais for the rest of the day. While Warwick and Clarence paced the deck of Warwick's flagship, unshaven and red-eyed, the Earl, a man less given to swearing than many of his fellows, gave vent to a string of oaths which graphically described the parentage of every man in the Calais garrison.

Towards evening, Anne came to them to say that Isabel's child, a boy, had been born dead. Isabel, herself, was very ill.

Next day, as he watched the tiny, shrouded body being dropped into the sea, it seemed to Warwick that he was watching the burial of his own hopes. The English people had refused to rally to George of Clarence; had rejected him in no uncertain terms as their prospective King. Isabel might not live, or, if she did, might not be able to have any more children after this terrible ordeal. And so his hopes of founding a Neville dynasty through her and her husband were as evanescent as his hopes of ruling through Edward had been.

There remained to him, therefore, his other alternative; his last hope of becoming England's dominant political force. He lifted his face, taking a deep breath, savouring the salty tang of the sea. If Edward thought him beaten, he was wrong. The Earl might be exiled, a fugitive, wanted for treason, but he was not finished yet. He would make for France; throw himself on the mercy of his good and admiring friend, King Louis. Henry of Lancaster might be miles away, shut up and guarded in his room in the Lantern Tower; but here, in France, was Henry's wife and Warwick's old enemy, Margaret of Anjou.

17

At Amboise Castle, where, not so long before, his spy, John Boon, had demonstrated to the French King his master's enduring friendship, Warwick and Louis met once again.

They embraced like lovers, tears in their eyes, and the French Queen, eight months pregnant with a child whom, it was hoped, would be a boy to take the place of the dead Dauphin, came forward to kiss Warwick on the cheek as though he were a Prince of the Blood. Clarence, standing behind his father-in-law, felt the first prickings of doubt as to his place in Warwick's future scheme of things.

It was early May and the stormy morning showed patches of azure radiance between clouds whose edges gleamed with a golden fire. The last few weeks had been crowded with incident and there was not one of Warwick's party who was not glad to be safe at last upon dry land and partaking of the lavish hospitality of the French court.

Hardly had Warwick's fleet left the vicinity of Calais, than it had been attacked once more by Anthony Woodville and Lord Howard. As before, the Earl's brilliant seamanship had saved the day, together with reinforcements under the command of little Fauconberg's bastard son, who came to his cousin's support. The fighting had been bitter and many of Warwick's men had been killed or captured, but the rest had won free and inflicted severe losses on the enemy.

In an elated and vindictive mood, Warwick had ranged back and forth through the Channel, seeking English stragglers, but unsparing, also, of any other ships which came his way. The result of these weeks of piracy was that, while Edward's vessels had gained the sanctuaries of Dover and Southampton, a large number of unsuspecting Burgundian and Breton ships fell prey to the marauding Earl. By the time he reached Honfleur, with his prizes in tow, Louis was being inundated with protests from Duke Charles and many of his other subjects concerning Warwick's depredations. To make matters worse, the Earl's followers, landing at Honfleur and finding themselves among women for the first time in weeks, had gone on the rampage through the Normandy countryside, looting and raping and confirming the French in their opinion that the English were the children of the Devil.

Louis, however, sending placatory messages in all directions, insisted on greeting Warwick personally and treating him as an honoured guest. In the castle of Amboise, the two men talked into the early hours of the morning on this, their first meeting for nearly three years. As Warwick unrolled for Louis the swiftly moving events of the last twelve months, sating his curiosity and setting him right on many details which had been misreported abroad, the French King nodded and clucked sympathetically. In the light from the cressets and torches, his eyes gleamed round and glassy with cunning.

When Warwick had finished speaking, Louis said eagerly: 'Your brother, the Archbishop, will presumably keep you informed of events in England.'

Warwick laughed. 'Not only will George do so, but my brother, John, as well.' Carried away by the intoxicating intimacy of Louis' smile, he went so far as to tap the French King familiarly on the wrist. 'I've told you how John remained loy . . . ah . . . supported the King throughout all those months. Word reached me this morning, from John, himself, that Edward has released Henry Percy from the Tower and restored him to the earldom of Northumberland. John has been fobbed off with a marquisate.' He sneered. 'Marquis of Montagu!'

'But surely, a marquis ranks higher than a mere earl,' Louis said, puzzled.

Warwick was affronted. 'So it may,' he answered, withdrawing his hand, 'in theory. But it depends upon the possessions which go with a title, as you, Sire, will appreciate. The two greatest earldoms in England are my own and that of Northumberland. They are not only extremely rich, but have a — what shall I say? — an importance, a standing, which no one would trade, even for a dukedom.'

Louis, realising that his thoughtless words, 'mere earl', had deeply wounded his guest's pride, hurriedly pressed more wine upon him. 'And Edward has been so stupid as to withdraw this honour from your brother? Now? At such a time?'

'I warned John against Edward's ingratitude,' Warwick said. But even in the midst of his jubilation, he was amazed at his former protege's unbelievable foolhardiness in making an enemy of so powerful a friend. By this wanton act, Edward had thrown John Neville straight into the waiting arms of his brothers.

There was more good news as well. 'I have also received a letter from Lord Wenlock at

Calais,' Warwick told Louis. 'He apparently had no choice but to refuse us entry. Two of Edward's captains were with him and he would have been arrested immediately had he disobeyed their orders. But they have gone now and he assures me of his and the garrison's support in my future enterprises.'

'Ah!' The monosyllable fell from Louis' lips in a long drawn-out sigh and he unconsciously rubbed his hands. 'Your future plans! I received your letters, of course, and I think that I read them aright. I despatched messengers to Queen Margaret on her father's estate at Barre. I hope she will meet you. Indeed, I have no doubt that she will do so. But in what frame of mind? Not an easy woman to deal with, my dear Warwick, at the best of times — and you have said some harsh things about her in the past.'

Warwick agreed. 'I realise that I may have to . . . to 'eat humble pie' is our English expression, but I am prepared for that. For there is something else I want. I want the marriage of my daughter, Anne, to her son, Edward of Lancaster.'

Louis drew in his breath sharply. 'You ask more than she will be prepared to give.'

The Earl shrugged and his mouth set in a hard, determined line. 'She may argue and rage, but she will give in at the end.' He smiled into the King's eyes. 'She must, if she wants to regain the throne for Henry and her son. She cannot do without me, any more than I can do without her.'

'And your son-in-law, Clarence?'

Again Warwick shrugged, the red velvet of his doublet moving in ripples of scarlet and crimson against his powerful arms. 'He will see that this is for the best,' he said. 'The only way! He must realise by now that the English will not accept him as King. The only course now is a complete change of dynasty; a reversion to Lancaster. Oh, George will be reasonable enough.'

★ ★ ★

Lord Wenlock stared suspiciously at the handsome woman before him. She had been brought into his presence almost as soon as she had stepped ashore at Calais. Knowing that he had committed himself to Warwick's cause in writing, he was terrified now that one or other of Edward's many spies would find him out, and this forceful young woman was undoubtedly one of Edward's agents.

'You are on your way to Normandy?' he asked.

She inclined her head. 'I am,' she replied

with composure. 'I have letters for the Duke of Clarence.'

'Ah!' Wenlock saw a way of serving his friend, the Earl of Warwick. 'I should like to see some of them.' He added hastily: 'Just to prove your good faith, of course.'

'Of course!' the lady agreed, suavely. With much fluttering of plump white hands, she extracted from the pouch on her lap, one or two documents, but, even as she did so, she was aware that it was obvious that she had selected them with care.

Wenlock glanced through them quickly. Nothing there to suggest that the Duke of Clarence was plotting to return to his brother's side; only some brief, business-like letters from the stewards of his vast estates.

'I am merely travelling in France,' the lady said with a deprecating smile, 'and agreed to carry these letters from the Duke's men-of-affairs.'

Wenlock allowed his incredulity to show. In a moment, he would demand to see more of the letters and could easily have them wrested from her by force. He was as suspicious of her as she was of him.

Before she left England, the Earl of Worcester had instructed her: 'Whatever you do, don't let Wenlock know what you are up to. We suspect him of being in league with Warwick.'

She watched now as Wenlock's mouth opened to speak, his hand already stretched out for the silken satchel within her grasp. So, staking all on her last gamble, she leaned forward, confidentially.

'It's true,' she murmured, lowering her lashes and inflating her fine bosom. 'I am from the King. It was foolish of me to attempt to deceive such a clever man as you.' She was rewarded immediately by seeing Wenlock grow more affable towards her. 'I have letters here, not only for the Duke of Clarence, but for Lord Warwick, himself. The King is desperate to make his peace with the Earl. He offers almost anything that my lord desires, if only he will return as His Grace's friend.'

She had hazarded all and won. Wenlock was delighted, for nothing would suit him more than a reconciliation between his friend and the King. All necessity for involving himself in treasonable plots would then disappear. Smiling, he returned the two papers which he was holding and hastened her on her way with his blessing.

The lady, however, went nowhere near the Earl of Warwick. She went, instead, straight to the house in Normandy, placed at the disposal of George and Isabel by the King of France. It was odd, reflected this astute young woman, how alike in many ways were Warwick and his cousin, Edward. The King assumed that he could snatch back from John Neville the princely earldom of Northumberland and still command his loyalty. Warwick's assumption was that he could offer his son-in-law a crown, then cast him aside without incurring his ill-will.

One look at Clarence's sullen and moody face as she was ushered into his presence, was sufficient to assure the lady that her task was already more than half-done. As he read the letters from his brothers, his mother and his sisters, the Duke nodded and muttered to himself and tears of self-pity stood in his eyes.

At length he stood up. 'You may tell my brother, the King,' he said, 'that should the opportunity arise, he will hear from me. I cannot say where or when that will be. I am closely watched.' He picked up a candle from the table and started to burn the letters.

'Is it true,' probed the lady, her hands folded primly in her lap, 'that your sister-in-law is to marry Edward of Lancaster?'

'Oh yes, it's true,' hissed George and for a moment, he looked like an animal set for the kill. 'My father-in-law is determined to have one of his daughters Queen of England. As the people won't have me, and as he plans to restore Henry to the throne, he must, of necessity, marry Anne to Edward of Lancaster. Edward of Lancaster!' He repeated the name and, in a fury of frustration, banged with his fist on the chair.

The lady could not know what bitter childhood memories that name conjured up for George of Clarence; the pictures of humiliation at Ludlow market-cross which flashed across his mind. She only knew that she had achieved her object and could report success to the Earl of Worcester on her return.

And she was relieved, for, like most people, she feared that cold and rigorous man. He had personally supervised the execution of Warwick's captured sailors and his order to impale on stakes, not only their severed heads, but also their mangled bodies, had earned him the title 'Butcher of England' from an outraged populace.

★ ★ ★

The floor was hard to the Earl of Warwick's knees and his back hurt. If he lifted his eyes a little, he could see the threadbare brown skirt of the Queen's dress.

When he had told Louis that he was prepared to eat humblepie in order to further his long struggle for power, he had not lied. He had not, it was true, envisaged at the time that it would entail going on his knees to the woman whom he had, at various times, stigmatised as 'murderess' and 'hell-cat'. Nevertheless, it had become necessary to do so, and here he was in the great hall of the castle at Angers, in obeisance before Margaret of Anjou.

It never entered his mind to question the process of events that had led him to this humiliating posture in front of a woman he detested; nor did it occur to him to wonder what his wife and youngest daughter were thinking as they stood beside King Louis. Richard Neville had never lingered over the past; the present moment was everything. His greatest natural asset was his resilience; his ability to shrug off disappointment and disaster and press on towards a new tomorrow.

Margaret's voice sounded above his head. 'No! I refuse!'

King Louis hastened forward, motioning with him Count Rene of Anjou, the Queen's father, whom he had commanded to Angers to do battle with a recalcitrant daughter.

The Count's face, red and sweating, bobbed forward on his short bull-neck.

'My dear child,' he said, thickly, 'this might be your last chance to regain your rightful place.'

'And what proof have I,' Margaret demanded, her voice high-pitched and querulous, 'that Lord Warwick will keep his side of the bargain?'

Louis was shocked. 'Has he not promised to swear an oath with you on the Cross of St. Laud d'Angers? Who would dare to break an oath sworn to upon a piece of the one True Cross?'

Margaret shuffled her feet. Warwick noted that her shoes were as shabby as her gown. Her brother, John, the long-faced Duke of Calabria, came forward to add his persuasions to those of his father and cousin. Warwick could not see the Queen's face, but he could well imagine the conflict of emotions raging in her mind; her deep-rooted hatred of himself at war with her suddenly reawakened hopes.

'Very well,' she grunted, after what seemed an age. 'I agree to an alliance with Lord Warwick, but I shall not allow my son to marry his daughter.'

There was a pause and, for a moment, it seemed that the argument must collapse in the sweltering July heat, which had given the hall the temperature of a bake-oven. Then Louis, knowing the marriage to be Warwick's chief condition, anxious for this alliance and in splendid humour since the birth of his son some weeks before, put his arm caressingly about Margaret's shoulders.

'What are your objections?' he asked gently. 'Here is a young girl, a very lovely young girl' — his eyes rolled lasciviously in Anne's direction — 'who is a descendant of kings. Besides,' he continued, squeezing the Queen's shoulders and lowering his voice to a whisper, 'by this marriage and the children of this marriage, you ensure Lord Warwick's permanent support. You will be co-founders of a dynasty.'

Margaret closed her eyes. Suddenly, she felt unable to resist any more. The cogency of Louis' arguments persuaded her against her natural instincts and better judgement to accept the full terms of the alliance. After all, what alternative did she really have?

'Very well,' she said, wearily. 'But I make one condition.' Her eyes flashed open again and she stared around her, defiantly. 'My son waits here, in France, with me, until Lord Warwick has ousted the usurper and restored my husband to his throne.'

There was a general sigh of relief. Only

the Countess of Warwick and her daughter averted their eyes from the scene of rejoicing.

★ ★ ★

In the valley of the Dart, the first golden haze of autumn lay upon the slopping banks of trees, the summer's green a-shimmer with bronze and red. Mist curled like plumes of smoke above the tiny village which Warwick had left as a fugitive five months before. Now, on this mid-September day, he returned with men and munitions, supplied by Louis of France, to drive King Edward from his throne and replace the man whom he had helped to depose nine years earlier.

At the end of July, he had seen his youngest daughter betrothed to her cousin, Edward of Lancaster, at Angers. It had been an occasion of double ceremony, for, at the same time, he and Margaret of Anjou had sworn to their compact on the True Cross. If he had had, at the last, any qualms about marrying his quiet, fragile, little daughter to a young man of whom it had been said that 'he speaks and thinks of nothing but war and the cutting-off of heads,' the Earl had suppressed them. He was very fond of both his daughters, but somewhere in the maelstrom of his life, he had learned to subordinate all other feelings to his driving ambition for power.

He and his men came ashore, clattering through the sleepy village where John Boon had grown up, and startling the inhabitants by his appearance among them for the second time that year. Many of the people did not even know who he was, neither did they care, staring at him and his heathenish foreigners with heavy, indifferent eyes and answering his questions in the slow, thick dialect which he found almost impossible to understand, and which caused the Frenchmen to throw up their hands in despair.

Warwick marched towards Exeter, joining up on the way with the remainder of his troops, under the command of the Duke of Clarence, who had landed at Plymouth. Also with him were his brother-in-law, Oxford, and Jasper Tudor, still styling himself Earl of Pembroke. Warwick sent messengers galloping throughout the countryside, proclaiming the readoption of King Henry the sixth, and was rewarded by the recruitment of such notables as the Earl of Shrewsbury — who had refused to rally to King George — and the most cautious of his brothers-in-law, Lord Stanley.

'What about Hastings?' the Earl enquired

of Stanley, but received only a laugh in reply.

'That's one brother-in-law he will never recruit to the Bear and Ragged Staff,' Shrewsbury remarked later to Oxford.

General pardons were lavishly promised in Warwick's proclamations to all but King Henry's chief enemies, and the troops were threatened with death as the penalty for rape and pillage. Their numbers increased as they advanced northwards, but the questions uppermost in everyone's mind were: Where would Edward bring them to battle? And what would be the outcome?

Then, suddenly, it was all over. At the time of Warwick's landing, the King, with Richard of Gloucester, Hastings and Anthony Woodville, had been at York, but on receiving news of his cousin's arrival, had started south without delay, recruiting men as he went. Confidently, he had summoned John Neville to his aid. Apparently complying, the new Marquis had advanced from Pontefract, but, on reaching Doncaster, where the King's army was spending the night, had repaid Edward's ingratitude in kind and fallen upon the unsuspecting Yorkists.

The King, his brother, Hastings, Earl Rivers and a handful of loyal supporters had barely escaped with their lives. Fleeing through the night, they had reached Lynn and, on October the second, had sailed for Burgundy.

★ ★ ★

Saturday, October the sixth, in the year 1470, was to prove the zenith of Warwick's career. On that day, he entered triumphantly into London to be greeted by his brother, the Archbishop, and the shambling, vacant-eyed man who had once again become King of England.

As they knelt side-by-side in St. Paul's, Warwick hissed in his brother's ear: 'Couldn't you have found him something more suitable to wear than that ancient, blue velvet gown? It's the same one he wore when we brought him back from Islington.' Here, he received a pained and indignant look from the Archbishop of Canterbury who was conducting the service, but he cared nothing for the disapproval of Thomas Bourchier. 'And another thing,' he continued, 'he's dirty.'

'I know, I know,' George Neville whispered back, 'but he won't let anyone touch him. We shall have to wait until he is more amenable.'

'Does he understand what's happening?'

'God knows! If he does, he gives no sign.'

After the service was over, Henry was conducted to the Bishop of London's palace, where Warwick also installed himself, as indication of his rightful position. It should be clearly understood from the beginning that the Earl of Warwick's place was with the King. The Duke of Clarence, having paid homage to Henry, departed for 'The Erber', once the London home of his uncle, Salisbury.

'Can we trust him?' George Neville asked as he watched his namesake's retreating back.

'Oh, implicitly,' answered his brother in surprise. 'What makes you ask that? Hasn't he been committed to our cause from the very start? Long before he married Isabel!'

The Archbishop looked wonderingly at the Earl. 'That, my dear Richard,' he said carefully, 'was before you offered him a crown, then took it away to give to his arch-enemies.'

'Rubbish!' Warwick exclaimed airily. Turning the subject, he asked: 'What's all this trouble in London that I've been hearing about?'

'For a start,' replied the Archbishop, 'the Kentishmen have used the general unrest as an excuse to attack the Flemings and the

Dutch. And then every felon in sanctuary has issued forth, proclaiming himself a Yorkist political prisoner and a Lancastrian sympathiser. They've thrown open the gaols and let out all their fellow criminals on the same pretext. Looting and murder have been the natural outcome.'

'Never mind!' Warwick murmured comfortingly. 'We can soon deal with them. And it's left the sanctuaries empty for the Yorkists to get in. Where's Elizabeth?'

'In Westminster sanctuary with her daughters and Gloucester's two children. And about to produce her latest offspring at any minute by the look of her.'

'We must see to it that she gets proper attention,' Warwick grunted, reluctantly, and George nodded agreement.

'Naturally! We must overlook nothing that will add to our popularity.'

'Edward got safely away, I suppose?'

'Completely! He sailed from Lynn four days ago. I heard this morning that his fleet was attacked by the Easterlings, but unfortunately, the Seigneur de la Gruthuyse sent ships to his aid.'

'A pity,' said Warwick. 'If he had been killed or drowned it would have solved everything for us.'

'Never mind,' answered his brother, echoing

his own words. 'We have Tiptoft. Our 'Butcher' was found hiding in a tree somewhere in Huntingdonshire.'

'He's here? In London?'

'He is. And the people will soon he howling for his blood.'

The people did howl for the Earl of Worcester's blood. It would have provoked a full-scale riot if, at his trial, he had been acquitted. But his judges were no fools: they valued their own lives too much. On October the seventeenth, Tiptoft left Westminster under heavy guard for the scaffold on Tower Hill.

The crowds in the streets, however, were so dense and so hostile that the terrified officers could not reach Tower Hill and took refuge in the Fleet Prison for the night, urgently sending for reinforcements. All night the mob howled and prowled outside, screaming hatred and abuse at this man whom they loathed above all others.

The only one unmoved was the prisoner. In response to the accusation of one of his guards: 'You have brought this upon yourself by your own cruelty,' he merely smiled.

'When one is an officer of the state,' he replied calmly, 'one must do that which is best for the government of the country. If it is necessary to use harsh and cruel methods, then one must do so.'

'You don't have to enjoy it,' snarled another of his gaolers, but again, John Tiptoft only smiled.

'We are all made in our own mould,' was all that he would answer.

The following day, a path was forced to Tower Hill and the people, still hurling filth and obscenities, milled around the scaffold, their hysterical fury heightened by the Earl's unconcerned demeanour.

'He was as calm,' wrote an observer later, 'as though he had been going to his breakfast.'

Placidly he made his confession. Smilingly, he requested the headsman to use three strokes of the axe — 'in honour of the Trinity.'

At almost the last moment, an Italian friar pushed his way forward and shouted: 'What of the two children whom you murdered?'

'It was for the good of the state,' Worcester answered, and, kneeling, laid his head on the block. A second later, the axe fell.

(And in far-off Italy, a baby, whose name was Niccolo Machiavelli, slept the deep, untroubled sleep enjoyed by the very young.)

18

Jasper Tudor, who had gone to Wales to visit his estates after his many years of exile, returned to Westminster on November the first, bringing with him his nephew, the thirteen-years-old Henry Tudor, for whom he demanded the restoration of his father's title, Earl of Richmond. Warwick hedged.

'Why not?' flared Tudor. 'My brother held the title until his death and you know it.'

Warwick, a man beset by many problems, was annoyed at having another one thrust upon his already over-crowded plate. 'There are titles just as good,' he said, 'and the boy shall have his pick.'

Jasper laughed. 'Don't stall with me, Lord Warwick. I know that the Duke of Clarence' — he fairly spat the name — 'is styling himself Lord and Earl of Richmond. How many more sops does that bastard have to have to keep him quiet?'

Warwick rose angrily to his feet, but before he could think of a suitable retort, the door to the adjoining room was pushed tentatively open and Henry shuffled into the presence-chamber. Jasper and Henry Tudor fell to their knees, but Warwick, although giving a slight bow, remained standing.

'Oh! People!' The King, like a startled rabbit, was preparing to withdraw, when his half-brother got quickly to his feet, gently calling him by name.

Henry paused, looking anxiously over his shoulder. 'Who . . . who are you?' he quavered.

Jasper moved forward and took one of the trembling hands in his own. 'It's Jasper! Your brother! And this' — he beckoned Henry forward — 'is our nephew, Edmund's boy.'

'Edmund's boy,' Henry repeated stupidly, and the two Henrys stood for a moment, looking into each other's faces; one young and curious, the other middle-aged and vacant.

Watching the little group by the door, Warwick, who was not much given to pondering the workings of fate, could not help thinking how ironic it was that of all the sons of Catherine de Valois, it should have been her eldest and only important son who had inherited to the full the madness of her father. There had been rumours that Owen Tudor, the son who had become a monk at Westminster, had done so because he had been afflicted with the taint of his grandfather's insanity, and young Henry's

334

father, Edmund Tudor, had not been strong. But Jasper Tudor was as normal and healthy as any man alive. Indeed, reflected Warwick sourly, one could almost imagine that it was he, and not the King, who was Monmouth Harry's son.

'Edmund's boy,' the King repeated yet again. Then, like a man who has fought his way through a dense fog into sunlight, his face suddenly cleared. 'Edmund is dead,' he said.

Jasper nodded and his young nephew silently marvelled at the patience which his normally choleric uncle was showing to this silly old man.

'That's right,' Jasper said gently, patting his half-brother's hand. 'Edmund is dead. But Margaret's not. We should like to see Margaret. The boy ought to see his mother.'

The King's mind struggled desperately to stave off the darkness which threatened it. 'Margaret Beaufort,' he muttered. 'Edmund married Margaret Beaufort.' Jasper nodded again and Henry smiled, pleased with himself. 'My cousin,' he added.

'Quite right! We should like to see her.'

'Lady Stafford is not in London,' Warwick broke in, tired of this affecting little scene and anxious to get on with his work.

He had enough of it, Heaven knew! His

biggest headache at present was a complete reversal of foreign policy; an alliance with France which would entail a war against Burgundy. It might have appeared to him an enormous problem had he ever really bothered to understand the minds of his countrymen. Had he taken this trouble, he would have realised the depth and extent of the average Englishman's hatred of France; the cradle of the Norman Conqueror, the home of the men who, from time immemorial, had ravaged England's coast; and of Frenchmen, themselves, the recent victors who had thrown the all-conquering English out of France and sent them, in humiliation and defeat, back across the Channel.

But even without comprehending any of this, Warwick realised that the merchants, a class getting stronger and more numerous every day, would violently oppose his policy as being ruinous to their trade. The weaving of cloth, at which the Flemings excelled, was vital to the export of wool. Moreover, Burgundy had always been one of England's best customers for many other commodities, and there was already much grumbling in the city about the proposed treaty with France.

There were other problems, as well. As

Warwick, sighing with relief, saw the door close behind Jasper and Henry Tudor, he knew that he would never be whole-heartedly accepted by the true Lancastrians. And, in the deepest places of his heart, he had no wish to be. Now that he had been put to the test, he found that, apart from Tiptoft, he could not turn his hand against any of the Yorkists. He granted an amnesty to Robert Stillington and Edward's physician, William Hatcliffe; he accepted the presence at court of such known partisans of Edward as Thomas Mowbray, Duke of Norfolk, and Henry Bourchier, Earl of Essex. More significantly, he offered no government places to Shrewsbury and Jasper Tudor, nor even to his brothers-in-law, Stanley and Oxford. And if conclusive proof of his sub-conscious feelings was needed, either by himself or the world at large, he granted a pardon to Elizabeth's brother, Sir Richard Woodville.

★ ★ ★

The day following Jasper Tudor's meeting with King Henry, Friday, November the second, Lady Scrope was admitted to Elizabeth Woodville's lying-in chamber in Westminster sanctuary.

'I have been sent,' she said austerely, 'to

assist your ladyship, by the King's Lieutenant of the Realm.'

Elizabeth, whose labour had already begun, stopped pacing the floor and turned viciously on Lady Scrope. 'If you mean Warwick, say so,' she snarled. 'King's Lieutenant of the Realm, indeed! God's Bowels! What King? That doddering, half-witted old fool, Henry of Lancaster?' She laughed, hysterically and clutched at her stomach.

The midwife, Mother Cobb, came hurrying up, but Elizabeth waved her aside and lowered herself heavily into a chair.

'I'm overwrought,' she said. 'Forgive me. So much has happened in the last few months.' She pushed her hair back from her sweating forehead and patted the seat beside her. 'Tell me the news,' she invited. 'Are my sons both safe?'

'They are both in St. Martin's sanctuary, along with many more,' Lady Scrope answered, mollified.

Elizabeth only grunted, but relief showed in her face. 'And the gossip?'

'Oh, there's plenty of that.' Lady Scrope smiled. 'Lord Stanley's brother, Sir William, has married Tiptoft's widow. Off with the old, on with the new, eh?' Even as she said it, she remembered that Lord Grey had been dead only a few months when

338

Elizabeth had first met Edward.

Elizabeth saw the thought written on her companion's face and laughed. 'One has to take care for the future, Lady Scrope. Always take care for the future.'

Her eldest daughter, now nearly five years old, came in, followed by her two sisters. Elizabeth regarded them with dissatisfaction.

'Girls! Girls! Girls!' she muttered, getting abruptly to her feet. 'I provided sons for my first husband. Why can't I do so now?'

'Hush, hush, Your Grace,' soothed Mother Cobb, coming swiftly to her side, using the regal form of address and glaring defiantly at Lady Scrope as she did so. 'This may well be a boy, and if not — well, you're young and strong.'

'I'm thirty-three. That's not so young,' Elizabeth said, petulantly. Then: 'Take the children away,' she muttered. 'Quickly!'

Two hours later, it was over. Elizabeth Woodville lay back on her pillows, holding her new-born child in her arms. Between laughter and tears, triumph and despair, she gazed into the tiny, crumpled face with its fringe of pale hair and close-shut eyes.

For here, in sanctuary, in the hour of defeat, seemingly at the nadir of her fortunes, she had given birth to the son for whom she and Edward had waited so long.

* * *

The news of the birth only added to
Warwick's difficulties. Here was the incentive
— if, indeed, his cousin had ever needed
one — to spur Edward on in his plans for the
reconquest of his realm, and to this possibility
Warwick was ever alert.

He was also unhappily aware that he
could delay, perhaps even prevent Edward's
plans if he would but assure Duke Charles,
of England's friendly intentions towards
Burgundy. Charles had always had a marked
preference for the cause of Lancaster, because
his mother, a princess of Portugal, had been
a descendant of John of Gaunt. He had been
forced into an alliance with Yorkist England
by King Louis, but was now showing himself
more than willing to treat with King Henry,
even though this meant treating with his
old enemy, the Earl of Warwick. He had
received neither of his brothers-in-law at the
Burgundian court and had even forbidden his
wife to visit the house of Gruthuyse where her
brothers lodged.

But Warwick could not bring himself to
abandon King Louis, nor was it in his nature
to perform the complicated double game,
which his cousin knew so well how to play.
Moreover, the golden bait, Prince of Holland

340

and Zealand, still had the power to land him, squirming and wriggling with delighted anticipation, in King Louis' basket.

Other worries beset him. He was beginning to be as uneasy as the Archbishop about the Duke of Clarence, and, in his first Parliament, an act was passed at Warwick's instigation, naming his son-in-law as heir to the throne should Anne Neville and Edward of Lancaster die childless. But the sop was indignantly spurned.

'Much good may that do me,' George shouted furiously to Isabel. 'They are both young and not unhealthy, even though Anne looks weak. It's like throwing a scrap to a starving dog. Mark my words! Your father will now insist on Anne's marriage.'

And as, with a very bad grace, George joined in the Christmas festivities at Westminster, news reached him that his sister-in-law and Edward of Lancaster had been married at Angers. As the New Year approached, he withdrew sulkily to his west-country estates.

'He will guard the southern and western coasts in case Edward should make a landing there,' Warwick told his brother, but George Neville looked doubtfully down his nose. The Archbishop was also unhappy about his brother, John. Anger and bitterness had brought Montagu over to their side, but could they count on him in the future? Violent emotions had a habit of lessening in intensity as time passed and loyalty to Edward had long been a habit with the Marquis.

The Archbishop, now restored to his old position as Chancellor, forbore to communicate this particular worry to his eldest brother. He felt that Warwick had enough cares of his own and merely wished the Earl a pleasant journey to Sandwich and a happy meeting with Queen Margaret.

The Queen, however, did not come. While Warwick chafed at the delay and spent the short February days staring vainly out to sea, hoping hourly for a sight of Margaret's sails on the horizon, her messenger arrived, having landed at Dover. The Queen had received word that Charles of Burgundy, convinced at last that he could hope for nothing from Warwick's government, had met Edward at Aire in January and was now equipping him with money and men. Margaret would not risk her precious son until the Earl had dealt with the invaders.

Warwick swore, but had the consolation of knowing that his wife and equally precious youngest daughter would be safe in France until all danger had passed.

He returned to a London caught in the grip of mounting tension and fear. The factions of Neville and Woodville had simply been exchanged for the factions of Neville and Lancaster, for it was becoming daily more obvious that the old Lancastrians refused to trust the new, and that Warwick was only tolerated because of the support he commanded in France. This meant that Warwick could never afford to break with King Louis, or Margaret's friends would immediately sweep him from power. The merchants, not only in London, but throughout the country, viewed the future with despondency and alarm.

News filtered through from Burgundy of a fleet being assembled at Flushing under the supervision of the able young Duke of Gloucester; of large sums of money cajoled from Charles by the diplomacy of Hastings and Anthony Woodville. Warwick waited in daily expectation of news of Edward's arrival and sent out his commissions of array. The Bastard of Fauconberg patrolled the seas, but he could not be everywhere at once and it was anyone's guess where the Yorkists would land.

Toleration was at an end. All known Yorkists such as the Duke of Norfolk and the Archbishop of Canterbury were put under arrest. Jasper Tudor was rallying Wales; the Earl of Oxford and Lord Scrope were keeping watch in the east; Clarence was presumably levying troops in the west; and the men of Kent and Yorkshire, Warwick could surely rely on as he had always done in the past. The Earl, himself, abandoning London to the care of his brother, George, left for the midlands, ready to strike in any direction as soon as news of Edward's landing was received.

The two brothers embraced at parting.

'Our defences are very strong,' the Archbishop said. 'We should have no difficulty in driving Edward out.'

'No, but send a messenger to France without delay. Stress the importance of Margaret's arrival as soon as possible. Wherever Edward lands, another army can only be an advantage.'

George agreed. 'It shall be done today. I shall be in constant touch.' They clasped hands for a moment, then Warwick mounted his horse and rode out at the head of his troops. They were never to see each other again.

★ ★ ★

On the fourteenth of March, Edward and his storm-driven ships arrived at Ravenspur in Yorkshire; that same wind-blasted strip of coast which had seen the start of Bolingbroke's invasion some seventy years earlier. And, like Bolingbroke, Edward declared that he came only to claim his dukedom, not the crown.

Warwick, at Warwick Castle, waited confidently for news of his cousin's defeat, but none came. Instead, the city of York entertained the invaders with lavish hospitality, and, as Edward struck south, many sympathisers issued forth from hiding and joined the White Rose banner. Henry Percy did not go to Edward's assistance, it was true, but neither did he strike a blow for Warwick: he sat at home upon his estates and awaited the outcome of the struggle.

John Neville made threatening movements, but, somehow or other, never quite managed to bring his cousin to battle. The Yorkist army drove off the Earls of Oxford and Exeter before pushing still further south, whilst Lancastrians such as Jasper Tudor, Wiltshire, and Somerset, refused to rally to Warwick's side, determined to wait for Queen Margaret's arrival.

Warwick removed to the city of Coventry and saw Edward's host surround its walls.

His cousin sent a herald to offer him trial by combat, but the Earl disdainfully refused. George of Clarence was approaching from the south and each day brought Margaret and her army nearer embarkation.

Then the blow fell. On April the second, near Banbury, a grand reconciliation took place between Edward and Gloucester and the Duke of Clarence. George, as he had promised his brothers the previous year, had taken the first possible opportunity to return to his rightful allegiance.

And on April the eleventh, Maundy Thursday, George Neville, compelled by the City Fathers, surrendered London to Edward, and the Yorkist army entered in triumph. Within a month, Edward had marched almost the entire length of the country and taken the capital without one serious engagement having been fought.

★ ★ ★

Warwick sat in his tent, writing far into the night.

His army lay across the main Barnet-to-London road and it was here, on the preceding evening, that the Yorkist troops, issuing forth from the capital, had halted him in his tracks. It had been dark when

346

his advance party had come rushing back to the encampment, ignominiously driven out of Barnet by the van of Edward's army.

In the gathering dusk of that Saturday evening, the thirteenth of April, the Yorkists had deployed across the open heathland. Warwick had opened fire upon them, but how much damage he had done, he had no means of knowing, for he could not judge the enemy's distance, Edward having ordered no noise and no fires.

One thing the Earl did know, from one of Edward's captured men, was the position of their leaders: Gloucester commanded the Yorkist right, opposite his brother-in-law, Exeter; Hastings the left, opposite Oxford; whilst Edward and George of Clarence were in the centre. His own centre Warwick had entrusted to his brother, John, who had joined him some days before, lame excuses for his failure to waylay Edward hovering on his lips. Warwick, himself, would command the reserve.

The Earl laid down his pen and rubbed his tired eyes. Everything had gone awry, but nothing, not even the wound of Clarence's betrayal, could hurt him now, for he had received the most numbing blow of all. A messenger from George Neville had reached him with a letter from King Louis, in which the French monarch calmly announced that he had signed a truce with Charles of Burgundy.

Warwick looked with bleary gaze upon the sheet of paper before him. The words ran together and danced under his eyes, but he knew by heart what he had written. Perjurer, liar, false friend; these were some of the epithets which Warwick had heaped on Louis' head. Did Louis know that if his letter had arrived a few days earlier, Warwick could still have made his peace with Edward? Worse still, had Louis deliberately waited until he felt assured that the Earl had finally tried his cousin's patience too far? Warwick summoned a messenger.

'This must reach France as soon as possible. Go tonight! Get past the enemy lines somehow, even if it means a detour of several miles.'

The man was dubious. 'I'll try, my lord, but the weather . . . ' He broke off, waving a hand, vaguely.

Warwick got up and went to the entrance of his tent. A thick mist lapped the world in an all-embracing silence. Warwick cursed, but: 'You must get through somehow,' he snapped. He burned to have that letter placed in Louis' hands.

John Neville came in, his face pale and

strained. He was already partially armed, but Warwick knew that his heart was not in this forthcoming fight. Whatever ingratitude Edward had shown him, and it had indeed been great, Montagu found it too difficult to change his loyalties easily. To be fighting for Henry and Margaret seemed to him to be terribly wrong.

Warwick turned away. His brother was a fool, he told himself desperately. What future could they have had at Edward's side?

But what future did they have with Henry? When Margaret arrived, what then? How long before Warwick found himself eased from his position of power, now that he could no longer rely on Louis? And where to turn now? All his alternatives were used up; all his schemes gone astray.

He shook off these depressing thoughts. It was time to arm and take his place on that fog-bound plain. In the distance, he could hear the Barnet bells calling the faithful to prayer on this Easter Day. The priests moved slowly amongst the men, ghost-like figures in the clinging, wet mist.

The trumpets sounded. The two armies groped their way towards each other and met with a shuddering impact. At first, all seemed to be going Warwick's way. In the dark, Edward had assumed the Earl's centre to lie directly across the road, itself, and, consequently, Richard of Gloucester overlapped the Lancastrian left, while Oxford overlapped the Yorkists. But whereas Oxford was on level ground and could, therefore, turn his men with ease to take William Hastings on the flank, the young Duke of Gloucester found himself going down into a hollow, out of which he could only climb with difficulty.

A messenger pushed through the increasing carnage to Warwick's side, where he stood directing his reserves against Gloucester, who, having dragged himself and his men out of the pit, was fighting with a tenacity and ferocity that resisted all Exeter's attempts to push him back again over the edge.

'My lord!' The man licked the salt sweat from his lips. 'The enemy is completely swept away on the right. Lord Hastings has failed to rally his men. Our troops under Lord Oxford, have reached as far as Barnet.'

'Fools!' stormed the Earl. 'Go after them and fetch them back at once. We need every man on the field.'

The plain was now a treacherous mass of churned mud and broken bodies, slippery with blood. In the centre, John Neville peered through the shrouding mist in an effort to spot the Sunbanner of York. Wherever it appeared, there would be Edward.

Suddenly he saw it and shouted to his archers to let their arrows go. As the vicious humming filled the air, his arm was seized by Lord Wenlock.

'That's not the Sun-banner,' he shouted, above the din of clashing steel and screaming men. 'That's Oxford's banner of the Star-with-Streamers.'

'But those men are facing us!'

'They'd reached as far as Barnet, but Warwick had them recalled.'

Even as he spoke, it was too late. With yells of 'Treason!' Oxford's men set upon Montagu's. The cry was taken up and echoed throughout the Lancastrian ranks. Unable to see what was happening, they only knew that somehow, somewhere, something had gone wrong. They had been betrayed.

Flinging down their arms, they ran headlong from the field. Vainly Warwick and his brother tried to shore up their disintegrating lines, but to no avail. Exeter fell as his men rushed past him in their flight. John Neville, turning to catch at Warwick's arm, was felled to the ground even as he opened his mouth to speak.

Dazedly, unable to believe that Fate had dealt him this final blow, Warwick lumbered for the rear of the battle-line, where pages were waiting with the horses.

The mist wreathed about him. He stumbled and nearly fell, but managed to save himself and staggered blindly on. He could see the dim shapes of the trees and hear the faint whinnying of the horses. He was almost there . . .

A man leapt from behind a bush, dagger poised. His jacket bore the Fetterlock of York. Warwick pushed up his vizor and shouted to him.

'No! No! I am the Ear . . . '

But the man did not wait to hear. He would not know until too late, what a splendid prize might have been his. Drunk with the lust to kill, he plunged his dagger into the open mouth, saw the rush of blood, the glazed eyes staring into his; then, was off, looking for further prey.

Behind him, the once mighty, proud and conquering Warwick, the man who had lived out his life in a struggle for power, the descendant and friend of kings, lay dead on the mist-soaked ground. It was his greatest tragedy that, except for his wife and daughters, there were very few who would shed a tear at his passing.